Deadly
Summer
Nights

A Catskill
Summer Resort Mystery

"Vicki Delany is one of my
favorite mystery authors."
—Kate Carlisle

VICKI
DELANY

National Bestselling Author

$7.99 USA
$10.99 CAN

ISBN 978-0-593-33437-9

5 0 7 9 9

**BERKLEY PRIME CRIME TITLES
BY VICKI DELANY**

The Catskill Summer Resort Mysteries

DEADLY SUMMER NIGHTS

The Year-Round Christmas Mysteries

REST YE MURDERED GENTLEMEN
WE WISH YOU A MURDEROUS CHRISTMAS
HARK THE HERALD ANGELS SLAY
SILENT NIGHT, DEADLY NIGHT
DYING IN A WINTER WONDERLAND

Deadly Summer Nights

VICKI DELANY

BERKLEY PRIME CRIME
New York

BERKLEY PRIME CRIME
Published by Berkley
An imprint of Penguin Random House LLC
penguinrandomhouse.com

ISBN: 9780593334379

First Edition: September 2021

Printed in the United States of America
1 3 5 7 9 10 8 6 4 2

Book design by George Towne

To Mom

Chapter 1

"MY NEIGHBOR MRS. FRANCESCO HEARD HIM AT A CLUB in the city. *Vulgar, unamusing,* and *all-around offensive* were the words she used. As if that wasn't bad enough, he was even worse the second night!" Mrs. Brownville blew a plume of smoke into my face. I gave her my best professional smile, but it wasn't easy.

"She was so offended she went a second time?"

"They were taken by friends. Please keep up, dear. One doesn't refuse the hospitality of friends." Another plume of smoke lunged toward me.

I tried not to cough at the same time I struggled to keep my smile fixed to my face. Mr. and Mrs. Brownville were here for four weeks. They'd taken one of the best lakefront cabins in order to have room for a rotating roster of visiting friends and relations. At Haggerman's Catskills Resort we were not so flush with high-paying guests I could afford to offend one.

"Don't just stand there gaping, girl. What are you going to do about it?" Mrs. Brownville was in her sixties, and she was a woman not to be trifled with: approaching six feet tall, broad-chested, broad-shouldered, midnight-black hair sprayed into an unmovable object, small, dark intense eyes. She wore a powder-blue wool suit over a blue blouse with a floppy bow tied at the neck, and blue shoes with kitten heels. Not what most people would consider appropriate attire for a hot summer's day in the Catskills, but I'd never seen her in anything but a designer suit of one shade of pastel or another.

I glanced around, seeking escape. To my dismay, none was forthcoming.

"Elizabeth Grady, are you listening to me? Or must I speak to your mother?"

"No need to bother Olivia, ma'am," I said. "She trusts me to make decisions regarding the running of Haggerman's." I cleared my throat. "I'll have a chat with our entertainment director and with Mr. Simmonds himself to ensure he's fully aware that at Haggerman's Catskills Resort we're proud of our family-friendly reputation." We didn't actually employ an entertainment director, but I decided not to mention that the task of hiring entertainers, along with so many others, largely fell to me.

"You do that. I will, of course, be in the audience to be sure that his entire act is acceptable for young people and ladies."

Not a good idea. Charlie Simmonds was a rapidly rising comedian in the smoke-filled clubs of New York City and in the equally smoke-filled lounges of the Catskills precisely because he was, supposedly, cutting-edge and risqué. New York City comedians weren't normally hired as children's entertainers. Or to pass muster by the likes of Mrs.

Brownville, always on the lookout for something to be offended about.

I shifted from one foot to the other. Mrs. Brownville had waylaid me on the lakefront path at midday. The hot sun beamed down, the air almost dripped with humidity, and I was dressed in work attire of stockings and a girdle under a blue-and-yellow-print dress that fell slightly below my knees, with a Peter Pan collar and long sleeves. I thought fondly of the pretty sundress I hadn't had a chance to wear yet. Too informal for a professional woman on a working day, my mother sniffed when she suggested (*ordered?*) that I change.

"I have to point out, Mrs. Brownville," I said, "that Mr. Simmonds will be doing two shows each day for the three days he's engaged to be at Haggerman's. A family-friendly performance at nine and a more . . . adult-oriented one at eleven, following the dessert buffet."

Surely Mrs. Brownville would be long abed by eleven. A day spent finding fault with everything and everyone had to be exhausting.

"Adults," she pronounced, "also need to be protected from filth. I will attend both shows this evening. Now, about the other matter I wanted to discuss with you." She dropped the end of her cigarette onto the path and rummaged in her cavernous handbag for the pack.

Attempting to be discreet, I moved my right foot and ground out the still-lit end before it could set the whole place on fire. I checked my watch. "Will you look at the time. I have to be off. I have . . . uh . . . something important to do."

"Won't take long." She popped a fresh Lucky Strike into her lipsticked mouth, flicked the gold engraved lighter, lit the cigarette, and took a deep breath.

Unfortunately, Mrs. Brownville can talk while smoking.

I suspect Mrs. Brownville can talk while sleeping. Another smoky plume wafted my way. I held my own breath.

"I'll walk with you, Elizabeth," she said. "The exercise will do me good. Don't just stand there, girl. Let's go. About the chicken à la king served last night at dinner. I myself am blessed with the constitution of my Scottish forebears. Hearty Highland stock the lot of them, but Mr. Brownville is not so fortunate. He—"

My heart leapt for joy as I spotted salvation heading my way. "Randy! Randy!" I waved my arms and called.

Randy Fontaine, the resort's aquatic director, swimming instructor, and head lifeguard, saw me, and who I was with, a second too late. He knew I knew he'd seen me and turning tail and fleeing would not be a good career move. His eyes stopped darting about, seeking escape, and he slapped on a big smile. "Good morning, Mrs. Grady, Mrs. Brownville. Beautiful day, isn't it? Don't let me keep you."

"Randy," I said. "It's almost lunchtime, so you have no appointments for the next while. Mrs. Brownville and I were chatting about the meals. You know that's primarily the domain of Chef Leonardo and Rosemary, but I'm always happy to hear what our guests have to suggest about the food we serve here at Haggerman's. Why don't you escort Mrs. Brownville to lunch and report back to me later?"

"Uh—" he said.

"Excellent idea." Mrs. Brownville grabbed Randy's bare arm and hauled him away. I couldn't help but notice they didn't take the most direct route to the main building. She'd want all her friends, and all her enemies, to see her hanging on the arm of our tall, blond, tanned, muscular swimming instructor. He'd pulled a shirt on over his bathing suit to take his break, but he hadn't done up the buttons.

A slim figure slipped out of the bushes lining the path

and fell into step next to me. "I saw that. Nicely done. Let Randy earn his wages for a change."

"I think Randy more than earns his wages," I said. "I'm convinced some of the young women, and the older women, too, rent other people's kids so they can watch them taking Randy's swimming classes."

Velvet McNally laughed. "You're probably right about that. I've had a couple of the daughters ask me if he gives *private* lessons."

I didn't laugh in return. "I hope you squashed any mention of that. I do not need trouble from irate fathers."

"Even Randy, as confident as he is about his supposed appeal to women, knows better, Elizabeth. That is, I hope he does."

"'Supposed appeal'?" I asked.

Her eyes, the color of lake water on a sunny day, slid to one side. "I've been told women find him attractive. Can't see it myself."

We walked up the path together, taking our time, enjoying each other's company. Velvet had been my best friend all through school and into our adulthood, and I'd managed to lure her away from her dreams of stardom to join the staff here at Haggerman's. Velvet's ambition in life was to be a professional show dancer, like my mother. Like my mother, and totally unlike me, she was graced with the perfect dancer's body: all sharp angles and jutting bones atop endless legs. Unlike my mother, but exactly like me, Velvet had not one ounce of grace. She could, and often did, trip on a flat stretch of pavement. She worked here as the director of our outdoor recreation programs. When I offered her the job, she said it beat slinging hash in a Bronx diner while waiting for her big break, which she'd finally admitted to herself wasn't going to happen.

My desk was piled high with papers needing attention, but I was in no rush to get back to it. It was a perfect Catskills day: hot and humid, but the humidity was cut somewhat by a light breeze blowing off Delayed Lake, bringing with it the scent of fresh water and the forested hills surrounding us. Children's laughter came from the swimming pool enclosure and the small sandy beach. A woman called lunchtime, and a screen door slammed. One of the grounds staff nodded politely to us as he came out from behind a bush, straw hat low over his eyes, pruning shears gripped firmly in his hand.

I returned his nod, and then took a deep breath and looked around me, wanting to enjoy the moment before I headed back to my crowded, hot, stuffy office.

The yellow ball of the sun shone in a sky dotted with fluffy white clouds, and we were surrounded by every shade of green imaginable. The dark greens of the trees on the hills, the emerald green of the well-maintained lawn, variegated greens in the foliage of the flower beds and the iron pots lining the lakefront path. Even Velvet's lime-green exercise shorts and matching shirt. To our left the blue waters of Delayed Lake shimmered. Two paddleboats went past, the laughter of the passengers echoing through the hills. Further out, teenagers leapt into the lake from the diving platform, screaming their enjoyment.

"What are you smiling at?" I said to Velvet.

"You. You love it here, don't you?"

"I love it here, yes. I don't love all the work I have to do. When Olivia suggested I join her in running this place she so unexpectedly inherited, she neglected to mention that I would manage the entire resort and everything to do with it while she sips cocktails, looks gracious, and pops up now and again to charm the guests."

"Such is life." Velvet laughed. "Someone has to do the charming. Would you want your mother doing more?"

I shuddered. "Heavens no. Half the staff would quit the first week, and the other half would sit back, light a cigarette, and ask me to fetch them a cold drink."

"You have your aunt Tatiana."

"Tatiana." I felt a warm rush of pleasure at mention of the woman who'd been largely responsible for raising me. "And you. You both keep me sane." Enough lollygagging. I picked up my pace. "What have you got on this afternoon?"

"After lunch it's calisthenics on the dock for the women over fifty and then the teenagers. I'm not planning to play in the handball tournament, but I'll pop over to the court and make sure it's under control. This evening we have the nature walk."

"Be sure and let me know how that goes." The nature walk was a new idea for this year, and today was the first time. We'd invited a member of a local nature lovers' society to lead the walk and give a talk on flora and fauna of the area. Randy and Velvet would tag along, to ensure none of our guests got lost or, in the case of teenage couples, deliberately fell behind.

We stopped walking when we reached the spot at which the lakefront path branched out in several directions. A sign bristling with arrows pointing every which way was planted in the center of a small flower bed: to the swimming pool, to the tennis and handball courts, to the cabins, to the parking lot, to the main building. Behind us lay the guests' boat dock and the beach, at this time of day crowded with brightly painted wooden chairs, beach towels, sunbathing guests, and pail-and-shovel-toting toddlers. In front of us, a brand-new bright red four-door 1953 Hudson Jet pulled up to the steps of the hotel, and uniformed bellhops came running from all directions to help unload the luggage.

"I'm looking forward to hearing that comedian tonight," Velvet said. "The nature walk will be over in time for me to run back to my room and change and catch his show. I could use a good laugh."

"You're always laughing," I said, "and so you should. You have a great job, fresh air, and healthy exercise all day long."

"I always appear to be laughing," she said. "There's a difference." She settled her face into serious lines, but she couldn't hold the expression. With her porcelain complexion, huge cornflower-blue eyes, and long golden hair, Velvet attracted her share of male admirers. During the day, when she was in the water or leading exercise classes and games, she tied her hair into a bouncy ponytail.

"Okay," she admitted. "I'd rather have my job than yours, although I do have to worry that some of the older women in my classes are going to think they're younger than they are and do too much and have a heart attack in front of me."

She turned, saying "See you later, alligator" as she skipped down the path leading to the guests' parking lot and the staff quarters behind.

A teenage boy stepped into the flower bed and walked straight into the direction sign, so intent was he on watching her go.

I smiled to myself and hurried over to make sure he was all right.

Chapter 2

HAGGERMAN'S CATSKILLS RESORT SPECIALIZES IN "heathy outdoor exercise during the day and the stars of entertainment at night."

Before my mother inherited it, Haggerman's didn't specialize in anything at all. It was just one of a hundred Catskills resorts New Yorkers flocked to all summer long.

The problem with Haggerman's had been that not many New Yorkers had been flocking *here*.

My mother, Olivia Peters, had been a Broadway and Hollywood dance star in her prime. The professional life of a dancer isn't long, and after one injury too many, Olivia hadn't been able to slip comfortably into straight acting or teaching dance. The daughter of solid Russian immigrants, she'd saved a lot of money over the course of her career and when she had to retire, she set herself up as a patron of the arts. Young dancers, singers, and actors flocked to her luxury apartment on East Sixty-Fifth Street near Central Park to bask in her fame and meet the directors and producers she also cultivated.

Unfortunately, as well as being taught to watch her pennies, my mother had been taught that a respectable woman let her husband handle the details of their financial affairs. Olivia's third husband, the cursed Jack Montgomery, emptied out her bank accounts and skipped town. She lost the Manhattan apartment, most of her jewelry, designer dresses, and fur coats, and would have been on the street had a longtime admirer not conveniently up and died and left her the only thing of any value he owned: Haggerman's Catskills Resort.

The one thing Olivia hadn't lost was her address book and the respect of her peers. With her influence, we were able to attract top-notch entertainment to our stage. That, plus Olivia's own name and fame, kept guests coming. I've been told some people book their vacation at Haggerman's rather than one of the better-known resorts in the hope of meeting Olivia Peters herself.

"I dance, my darling," Olivia had said to me when she invited me to join her in this endeavor. "I leave the trivialities to other people." She might as well have said "to the little people." That meant me.

This is our second year here, and so far the concept seems to be working. It's late June, the start of the season, and bookings are looking good for most of the summer.

The phone on my desk rang, and I glanced up from the payroll balance sheet I was trying to whip into some sort of shape. I threw down my pencil and leaned back in my chair, circling my shoulders and rubbing at the back of my neck in an attempt to work some of the kinks out. I could use some healthful exercise myself right about now, but these books weren't going to balance themselves, and no one else would do it. I sighed and wiped sweat off my forehead. A dusty fan propped in a corner on top of an out-of-date New York State map book accomplished nothing but stirring the sticky heat around.

I answered the phone. "Hello?"

Darlene at the reception desk. "The Carletons in four-oh-five are threatening to check out and demanding a full refund. Mrs. Carleton says she saw a rat on their windowsill. If she wants to see rats, she'll go back to the city."

"Mrs. Carleton wouldn't know a rat from a squirrel. Isn't Mr. Carleton the one who threatened to sue us last week because he tripped over a branch while taking a shortcut through the woods?"

"Yup."

"Yet here they still are. In the Catskills, where it's been known to have an occasional tree branch fall onto the forest floor or a fluffy-tailed creature searching for sustenance. Okay, I'll get Olivia to drop into their room and make soothing noises. That's all they want anyway."

Darlene chuckled. "Thanks, Elizabeth."

We hung up, and I gave my shoulders another stretch. I glanced around the dark, tiny room that passes for my office. Guests never come in here, so no money had been spent on fixing it up. The green-and-brown wallpaper was yellowing and peeling in places, and when it rained, water dripped down the southern wall. After the first incident had soaked the reservations book so that the ink ran enough to be almost unreadable, I learned where not to place important papers. The only advantage my office has is the stiff, creaky back door that opens directly onto an overgrown, no-longer-used service path heading into the woods. I can sneak out without anyone knowing.

A tray had been placed on top of a stack of advertising materials from other resorts, which I planned to look through one day, when I had the time, to see what our competition was up to. I vaguely remembered hearing a server coming in at one point, but I'd been on the phone yelling at a delinquent meat supplier at the time. It looked as though the waiter had brought soup and a sandwich for my lunch. The soup was beef and vegetable, now gone stone-cold with an unappetizing greasy skin forming on the top.

I glanced at my watch. Quarter to four. Yet another day without a lunch break. A stack of envelopes sat on the corner of my desk, along with checks needing to be signed and mailed. I grabbed the phone and asked the switchboard operator to put me through to the house. All I got was a busy signal. If Olivia was on the phone chatting with one of her retired show business friends, she could be on for hours. Right now, a walk would do me good.

I grabbed the sandwich as I passed. Tuna fish. I hate tuna fish. The kitchen knows I hate tuna fish. I left through the central business office, chomping on my sandwich, folder of checks tucked under my arm. Our guests must hate tuna fish, too, if this was the leftovers from today's lunch offerings.

Heads were down, phones were ringing, and cigarette smoke filled the air. At least this room was moderately cool: the fan actually worked.

"I'm so sorry, but we have no availability that week," the reservations clerk said as she lit another cigarette. I don't think I've ever passed her desk when she hasn't had one on the go. "We have space the following week, in one of our best rooms, if that would suit."

All of our rooms are "one of our best."

"Yes, Mrs. Johnstone," another woman was saying. "You need to reserve a table for the evening entertainment. It's very popular, and guests come from resorts all over this part of New York. We do have a few good seats available for this evening. Shall I put you down for two?"

The business office opens onto a dark hallway. To my left there were more offices and the kitchens, and a few steps to my right, a door tucked unobtrusively under the wide, sweeping staircase that led directly into the lobby.

It was a Wednesday afternoon, so not many guests were arriving, and no one was checking out. The receptionist was leaning against a wall, studying her nails. She leapt to attention when she saw me, as well she should. I gave her a glare of disapproval and hoped that would frighten her into sharpening up. It was her first summer with us, and early in the season. She wouldn't yet know that my glare is far worse than my actions. I'll do just about anything to avoid firing someone. I leave that up to the department heads, coward that I am. The only time I've personally fired anyone was when a cocky young waiter from Westchester came to work so drunk he threw up down the front of the Christian Dior day dress worn by one of the lakefront-cabin guests as the lady was enjoying her breakfast.

Fans were swirling slowly in the lobby, and a wave of sticky heat hit me as the bellboy—handsome in his red-and-blue jacket with big gold buttons, and on the breast pocket the Haggerman's logo of two pine trees forming an *H* silhouetted against an orange sun rising over the lake—leapt to attention to hold the door open for me.

Heat was good. Anything that had the residents of New York City fleeing their sweltering apartments for the forested hills and cool blue lakes of the Catskills was good.

The main building is surrounded on two sides by a spacious veranda of wide golden wooden planks, white railings and pillars, and flower boxes overflowing with geraniums and cascading ivy. A row of slatted-wood rocking chairs lines the walls, and much of the space is dotted with small tables and chairs where guests can relax and enjoy the view, have a drink, or meet with their friends. The regular four o'clock duplicate bridge tournament was getting started.

I skipped down the steps and headed for the lakefront path. Laughing, splashing children filled the pool while not-very-watchful mothers in giant sun hats relaxed on lounge chairs, smoking and reading or gossiping while sipping iced tea or cocktails. Velvet stood on the beach, watching Randy give swimming lessons to a group of women. These women were mostly elderly and having a great time, laughing and splashing with as much enthusiasm as the children in the pool, their brightly colored swim caps bobbing above the surface of the water. Farther out in the lake, teenagers dived off the floating platform into the cool water, orange paddleboats skimmed across the surface of the lake, and a rowboat took guests out to try to catch some fish. A game was ending on the handball court, and a doubles tennis match was underway on that court while two elderly men watched with half their attention and argued politics with the other half. Several of the cabins lining the lake had beach towels and wet bathing suits draped over porch railings to dry in the sun.

The well-maintained public path curves along the western shore of Delayed Lake, ending at the line of trees protecting guests from views of the boathouse, service dock, and equipment and maintenance sheds. From there, I turned into the narrower, overgrown walkway that heads uphill, skirting the woods, toward some of the staff dormitories and more equipment sheds. Olivia and I live in a small house at the rear of the property, set well back from the lake in a patch of thick woods. It's quiet and secluded, and even at the busiest times I can sit on the front porch during the evening with the hope of not being disturbed. Unfortunately, it's necessary to have a telephone in the house, and I am often disturbed by one crisis or another.

As I turned up our small private path I heard a rustle in the undergrowth. Far too large to be a rabbit or a squirrel. "Hello?" I said.

A man popped out from behind a pine tree. He was in his sixties, small and thin, a couple of strands of greasy hair plastered to his scalp with copious amounts of hair oil. He held his hat in one hand and a cane in the other, and his eyes darted nervously about. A Brownie camera hung around his neck. He gave me a weak smile. "So sorry. I hope I didn't frighten you."

I didn't recognize him, but that didn't mean anything. I work largely behind the scenes, and so many people come and go at Haggerman's I can't be expected to remember them all. "Can I help you with something, sir?"

"No. No. Nothing at all. Just out for a stroll. Lovely day." He didn't look at me. His eyes kept flicking toward the front porch of my house. There was something almost feral about him, and the hairs on the back of my neck started to rise.

"This area is off-limits to guests. Didn't you see the signs?"

"Signs? No. I didn't see any signs. So sorry. I'll be off now." He threw one last glance at the house before scurrying away.

I watched him go, gave my head a shake, and climbed the steps.

"Only me," I called as I came in through the screen door.

My mother was stretched out on the sofa, feet up, drink at hand, flipping through *Life* magazine. She gave me a warm smile.

I nodded to the black telephone on the piecrust table near the kitchen. "I tried to call, but the phone was busy."

"I've been on the line with darling Geraldine. Poor dear. She's not doing very well."

I didn't know anyone named Geraldine, but that didn't matter. I didn't know most of the people my mother talked about.

A squat, round English bulldog waddled out of the kitchen to greet me, spreading drool everywhere he went. I bent over and gave him a scratch between the little brown ears on his brown-and-white head.

"Why's Winston here?" I asked.

"I have absolutely no idea," Olivia said. "Why is Winston anywhere? I went out for a walk after lunch, and when I got home I found him on the porch waiting for me."

"I don't like the idea of him running freely around the property. Not all people are dog lovers."

"He's harmless," my mother said.

I suppressed a sigh. We'd discussed this before, more than once. The bulldog isn't supposed to have the run of the property, but his owner, Olivia's sister, Tatiana, doesn't believe dogs should be confined, so she lets him pretty much go where he wants, when he wants. She'd always wanted a dog, but a tiny apartment above a corner store in Brooklyn isn't the best place to keep an exuberant animal. Not that *exuberant* is the word I'd ever use to describe the quiet, slow-moving Winston. I don't quite know where Winston came from, but when Aunt Tatiana stepped off the train that first day, come to run the housekeeping department at her sister's resort, the short, squat, crinkly-faced dog got off with her.

"As I was returning from my walk, I ran into a most interesting gentleman," Olivia said. "He's taken a cabin until the end of July. We had a nice chat on his porch."

"How interesting?" I asked.

"Rest assured, he was not interesting enough to be husband-number-four material, dear. He's here by himself, which is unusual, but he's wanting privacy and peace. I'm happy to grant him that, and I left him to it."

"Speaking of men . . . A man was outside just now," I said. "Behaving rather strangely."

My mother's eyes narrowed. "What did he look like?"

"Small, weaselly, greasy. Early to midsixties, at a guess. Walks with a cane."

"Not my new friend, who's tall and distinguished-looking. The man you saw sounds like Louis."

"Louis?"

"Louis Frandenhelm. Frandeheim? Something like that. He waylaid me—that's the only word I can think of—when I was having my walk. Overly enthusiastic followers are, of course"—she patted her hair modestly—"one of the burdens of fame. Louis told me he's with his sister and her family for two weeks, and it was his suggestion they come to Haggerman's this year, specifically hoping to meet me. He then regaled me with a comprehensive list of all the Broadway shows and Hollywood movies I've been in. He has, according to him, seen every one. I was only able to escape his . . . outpouring of adoration by joining a group of ladies also out for a stroll."

"I'll tell security to keep an eye out. We can ask him to leave if he's bothering you."

She waved her hand in the air. "He's harmless."

"I wouldn't be so sure."

"After all these years, I have an instinct for the dangerous ones. Now what brings you here in the middle of the day, Elizabeth?"

I wasn't as confident as my mother about the "dangerous

ones." I made a mental note to have a word with the security guards. "I've brought some checks for you to sign." I put the folder on the dining room table. "And to tell you that you need to make nice with the Carletons."

She swung her legs to the floor and stood in one smooth liquid movement. A flash of pain crossed her face. I pretended, as I always did, not to notice. Olivia pretended, as she always did, that it hadn't happened.

Her figure is one a woman half her age would envy—come to think of it, I'm half her age and I envy it. She's graced with the perfect dancer's body: tall, lean, and trim, topped with a long neck, pointed chin, sculpted cheekbones. Her lips are plump and her eyes so dark they're almost black. Her flawless pale skin's beginning to show a few signs of age around the eyes and the corners of the mouth, and these days her thick black hair owes more to the skill of her hairdresser than to her (supposedly) aristocratic Russian ancestors.

I, on the other hand, do not take after my mother's family but my father's Irish peasant forebears. People sometimes tell me I'm cute: curly red hair, green eyes, masses of cursed freckles, of average height, with a tendency to put on weight if I'm not careful.

"Them again," Olivia said, referring to the Carletons, not the checks. Although she might have been meaning the checks. "What a bother."

"Them again. They came last year. That means they're regulars, and they need to be soothed. A squirrel got onto their window ledge, and they say it was a rat."

My mother snorted. "Stuff and nonsense. They're from New York City. They should know a rat when they see one."

"This year they brought another couple with them. All the more reason to keep them happy."

"I'll drop into the cocktail hour and sit at their table. The Carletons are always quick to attend anything at which drinks are being served." She settled herself at the table, Winston curled up at her feet, and I opened the folder, uncapped my pen, and handed it to her. She let out a mighty sigh. "I find this business of paying bills so tedious."

"Which," I said, "is why I collect the bills, prepare all the accounts, write the checks, and all you have to do is sign them."

"Why don't you sign them?" she said, not for the first time.

"Because I don't own Haggerman's Catskills Resort, Olivia," I replied, not for the first time. "You do."

"If there's a check in there with my name on it, add an extra zero while you're at it." The screen door squeaked, and Aunt Tatiana came in without bothering to knock. Winston stretched every muscle in his body and slowly rose to greet her. "I was wondering where you got to," she said to the dog.

"You'll have to wait for that check," I said. "You're not threatening to foreclose or take us to court." A bit of an exaggeration; we were on track to break even and perhaps make a small profit this summer. But I must never forget that *on track* is a nebulous term. The hotel business is a tough one, and seasonal resorts even harder to keep profitable. A couple of bad days over the summer and we'd be set back irreparably.

"There's an idea." Tatiana coughed and took a drag of her cigarette at the same time. Winston settled himself at her feet.

I flipped the pages, and Olivia scrawled her signature across the checks: a giant *O* followed by a wiggly line that was supposed to represent Petrovia. The *O*, not many people knew, stood for Olga, which is her name. Not Olivia, which is what she calls herself onstage and off. These days, far more off than on.

She didn't bother to read what she was signing, and I let out a sigh. I'd tried to teach her to at least keep an eye on the business affairs, but she had no interest. My mother had been raised to believe a properly behaved woman controlled her household budget but otherwise left all financial matters to her husband.

Which—I could point out until the cows came home but why bother—is why she's here, trying to make a go of a midsize Catskills resort and not living in an apartment overlooking Central Park and being feted by the Broadway and Hollywood elite.

At last she reached the bottom of the pile, recapped the pen, and handed it to me. "There. Are you happy?"

"Ecstatically so." I closed the folder and scooped it up. "For this afternoon anyway. I want these to get into town first thing in the morning for the early mail." I turned to my aunt. "Everything okay in housekeeping?"

"Why would it not be?" she said.

"Just checking."

"If things were not okay, as you say, then I would tell you, *lastachka*."

I grinned at her. My aunt has always called me her little swallow. "That's what I like to hear."

"I heard some talk earlier, O," Tatiana said. "People are talking about that comedian from New York. They are saying they won't allow their daughters to attend."

Tatiana refused to use her sister's stage name; she thought it an insult to their parents. My mother refused to react to her birth name; she thought it too common, not to mention too Russian. So they compromised, and most of the time Tatiana simply called her O.

"Maybe booking him wasn't a good idea," I said. "Not if people are going to be offended."

"One thing you need to learn about show business, Elizabeth," Olivia said, "is that people love to be offended. Gives them something to get excited about. They might not let their daughters go to the show, but you can be sure they'll be there themselves. All ready and eager to be shocked—*shocked!*—and offended. I've asked Rosemary to print a sign to put by the ballroom entrance saying the show is not recommended for everyone."

"That'll have them breaking down the doors," Aunt Tatiana said. "Come, Winston. Time to go home." She clicked her fingers.

Winston yawned. I gave him a tiny nudge with my toe. He groaned, stretched, stood up, and waddled after Tatiana.

"It's almost five o'clock," Olivia said. "If I'm going to soothe the ruffled feelings of the Carletons, I'll have to dress appropriately."

Somedays Olivia could dress as though it were a costume change between scenes. Sometimes it could take an hour or more. Cocktail hour begins at six, and we have a strict dress code at Haggerman's. Women are required to wear dresses and men suits in the evenings.

I picked up the folder containing the checks. "I'll get these to the post drop now so George can take them into town first thing tomorrow. I'll pop into the kitchen and check on dinner preparation, and then I need to come back here and rest. I was up early, and I want to catch that comedian you arranged. If he really does offend anyone, I need to know. Do you want me to get the kitchen to send you something?"

"I'll eat at the cocktail hour. That will give me something to do while Mrs. Carleton drones on and pretends not
to see her husband constantly popping up and down to get
a refill of his whiskey glass. I think the purple satin would
be suitable for this evening, don't you, Elizabeth?" She
went into her bedroom without waiting for me to reply.

Chapter 3

IT WAS AFTER SIX BY THE TIME I LEFT THE MAIN BUILDING.
One of my responsibilities here is to listen to my department heads complain. The delivery truck wouldn't start, and George, from maintenance, made sure I was aware that the American vehicle industry had let standards slip since the war. Not one but two gardeners had quit this morning, lured away by nearby Kennelwood Hotel, and Mario, the head groundskeeper, told me we needed to pay more to get and keep qualified staff. We didn't need qualified gardeners, I told him. We needed someone to cut the lawn and dig up weeds. Wasn't that what local kids were for?

In the kitchen, I found that my threats to the delinquent supplier having failed, a big meat order hadn't arrived.

"We can't not have roast beef on tomorrow's menu," the head chef wailed.

Rosemary Sullivan, who managed food service and restaurant staff other than the saladman, the chef, and their helpers, rolled her eyes at me from behind his back. Our head chef was notoriously bad-tempered. When he wasn't working he always seemed as gentle as a pussycat. I assumed he put on the temperamental-chef act because he thought it was expected of him.

"Chef Leonardo," I said, "I know you'll do your absolute best with what's provided. First thing tomorrow, I'll call them again and threaten to change butchers if your order isn't here by noon."

He huffed and turned quickly around, almost colliding with a dishwasher passing with a load of pots. Chef Leonardo—real name Leon Lebowski—threw up his hands and began berating the boy. Although he wasn't really a boy. Late twenties, perhaps, small and nervous, with eyes as frightened as a rabbit cornered by Winston. The poor dishwasher looked as though he was about to burst into tears, and his entire body trembled. The pile of pots tottered dangerously.

Rosemary grabbed one off the top. "You're carrying too much, Francis. I've told you to be careful. Don't just stand there, get these out of the way."

He bolted beneath his stack of wavering pots.

"I'll get out of your hair," I said. "Looks like everything's under control."

"Ha!" Chef Leonardo roared. "Onions! Who has the onions?"

The kitchen was in full chaos mode. Dinner preparation for 350 famished guests plus another meal for live-in staff was underway, the extra desserts that would be provided at the buffet served during the late-night entertainment were being assembled, and finishing touches were being put on the canapés for the cocktail party.

Rosemary put the dirty pot on the counter, and she and I slipped into the empty dining room to finish talking.

A group of waiters came in, heading for the kitchen to get their evening's instructions. Several of them nodded politely to us and mumbled, "Good evening, Miss Sullivan, Mrs. Grady." One, a tall young man in his early twenties, face all sharp angles and deep-set eyes, gave me an insolent wink. He would have been moderately good-looking if not for the weak chin and curl of his lip. I returned the wink with a glare. He smirked and carried on his way.

The cold canapés had been arranged on serving trays and put into the empty dining room, to get them out of the way in the main kitchen before being ferried upstairs to the small kitchen off the ballroom. "Those look good," I said to Rosemary. "You've gone to a lot of trouble. Thank you for that."

She smiled at me. Rosemary wouldn't have done the cooking, but she prepared the cocktail hour menu in consultation with the saladman and Olivia. Olivia didn't concern herself with what was served at regular meals, but to her a cocktail party was a special thing and the food and drinks had to be special. She wanted food that would be the perfect accompaniment to cocktails, small and compact yet delicious items our guests could serve themselves to munch on before dinner. Silver trays held deviled eggs, smoked oysters, deviled ham on toast, and oranges pierced with toothpicks bristling with olives. A platter held small tomatoes that had been hollowed out, filled with mayonnaise, and a plump shrimp placed on top. Guests would also be offered pigs in blankets, crab cakes, a variety of melons cut into squares and skewered, an overflowing pickle tray, and celery sticks stuffed with the newest thing in American food: Cheez Whiz. The centerpiece was a fresh pineapple with perfectly cut squares of yellow and orange cheese attached to it with more skewers.

At Haggerman's, as at all the Catskills resorts, food was included in the weekly rate. Our guests were determined to get their money's worth, and we were determined no one would have cause to complain they were ever hungry.

"I'm hoping to get home and put my feet up," I said. "I'd better get going before another disaster strikes."

At that moment a man's shout came from the kitchen. "Francis, watch out!" followed by the sounds of crashing pots, shattering china and glassware, and a lot of swearing.

"Dishwasher not working out so well?" I said to Rosemary.

She sighed. "That's an understatement. Francis Monahan. He's a local boy and, dare I say, not terribly bright. Yesterday he dropped a tray containing a room-service order he was delivering to a cabin, and he fled without so much as apologizing or cleaning up, leaving the guest standing in the doorway wondering what was going on. Francis said he felt sick, and he had to go home. He works hard and he means well, and I really, really would hate it if I had to let him go."

"Do what you have to," I said.

Two waiters ran out of the kitchen, laughing, slapping each other on the back. "Oh boy! You've got a heck of a mess in there, Miss Sullivan."

"Then get back in there and help clean it up!" Rosemary yelled.

I made my escape before anything else could go wrong. The dining room was being laid for dinner. The waiters were all boys, mostly college students from the city mixed with a handful of locals who'd worked here for a few seasons before being promoted to the big-tip jobs.

I left the dining room and entered the spacious lobby. The long mahogany reception counter filled one side of the room; numbered pigeonholes dotted the wall behind it. The carpeting was brown, and chairs and sofas upholstered in shades of oranges and browns were strategically placed around low tables to allow for conversation. The front wall was mostly glass, giving a magnificent view over the curving driveway, across the lawn and flower beds, past the pool, and to the beach and the lake beyond. On the far side of the reception counter, a wide staircase with a deep red carpet and imitation white marble banisters curved up to the second floor, where the main ballroom was located.

Guests were streaming in for the cocktail party. Everyone was dressed to the nines, chatting excitedly. Jewelry, both genuine and costume, flashed. The scent of tobacco, perfume, aftershave, and far too much hair spray filled the air.

I nodded politely to our guests, wished them all a good evening, and walked rapidly through the lobby. The bellhop opened the door for me with the slightest of polite bows, and I stepped outside.

On the veranda, the bridge players were packing up and others were taking their places for the regular six thirty canasta game. Children were being called out of the lake and the pool, while mothers gathered up their beach bags. Paddleboats headed for shore, and rowboats carried fishermen out to try their luck. At the tennis courts an intense game was underway by four women in their seventies who didn't let age dampen their enthusiasm for the game. Two elderly men had set up a chessboard on a bench next to the court.

"I tell you, Morty, McCarthy's on to something." The player moved his knight as I passed.

"Reds under the beds. You're a bunch of frightened children," his partner growled. His bishop slid across the board.

"People like you are getting soft. You've forgotten how dangerous they can be. My brother's grandson's in Korea."

"This isn't Korea, this is America, and in America McCarthy's more dangerous than any communist. Check."

"And checkmate to you." The first man swept the white king off the board with a chuckle of triumph, while on the tennis court the women shook hands over the net.

I walked down the lakefront path, heading for home. Six thirty in New York State in late June meant it was still daylight, but some of the heat of the day had passed, and the air was clear and fresh. I heard children playing on the swings, and mothers calling them in to get ready for dinner. A group of preteen girls, bare arms and bare legs, screaming with laughter, ran past me, and a handful of older couples were enjoying a stroll before dinner. Porch swings squeaked, and screen doors slammed.

Where the public path ended, a man stood at the edge of the lake watching the small waves wash over the rocks and gravel. He was nicely dressed in a dark suit, and there was something about the way he stood, so quiet and so still, that had me stopping to watch him for a moment. The end of his cigarette glowed in the shadows cast by the big willow he stood beneath. Aware I was intruding on his privacy, I stepped back. A branch cracked under my foot, and the man swung swiftly around; his shoulders snapped to attention, and his hands tightened at his sides. His eyes were sharp and fully focused on me.

"Sorry to bother you," I said. "I'm Elizabeth Grady, the resort manager. I hope everything's okay?"

His face relaxed, and some of the tension left his body. He took the cigarette out of his mouth and gave me a polite smile. "Perfectly okay, thank you." He was tall and lean, in his early fifties, perhaps, with thick silver hair slicked to one side, a neatly groomed black-and-silver mustache, and startling blue eyes under black-framed glasses. "I'm enjoying the evening. The nicest time of day, I've always found. So peaceful and so quiet."

Behind us a teenage girl screamed in fake fear, and strong, young footsteps crashed through the trees.

The edges of the man's mouth turned up. "Some of the time, anyway. This is a beautiful place you have here."

"We think so. Will you be staying with us for long, sir?"

He breathed out smoke. "I've taken cabin nineteen until the end of July. Five weeks."

"I'll leave you to it," I said. "Good evening."

"Good evening, Miss Grady."

Chapter 4

WHEN I GOT HOME, OLIVIA HAD LEFT FOR THE COCKTAIL reception. I phoned the kitchen to ask them to send me dinner at eight fifteen, kicked off my shoes, and pulled off my girdle and stockings, and then I lay down on the couch and propped pillows behind me, intending to close my eyes for a blissful hour.

I was woken by loud banging. I groaned, called, "Be right there," and rolled off the couch.

Francis, the dishwasher, stood at the screen door, peering in, his face pink with shyness. I held the door for him, and he carried in a tray containing a mug of coffee, cutlery and a pressed white napkin, and a dish covered with a silver cloche.

"Thanks, you can put it on the table."

He did so, and then he backed out of the room. He caught sight of my undergarments, tossed on the floor by the sofa, and the pink face turned into a furious red. He left without having said a word. I lifted the cloche to see what they'd sent me. Fish in white sauce. I hate fish.

Outside, a strong young voice said, "Hey, Francis, I hope you're not sneaking around, peeping into windows. I wouldn't want to have to report you." A burst of male laughter and all was quiet again.

I ate my dinner quickly and then went into the bedroom to get changed. If we had a dress code for the guests, I had to abide by it. I'd bought a new dress for this season. It was a soft green that, I hoped, went some way toward taking the red out of my hair, with a tight bodice, thin straps, and a swing skirt that flared around my knees. I had a quick bath and tried to rearrange my hair, cursing as always at my frizzy curls. I'd recently had it done in a poodle cut, gathered at the sides and swept up into a roll above my forehead, like Lucille Ball. It looked better on Miss Ball than it ever did on me, but at least it was fashionable. I added a touch of pink lipstick and some rouge to my lips and face.

The screen door squeaked and then slammed. "Is that you, Olivia?" I called.

"Home from doing my duty. My goodness but the Carletons are bores. The both of them."

"Olivia, please remember the walls of this house are not soundproof."

"Oh, good, dinner's been brought up. So thoughtful of you. I didn't have anything at the party. I had a couple of cocktails, though. The new bartender is quite good, and he knows how to make all the newest drinks." The plate clattered as the cloche was lifted. "You ate it."

"Yes, I ate it. It was my dinner, not yours." I wiggled my hips into the hated girdle, sat on the edge of the bed to pull on my stockings and clip them to the garters, and then I got my dress out of the closet and slipped it on over my head and zipped it up. Lastly, I opened my tiny jewelry box. My wedding ring lay inside, framed by the green velvet lining. I reached out and picked it up. I rubbed the soft gold between my fingers and briefly thought of what had never been. I put the ring back and selected a pair of earrings containing stones of green glass and a matching necklace and put them on. I then slammed the lid on the jewelry box, hoping to trap the unwelcome memories inside. Last of all, I slipped my feet into black pumps with a thin strap and one-inch heels. I studied myself in the mirror.

Not a Broadway star, but I'd do.

I went into the living room to join the real Broadway star.

Olivia wore a dress I hadn't seen before. It had a cap-sleeved black lace top that fell to the top of her breasts where it joined luxurious purple satin. The dress clung to every angle of her body down to her hips, and from there it flared to the floor. Black gloves reached above her elbows, and the tips of open-toed black shoes peeked from beneath the hem of the dress. Her earrings and necklace were not made of gold and diamonds, but they'd fool anyone who wasn't a jeweler. She'd styled her hair into a loose black chignon, and her makeup was heavy and dramatic, her eyes rimmed with kohl, her mouth a deep red slash. She was overdressed for cocktail hour, but Olivia believed in making an impression everywhere she went. She certainly would have this evening.

"You look," I said, "absolutely amazing."

"I know," she replied. Modesty isn't one of my mother's virtues. "Do you think that particular shade of green is entirely suitable for your distinctive coloring, dear?"

"Yes, I do. Which is why I bought this dress. Velvet helped me pick it out."

"It'll do, then." My mother trusts my friend's taste better than she does mine. It doesn't bother me. I trust Velvet's taste better than I do mine.

"It's quarter to nine," I said. "The cocktail reception ended at seven fifteen and you didn't go to dinner. Where have you been all this time?"

"I'd like to say I met a handsome young man and he whisked me, along with a plate of oysters and a bottle of champagne, to his cabin, but sadly, I cannot. I paid a call on Tatiana."

"Are you coming to see the show?"

"No. I feel like an early night." The lines of pain etched into her face were prominent tonight, and the faint smell of Aunt Tatiana's special muscle cream mingled with my mother's perfume.

"I'll see you tomorrow, then," I said. "I hope this comedian is as good as you say he is."

"As good as I've been told," Olivia corrected me. "I've never seen him perform."

Y

HE WAS GOOD. HE WAS VERY GOOD. A LOT OF FAMILIES brought their teenage children to the early show, so Charlie Simmonds kept it clean.

The evening opened, as it usually did, with music and dancing. When I arrived, the seven-piece orchestra—piano, bass, drums, trumpet, alto and tenor saxophones, and trombone—had taken their place onstage. This was our house band that worked here throughout the summer. They were all men, dressed in black suits, white shirts, and black bow ties. On occasion, a female singer would come up from the city to join them.

The bandleader welcomed everyone to Haggerman's Catskills Resort and then, without further ado, they struck up the first tune: "Dancing in the Dark" by Arthur Schwartz for a fairly gentle foxtrot. Couples took to the floor.

A few younger members of the staff, dressed in black slacks or skirts and white shirts or blouses, circulated around the room. They weren't here to wait tables but to dance with the guests who didn't have a partner. Widowed women who'd come to Haggerman's with their families and friends, and what's known in the Catskills as "weekday widows": women here for a good part of the summer with their children, while their husbands work in the city and come up for the weekends or their week of vacation. Some of the women who weren't widowed simply couldn't persuade their husbands to dance. The girls would dance with those men whose wives couldn't or who wanted a lively young partner for one or two turns around the dance floor.

I stood at the back of the room, watching. The ballroom was full, every seat taken. Rows of round tables covered in white cloths circled around the shiny wooden dance floor in front of the stage. The big chandelier hanging from the ceiling threw sparks of light on the women's jewels and the sequins in their dresses. The line in front of the bar at the back of the room was long.

Rosemary came out of the swinging doors leading to the upstairs kitchen, a full silver ice bucket balanced in her arms. She nodded politely to the row of guests lined up at the bar as the two bartenders scooped ice, flipped bottles, and turned the mixing of cocktails into performance art. "You could use another bartender, Elizabeth."

"I know, Rosemary, I know. And I know you'd do as good a job as either of them."

"Better."

"Probably. But Olivia insists it isn't proper to have women tending bar, and she is the boss, after all."

I'd met Rosemary Sullivan years ago when she'd been working as a short-order cook at a diner in Manhattan, which was a favorite late-night, after-show stop for the Broadway elite and their hangers-on. She'd dreamed of being a chef in a fine-dining restaurant, but despite her drive, her qualifications, her experience, and her work ethic, she couldn't get a position at a place like that to do more than chop vegetables. Women cooked; men were chefs. And bartenders.

It was unfair, but that was the way it was, and Rosemary gave up the dream and reinvented herself as a restaurant manager. When I decided to join Olivia in her new venture, I'd persuaded Rosemary to come and work for us.

She gave me a wry grin and took her ice bucket behind the bar.

Randy, dressed in a pale gray suit, white shirt, and dark tie, danced past, partnering a young teen girl who was all big feet, ears, and pink embarrassment.

Scion of a blue-blood Boston family, Randy had scandalized his parents by going into the movies rather than following his father into the family law firm. Unfortunately for Randy, his acting skills were nonexistent. Only because of his blond all-American good looks, plus his family connections, he'd landed roles in a few Esther Williams movies. I don't know quite what happened, but he ended up back in Manhattan, drifting around the outskirts of my mother's circle. He was in his late thirties, but his indulgent grandmother still supported him financially. He didn't need this job, but he did need something to do with his life, and I suppose teaching swimming to the children of rich women impressed with his "aquatic movie star" credentials during the day and dancing with them in the evening beat hanging around a scalding-hot apartment in the city waiting for his agent to call.

"Full house," Velvet said to me.

"That's what we like to see."

Randy and his partner swung—her awkwardly, him smoothly—past us, and Velvet gave her head a shake. "What a show-off he is. Do you think he wore that suit so no one would mistake him for a common employee?"

"Probably."

Randy's light-colored suit did set him apart from the rest of the staff, who were expected to wear black and white.

"What have you got there?" I asked.

Velvet held a frothy pale pink concoction served in a martini glass accompanied by three bright green maraschino cherries on a stick.

"This, my *darrrr-ling*," she drawled, "is called a Pink Squirrel. Most delicious. I must tell the bartender so. He's anxious to try out all the popular new things, and I'm confident this will be an *eeee-normous* hit." She dropped back to her regular voice. "Any testing of cocktails you need done, Elizabeth, I'm your girl."

"I might try one myself later. Are you here to dance?"

"Not if I can help it. My toes still haven't recovered from that partner I had last week. I'm here to look good. Like it?" She tilted her head, half turned, and thrust out one hip.

"I do," I said.

Like the cocktail, her dress was a frothy pink concoction of polka dots draped over layers of pink tulle, with a deep square neckline and a huge dark red bow pinned to a thin shoulder strap. Her long blond hair was arranged to fall over her right shoulder in a series of golden waves, and her lipstick matched the bow on her dress. Open-toed silver dance shoes were on her feet.

Unlike the rest of the staff, as department heads, Randy and Velvet were allowed to wear outfits of their choice to social events.

"How was the nature walk?" I asked.

"Great. I enjoyed it. Some of the older kids pretended to be bored, but the younger ones liked it. They were disappointed we didn't see a wolf or a bear. I think we should put it on the regular activity schedule and aim it at parents as well as children. Most New Yorkers, like me, wouldn't know a pine tree from a squirrel."

"A squirrel moves," I said.

Velvet slapped her forehead with her free hand. "So that's it!"

A hugely overweight man, beads of sweat popping out all over his bald head, tentatively approached us. He bowed to Velvet. "May I have the honor of this dance?"

"Mr. Osmond, it would be my absolute pleasure." She shoved her glass into my hand. "Mind this for me, please, Mrs. Grady."

I don't dance with the guests. I'm tone-deaf and I have two left feet, so if anyone asks me for a dance, I politely demure and beckon one of the staff to take my place.

The evening went off without a hitch, leaving me without much to do, which is always good. Not long after I arrived, Olivia's "admirer" Louis came in. He wandered around the room, peering myopically at everyone. He spoke briefly to a solidly built woman about his age but didn't take a seat at her table. He shook his head and left, disappointment written all over his face. He didn't return.

After forty-five minutes of music and dancing, Velvet, armed with a second (or was it her third) Pink Squirrel, took the stage. She clapped her hands prettily in front of her while still holding the cocktail glass and indicated to the audience they should do so as well.

Applauding heartily, people took their seats. Ties were loosened, shoes kicked off, and cigarettes lit.

"The Haggerman's Catskills Resort Orchestra is going to take a much-needed break." Velvet spoke into the bandleader's microphone. "They'll be back later with more great tunes for more dancing."

Someone cheered.

"In fifteen minutes we're proud to present, straight from the comedy clubs of New York City, Mr. Charlie Simmonds."

Someone booed. People laughed.

"Ladies, you have fifteen minutes to freshen up, and gentlemen, you have fifteen minutes to get your lady another cocktail."

This time more than one person cheered, and Velvet lifted her glass.

Chairs scraped the floor, and the rush was on. Women streamed into the hallway, and men headed for the bar. I noticed more than a few Pink Squirrels being ferried to tables.

Velvet gave them the fifteen minutes and then she, this time accompanied by Randy, climbed back onto the stage. The lights were dimmed amid a flutter of fabric and the clanging of jewels and more scraping of chairs as ladies scurried to their tables.

"And now," Randy said, "let's give a big Haggerman's

Catskills Resort greeting to the hottest comedy star in America today, Mr. Charlie Simmonds."

The man himself bounded onto the stage. He shook Randy's hand, hugged Velvet, and then took the microphone off its stand. He took a drag of his cigarette and said, "So, folks, are you having a good time?"

Mr. and Mrs. Brownville and their friends had taken the table front and center. A cloud of cigar and cigarette smoke hung over their heads all evening, and I hadn't seen them dancing once.

It was early enough that some teenagers were still in the audience, sitting with their families. I wasn't worried Charlie would get too daring. Not yet.

I took advantage of the lull at the bar to order something for myself. "You've been busy," I said to the bartender.

"Yes, ma'am, Mrs. Grady." The round-cheeked boy nodded to the jar on the counter, overflowing with coins and even some bills. "Great bunch of big tippers tonight."

"It's early in the season. After they've been here a couple of weeks, some of the guests begin to realize they're spending more money than they'd planned." Food at Haggerman's was part of the rate. Alcoholic drinks were not. "What would you recommend I try?"

"The Pink Squirrels have been popular tonight," he said.

"Maybe something less . . . pink."

"If not pink, why not green? Match your dress. A grasshopper?"

"Perfect."

I accepted the drink and returned to my place by the wall to watch the rest of the show. I couldn't help but notice Mr. Brownville laughing along with everyone else, or that his wife's shoulders shook on occasion.

Charlie Simmonds was a thin, pale man of average

height, with short brown hair and bad teeth, dressed in a nondescript brown suit and shoes that had seen better days. Anyone would pass him on the street without a second glance. I had met him when he arrived at Haggerman's this morning and had frankly been unimpressed. He was soft-spoken, verging on mumbling, and nervous in my not-at-all impressive presence. I'd hired him because of his reputation, and tonight I was not disappointed. Simply put, the man came alive onstage. His voice strengthened, he brimmed with confidence, and he seemed to physically grow as he paced the boards, gripping the microphone in one hand and his cigarette in the other. He caught the audience's attention immediately, and aside from gales of laughter, no one made a sound. Even the bartenders, temporarily left with nothing to do, watched.

His act lasted for twenty minutes, and then he bowed deeply to a pretty girl sitting with her family at a front table, thanked the audience, accepted enthusiastic applause, said he'd be back later, and left the stage. The silence broke as people turned to their neighbors, or pushed back their chairs.

The audience didn't completely turn over between one set and the next, but most of the older couples left when Charlie finished, as did the families with children.

The orchestra took to the stage again. This time the dance tunes were faster, more energetic. Some swing for the younger people, mixed in with foxtrots for the more sedate dancers. I checked my watch. At ten thirty the desserts would be brought out, and Charlie would retake the stage at eleven.

"Single-man alert," Velvet whispered into my ear.

I was standing at the back of the room, watching as

Randy tried to convince an elderly gentleman that perhaps he should take a break. The man had obviously had more than a few drinks before the dance began and had been a regular figure at the bar since it opened. When I'd seen him stumble for the second time, kept upright only by the quick actions of the dancers near him, I'd interrupted Randy's dance and asked him to see to it. I'd be more than happy to throw out the drunk by the ear myself, and I was certainly capable of it, but I knew from experience some men can get even more argumentative when a woman tries to tell them what to do.

"A *young* single man," Velvet added.

Randy took one of the drunk's arms, an elderly woman took the other, and they maneuvered their way out of the hall, keeping to the walls so as not to interfere with the dancers.

Good job, Randy, I thought. That settled, I turned to Velvet. "Where?"

A single man. A *young* single man not employed by one of the hotels was as rare a sighting in the Catskills as a crocodile in Delayed Lake.

"At the bar. Good gray suit."

I looked. The man in question had his back to us as he waited his turn to be served. He was about six feet tall, with wide shoulders and a slim waist, black hair clipped short. He stepped forward to place his order, put money on the counter, accepted his drink, and turned. I caught a glimpse of thickly lashed hazel eyes, strong cheekbones, and a freshly shaven chin before I looked quickly away. I guessed he was in his early thirties.

"How do you know he's single?" I said to Velvet. "His wife might be sick, or she doesn't like to dance."

"No wedding ring."

"Lots of married men don't wear a wedding ring."

"He's the sort who would. Oh, he's coming this way. Try not to stare."

"I'm not the one staring, Velvet."

"Good evening," said a deep voice in an Upstate New York accent. He'd declined a fancy cocktail in favor of a glass of beer.

"Good evening," Velvet said.

"Having a good time?" I asked.

"Yeah," he said. "I'm not much of a dancer, though. I'm looking forward to hearing your comedian."

"Are you staying at Haggerman's?" Velvet asked.

"No. I'm . . . at Kennelwood."

Our main competition.

"A word to the wise," Velvet said. "Shake out your pillow every night."

"Velvet!"

"What?" she said, all wide-eyed innocence. "I'm not saying they have bedbugs, but I've heard stories."

He roared with laughter. "I'll keep that in mind, thanks."

"Excuse me," said a thin wavering voice. "May I have the honor of this dance, Miss McNally?" A gentlemen, well into his ninth decade, all of five feet five and 110 pounds, blinked watery eyes at Velvet.

"Mr. Moretti! It would be my absolute pleasure," Velvet declared as though a turn around the dance floor with this man was her life's ambition. "You're sure Mrs. Moretti doesn't mind?" she said as she linked her arm through his and led him away. "We wouldn't want to make her too dreadfully jealous now."

An equally elderly, equally tiny woman, almost weighted

down by her jewels and the sequins on her dress, smiled proudly around the cigarette holder clenched in her yellow teeth as she watched them take their places on the floor.

"You have good staff," the beer drinker said to me.

"Velvet's more a friend than a member of the staff. I didn't get your name."

"Richard."

"Richard Kennelwood, I presume."

He grinned. "I've been made."

"I assume you know who I am."

"Elizabeth Grady, of course. Olivia's daughter."

Kennelwood Hotel was the closest of the big resorts to Haggerman's. They were older than us, bigger than us, grander than us, situated on a bigger lake than us, and attracted better entertainers than us despite Olivia's contacts, because they could pay better.

When Olivia and I arrived last year to take ownership and management of Haggerman's, Kennelwood owner and hotel manager Jerome Kennelwood, son of the founder, came to welcome us to the neighborhood, so to speak. He'd oozed charm, offered us friendly advice, wished us well, and when he left he went straight to his office, where he placed phone calls to all the hotel booking agencies on the East Coast to tell them a place run by two dames—one of them a past-her-prime *dancer*—would never last the first season. He then proceeded to ensure we'd never last the first season by trying to poach our staff. Not by offering them more money but by warning them that if they stayed at Haggerman's, they'd be out of work by the middle of the summer. Unfortunately for Mr. Kennelwood, his head housekeeper, a widowed Russian lady from Brooklyn, was delighted to hear one Mrs. Rostov would be living at Haggerman's and paid a call on Tatiana. Mr. Kennelwood still didn't know we had an inside source at his hotel. I'd called all the hotel booking agencies on the East Coast myself to assure them I was in charge and I knew what I was doing. That might have been a little white lie, but I was determined to fight fire with fire. My department managers were instructed to tell new hires to think very carefully about any approaches they might get from Kennelwood. Last week, over Tatiana's samovar, open-faced rye-bread sandwiches, and homemade Russian tea cakes, her informant told her Mr. Kennelwood had been seriously ill over the winter and his son, Richard, had arrived from the city to take over the day-to-day running of the place.

"Don't," I said to Richard now, "even think about poaching Velvet or anyone else on my staff."

"I won't." The teasing twinkle faded from his eyes. "I'm sorry if my dad hasn't been a good neighbor to you. For him, business is a blood sport. I don't operate that way."

"That's good to hear," I said.

"Doesn't mean we're not in competition. None of us are making a ton of money around here, and we have to watch out for ourselves, but I believe rivals can, and should, work together to the benefit of all parties. I've been hearing a lot about this new comedian you've landed, and I came to see what he's about. Can I get you a drink? Is it Miss or Mrs. Grady?"

"Mrs."

"Does your husband help manage the resort?"

"I'm a widow." I used a tone of voice that meant the topic was not up for discussion. "Now, if you'll excuse me—"

"That drink?"

"I've had enough for tonight, thank you."

"A dance, then?"

"I don't dance when I'm working. Have a nice evening." I walked away, heading for the buffet table to check that it was ready for the desserts to be brought out. I felt Richard Kennelwood's eyes on my back.

He seemed nice; he seemed friendly. His father had also seemed nice and friendly, before trying to destroy us.

Chapter 5

I HAD A QUICK WORD IN VELVET'S EAR AS SHE AND HER newest partner danced past me. "That single man is Jerome Kennelwood's son. Stay away."

"Got it," she said before being whisked across the room.

The windows had been flung open and the fans turned on, but there were too many people in the enclosed hall, and the air was thick with cigarette smoke, alcohol fumes, and perfume too heavily applied. I went outside for a breath of fresh air. The excessive heat of the day had dropped fractionally, and a gentle wind blew off the lake. Lamps lighting the paths and shining above doorways threw a soft yellow glow into the night. The trees on the hills all around us were wrapped in darkness. A young couple walked past, holding hands, and a rowboat headed for the dock, returning from an evening fishing expedition.

I took a deep breath. Helping my mother run a Catskills resort, desperately trying to keep the place profitable, might not have been part of my plans for my life, but I had to admit I was happy here. It was a simple life in a beautiful place, and it suited me. It even suited me—at this point in time, anyway—to live with my mother. We'd never been close, to put it mildly, as I'd been raised by Aunt Tatiana and her late husband, Rudolph. While Olivia danced in pursuit of her dreams of stage and screen glory, Tatiana and Rudolph stayed in Brooklyn, ran their corner store and newsstand, and had loved and looked after me. Uncle Rudolph died a couple of years ago.

A few of the guests also in search of a breath of fresh air slipped out of the building. A dance partner–waiter came onto the veranda with his arm tucked into that of an elderly guest. She wore a straight-lined, calf-length red dress that would have been all the rage in the jazz clubs of the twenties and red elbow-length gloves. The jewels at her ears, throat, and wrists flashed in the lights from above the door.

"Such a lovely party," she said to me. "I'm sorry to leave early, but I'm not quite as young as I once was, and I'm all tuckered out." She walked slowly away, the waiter guiding her. I called good night after them.

A man stepped out of the shadows and climbed the stairs. The white bow tie and heavily starched white shirt under his immaculate black suit shone in the deepening dusk, and his heavy gold cuff links reflected light spilling from the windows.

He nodded to me, said, "Good evening, Miss Grady," and went inside. It was the silver-haired man I'd seen earlier, standing by himself at the edge of the lake, enjoying the silence.

I followed him across the lobby, up the grand staircase, and into the ballroom. The orchestra was having a break, and the lines at the bar and the food table were long. An angel food cake covered with a thick layer of pink icing dotted with maraschino cherries, platters of Rice Krispie squares, and a glistening pineapple upside-down cake were tonight's offerings. More than a few of our guests took a piece of everything on offer. Some helped themselves to more than one piece of each.

Richard Kennelwood leaned against a wall, smoking a cigarette, watching everyone and everything. The silver-haired man went to the bar and walked away with a high-ball glass containing one piece of ice and a splash of amber liquid. He made no move to find a seat.

Once the desserts were decimated, the trays replenished, decimated again, the side plates scraped clean, and the lights lowered, Velvet and Randy took the stage. They introduced Charlie Simmonds again, and once again he bounded onto the stage. Charlie shook Randy's hand, hugged Velvet—taking a bit longer over that than he had the previous time—lit a cigarette, lifted the microphone off its stand, and started to talk.

The Brownville party remained in their seats. Mrs. Brownville sat stiff and disapproving through the whole act, but her husband's shoulders shook with laughter. At one point I saw her turn her head and give him a ferocious glare. His shoulders slumped.

Charlie's act the second time around was slightly more risqué than it had been earlier, and a few of his jokes verged on the bluer side, but nothing I'd consider inappropriate for eleven at night. He was booked here for three days, and I wondered if he was checking out the mood of the room tonight, saving the riskier stuff for later in the week. His routine was very Catskills-centered. He said he'd been brought up in Monticello, not far from here, and had spent his summers working at a resort much like Haggerman's.

Except, according to Charlie, the staff members were a lot funnier and the guests a lot wilder. He even got in a couple of digs at management.

Richard Kennelwood had taken a seat next to a young married couple, and he appeared to be enjoying the show. The silver-haired man in the black suit stood at the back of the room, smoking steadily, laughing occasionally, not speaking to anyone. He finished his drink and did not order another.

"You've been a great audience. I'll see you again tomorrow night!" Charlie bowed deeply, and the guests applauded. He hurried off the stage.

The band resumed their places and immediately started an energetic Lindy Hop. I considered going home to bed but decided another grasshopper would not go amiss. We had some good dancers here, guests as well as staff, and it was fun to watch them going through their moves.

I was getting to the bottom of my drink, and the audience was thinning, when the bandleader thanked everyone for coming and told them they'd be back tomorrow with more great tunes.

Show over, people began gathering their things and getting to their feet. I put my empty glass on a table and went to stand next to the door, watching people file out, chatting happily. I heard more than a few say something along the lines of "great show" or "fun night."

Richard Kennelwood gave me an exaggerated wink as he left. I nodded stiffly, trying not to smile. I hadn't seen the silver-haired man leave. He must have slipped out, as silently as he'd arrived, when the comedy show finished.

Once the last of the lingering guests left, Rosemary helped the bartenders pack up their supplies, and the busboys came in to clean up the dirty dishes and glasses, discarded napkins, and food remains, and to stack chairs and sweep the floor.

One of the workers, I noticed, was Francis Monahan, who'd earlier caused such chaos in the kitchen. He saw me watching him, gave me a shy smile, blushed furiously, and ducked his head. He loaded his tray dangerously high, and as he turned to leave the ballroom, he almost tripped over one of the bartenders, who'd slid quietly up behind him.

"Whoa there, Francis! Watch where you're going," the bartender called. He turned his head and caught the eye of a third worker and smirked. They both laughed heartily.

I considered asking them what they thought they were playing at, but before I could move, Velvet handed me a coupe glass full of dancing bubbles. "You look like you could use this." She had one for herself also.

Busboys and bartenders forgotten, I accepted the champagne with a smile. "I've probably had enough, but thanks." I took a sip and sighed with contentment as the bubbles tickled my throat. "I'd say that went over rather well."

"It did. I overheard one man say to his wife, 'Maybe we should try staying at this place next year, honey.'"

"That's what we want to hear."

I glanced around the almost empty ballroom. Charlie Simmonds had disappeared the moment he stepped off the stage. I was surprised at that; the acts usually like to have a drink after their show, chat to members of the audience, and ask me what I thought of it.

"What did you think of the comedian?" I asked Velvet.

"I haven't laughed so hard in ages," she said. "All the people near me were roaring with laughter. Some people might not have cared for the joke about waiters creeping into the cabins when the housekeeping girls are cleaning them after guests have checked out, though."

"If anyone objected, I'll hear about it soon enough. Everything seems to be under control. We're not needed here. Let's grab a few minutes and go sit by the lake."

"Good idea," Velvet said.

We took our drinks and went outside. Some guests lingered on the veranda, talking; rocking chairs squeaked softly; couples strolled down the paths. Velvet and I turned left onto the lakefront path. We passed the silent and empty tennis and handball courts and the children's playground, the row of guest cabins, and eventually walked through the line of trees separating the public walkways from the working end of the lake. The bright lights of the path fell behind us as I jumped across the small, rocky creek tumbling out of the hills to spill into Delayed Lake. I turned at a low cry to see Velvet behind me, struggling to keep the contents of her glass from spilling as she tried to keep her footing on a wet rock. I grabbed her arm before she fell in, and she gave me an embarrassed shrug. I laughed, and we carried on. The wooden shacks stuffed full of life jackets and fishing equipment were locked, and canoes and rowboats secured to the service dock, rocking gently on the light waves. The paddleboats had been pulled up onto the shore for the night.

I turned at the sound of footsteps behind us to see Randy hurrying to catch up. "Mind if I join you?"

"It's a free country," Velvet said.

"I'll take that as an enthusiastic yes." He stepped between us and linked his arms through ours. "You should be pleased, Elizabeth. I heard nothing but compliments about the evening as the guests were leaving."

"I'll tell Olivia," I said.

A soft woof sounded to our left, and Winston broke out of the trees. He ran up to us and sniffed at our feet, his chubby rump wiggling in delight. Twigs and dead leaves were caught in the short hairs under the dog's belly and behind his ears.

He followed us to the end of the service dock and snuffled around the crumbling old wood as we lowered ourselves onto the planks. I kicked off my shoes and said "Don't look" to Randy, hiked up my skirt, and unfastened my stockings. I then swung my legs over the side of the dock, rearranged my skirt, and dangled my feet in the cool water. Velvet did the same, except she didn't bother to tell Randy not to look before she dropped into a puddle of polka dots and pink tulle.

He sat between us, his knees bent and his arms folded around them. Winston settled on the other side of me and nestled his head into my lap. I stroked his ears with one hand and sipped my drink with the other.

"What's the story with Richard Kennelwood?" Velvet asked.

"Checking out the competition, so he said. He tried to be friendly, but we've been tricked once by his father. I'm not falling for that again."

"Kennelwood?" Randy said. "From the hotel on the lake at the other end of the channel?" He pointed to his left.

"The very one. The son's taken over management. If I see him on the property again, I'll release the hounds."

Winston grunted.

"I thought your mother might come down tonight," Randy said. "But she didn't."

"She went to the cocktail party earlier, and that was enough for one day. Olivia can never simply relax and enjoy herself. Every time she steps out the front door, she's making an appearance, putting on a show for the delight of her public."

"Why do you call her by her name and not 'Mom'?" Randy asked.

"Is that any of your business?" Velvet said sharply.

"Just being friendly. Don't answer if you don't want to, Elizabeth."

"I don't mind," I said. "It's no secret. I was raised mostly by Aunt Tatiana and her husband while Olivia was dancing. Tatiana taught me to call my mother 'Mama,' with a Russian accent, the same as she'd called her mother. When I was ten Olivia suggested I drop the 'Mama.' So I did."

"Is it hard for her, not to be onstage anymore?" Randy asked.

"Hard? Yes, very hard. But it can't have come as a surprise. A dancer doesn't have a long professional life. Olivia doesn't have the temperament to teach dance students or to be the artistic director of a tiny dance company in the suburbs."

"I don't know that I've ever met two more different sisters than Olivia and Tatiana," Randy said.

I chuckled. "No kidding. Tatiana's seven years older. They say their parents were high-ranking aristocrats who got on the bad side of the czar and had to flee Russia with nothing but their lives, but every Russian immigrant I've ever met says something like that. Regardless of their background, their parents came over from Russia dirt poor and worked every minute God gave them. They had no other children, and Tatiana pretty much raised Olivia. One of their neighbors had been a great ballerina before the revolution, or so she claimed anyway, and she introduced Olivia to dance. Tatiana married the son of Russian émigrés, as was expected of her, but Olivia decided that life wasn't for her, and she went into theater. For all their differences, though, they're very close."

I breathed in the air and the silence, and felt as much as I saw Velvet and Randy do the same. A loon called across the lake, and the waxing moon threw rippling rays across the water.

Velvet sucked in the soft night air and spread her arms in front of her. "If I have to work for a living, rather than marry a rich, childless old man who conveniently drops dead on our wedding night, which is my ambition, I couldn't find a better place to work in."

"No," Randy said.

Winston leapt to his feet and began to bark.

I grabbed his collar. "Shush."

He was normally very placid. We couldn't have a dog making a fuss, particularly at night, and potentially frightening or disturbing the guests.

He kept barking and strained against my grip.

"He's sensed something," Velvet said.

Winston wrenched himself out of my hold and bounded away, running back to shore. Instead of quieting down, the barks got louder and more insistent. Reluctantly, I pulled my feet out of the lovely water, stood up, and slipped on my shoes.

"Don't look," I said to Randy once again, as I reached under my dress and stuffed my balled-up stockings into the waistband of my girdle.

"Maybe he's sensed a deer," Randy said.

"It's not a wolf, is it?" Velvet said, also getting up.

"Wolves would never come this close to the buildings," I said. "A duck perhaps. Could be anything. Winston! Winston! Stop that!"

Far from stopping, the barking increased.

"He doesn't usually fuss like that," I said. "We'd better go see what's gotten into him."

My friends and I made our way down the dock. A loud splash sounded to the left as something heavy hit the water.

"That's no duck." I raised my voice and called into the night. "Is everything okay there? Hello? Is someone there? Do you need help?"

"The silly dog's gone into the water," Velvet said. "He's chasing a log."

I could see Winston about five feet from shore, his head up as his thick body sliced through the water, heading for a long black shape floating in front of him. It looked very much like a branch that had fallen from one of the trees lining the shore, but I knew right away it wasn't. Moonlight shone on a flash of white fabric at the back of a neck and one pale hand drifting on the surface of the black water.

"That's not a log. Someone's in the water!" I ran toward the edge of the lake and kicked off my shoes. I realized I was still holding my champagne glass, threw it to one side, and heard it shatter as it hit the ground. I jumped into the lake. Seconds later, two splashes followed in quick succession: Randy and Velvet were behind me. I waded out, fighting the weeds trying to wrap themselves around my legs and the mud sucking at my feet. Winston paddled in circles, still barking. The man in the water was hunched over, face down, arms and legs drifting. I grabbed for him and struggled to flip him over. He moved with the waves but did nothing to help me.

"I've got him," Randy said. "Now!"

We shoved and flipped the man onto his back. Velvet reached us, and together the three of us pushed and pulled the unprotesting weight to shore. Randy and I clambered onto the bank, our feet struggling for purchase, and pulled at the arms while Velvet lifted the legs and Winston swam in excited circles. We dragged the top half of the body out of the water.

I stared into the open, unseeing eyes of the man I'd spoken to by the lake this afternoon, the one who'd stood at the back of the ballroom watching the comedy act. The man from cabin nineteen.

Chapter 6

RANDY DROPPED TO HIS KNEES, TILTED THE MAN'S HEAD back, and lowered his own mouth to the other man's.

"Is he alive?" I asked.

"Don't know," Randy gasped between breaths. "Got to try."

"What are you doing?" Velvet asked.

"A swimmer on a movie set taught me this trick." He took another breath. "I'm breathing for him."

"I'll call for help." I set off through the trees, conscious of my bare feet on the small rocks, broken branches, and dead needles, and my sodden dress clinging to my body. As I waded through the creek, I considered going back for my shoes, but I reached the paved path in not more than a few strides and I broke into a run. Winston dashed past me, enjoying the race.

"Mrs. Grady!" a man called. "Is everything all right?"

I didn't slow. "Perfectly fine. I . . . forgot to feed the dog."

Into the lights of the lakefront path, past the empty dark
courts and the quiet playground, a porch swing squeaked
in the wind, low voices came through an open window, and
the scent of tobacco drifted on the night air. Lights shone
from some of the cabins and rooms in the hotel, but most
windows were dark. I reached the intersection and ran up
the steps into the hotel. Bradley, the night clerk, leapt to his
feet when I came in.

"Mrs. Grady is everything—"

"Find the security guard. Tell him to go to the end of the
lakefront path by the boat shed. Fast!" I reached across the
desk and grabbed the phone. I looked at the clerk, staring
at me openmouthed. "Go!" I said. "Then come straight
back here. Wait! What's the number for the ambulance?"

The emergency numbers were taped to the underside of
the counter next to the phone. I couldn't see them from this
side.

Bradley rattled off the numbers, and I dialed the funeral
home that operated the ambulance service for our area.

"Has a guest taken ill?" Bradley asked me.

"Answering for Jackson Brothers' Funeral Home," a
voice said from the other end of the phone.

I made shooing gestures at the night clerk. I'd have a
word with him in the morning about the meaning of the
words *go* and *fast*. Finally he understood and ran off. I told
the person on the phone what had happened, and he told me
an ambulance would soon be on its way.

"I'll have someone meet them at the main entrance," I
said. "Pull into the unloading circle by the front doors."

I hung up the phone and took a breath. I heard puffing
and looked down. Winston sat at my feet, tail thumping on
the floor, smiling up at me. Winston was most definitely
never, ever allowed into any of the public buildings. Also at

my feet was a puddle of lake water, getting larger as I looked at it. I was suddenly, and unpleasantly, aware that I was soaking wet and freezing.

I glanced around the quiet lobby. I shouldn't leave the desk unattended; people were always wandering in no matter the time of night to report a blocked sink or wanting a glass of milk. I ran around the counter and dug in the drawer for the registration ledger. I opened it to the most recent page and flicked backward, running my finger down the column for room number until I found it. Cabin nineteen. The guest's name, Harold Westenham, was printed in blue ink with a scrawled signature next to it. Number of guests: one. That was unusual. We rarely, if ever, got people coming here on their own. Cabin nineteen was the smallest of the private cabins. It had only two bedrooms and wasn't situated on the lakefront but nestled in the woods not far from the house Olivia and I were occupying. That cabin was usually rented by honeymooners seeking seclusion and privacy.

Someone had to be told that Mr. Westenham was being taken to the hospital. If a guest needed help right now, they'd be out of luck. I hurried toward my office, as Winston trotted happily behind me.

I came to a wet screeching halt. The office was, of course, locked. I keep staff records in there and payment details for our guests. I'd dressed for a party tonight and didn't have the jangling set of keys tied to my belt that I usually carry around on me.

I hesitated. *Wait here for the ambulance or run up to the house for my keys?* I could phone and try to get Olivia, but if she'd gone to bed she'd have her earplugs in and her eye mask on and wouldn't hear a thing. Even if she did hear the telephone she might not answer. Not at this time of night.

My mind was made up when I heard the ambulance approaching, and I ran out to meet it. No sign of the night clerk or the security guard, and Randy or Velvet had not come running to tell me Mr. Westenham had recovered and was going to be okay.

The ambulance pulled to a halt in the circle used for unloading passengers and luggage.

"I'm Mrs. Grady, resort manager. We found a man floating in the lake. Unconscious." I pointed out the direction. "You can't get the truck up that path. You'll have to walk."

Two men in white uniforms got out. They walked quickly to the back of the ambulance and threw open the doors. One man jumped in and dragged out a stretcher.

"Show us the way," the other said to me. Winston sniffed at his shoes, and the ambulance driver said, "Nice dog."

He was a fairly young guy, and I noticed him checking me over. Before I could think he was admiring my feminine charms, he said, "Uh, ma'am? You need to do something about those feet."

I looked down. Lake water had stopped pouring off my dress but drops of blood traced where I'd walked. Only then did I realize I'd cut my foot. Both feet. "I left my shoes in the woods with . . . with them. My friends are still there. That way. Just past the end of the path, in the woods. It's only a few yards. If you shout, they'll hear you."

Lights were coming on in the rooms above our heads and in the cabins, and heads popped out of windows.

At last the security guard arrived, huffing and puffing and as red-faced as though he'd come last in a footrace. The night clerk was with him.

"What took you so long?" I snapped.

"Sorry, ma'am," the clerk said.

"Sorry, ma'am," the security guard said.

"I don't want people coming out of their rooms asking what's going on and getting in the way. You," I said to the security guard, "follow the ambulance drivers and ask Miss McNally to come here. You"—to the night clerk—"start calming people down."

The security guard, well into his fifties and about fifty pounds overweight, shifted his belt under his belly and trotted off down the path as quickly as he was able.

"How am I supposed to do that?" Bradley, in his early twenties, looking as though the rest of the year he was on the college football team, asked.

"You tell them a guest has taken ill, and we don't need anyone's help. Do you think you're capable of doing that?"

He shrugged. "I guess."

"You guess? Or you can?"

"I can."

"I can, *Mrs. Grady.*"

He blinked.

"I'll go inside and attempt to intercept any guests who come downstairs to find out what's happening. When the ambulance has left, come back and resume your post."

"Okay. I mean, yes, Mrs. Grady."

He trotted off. I limped up the steps and into the lobby, leaving a trail of blood drops in my wake. It wasn't too bad, so hopefully the police wouldn't arrive and think someone had been murdered on the hotel steps.

This wasn't the first time an ambulance had been called to Haggerman's, and it wouldn't be the last. A good many elderly guests stayed here, as well as middle-aged men who hadn't exercised in years eating giant meals immediately after a game of handball, or women who forgot what too much sun can do to a bathing-suit-clad body that's been inside all winter.

But it was the first time we'd had a guest taken ill who was here on his own, and I needed to contact his family, if I could.

Velvet came in. She gave me a quick shake of her head. "He's gone?"

"Randy tried, but got no response. The ambulance guys are there now, and some kid said you wanted me?"

"I need to get into my office to find the man's booking form, but to do that I need my keys, and they're at the house. To get to the house I need shoes, and my spare shoes are in the office. To which I don't have keys."

"Sounds like a brain puzzle," Velvet said.

"Exactly. Run up to the house. I didn't lock the door when I left, and Olivia won't have locked me out. My bunch of keys are in the top drawer of the telephone table. Once you've delivered the keys, take Winston to Aunt Tatiana's cabin. I can't have him running around all night."

Winston woofed in agreement, and Velvet left without another word. The dog and I stood at the front doors watching the activity outside as the ambulance drivers loaded their stretcher into the back and drove away. They did not seem to be in any sort of hurry.

I heard a creak on the stairs and turned to see Louis, Olivia's pesky admirer, still dressed—despite the lateness of the hour—in the clothes he'd worn to the ballroom earlier.

"Miss Peters, is everything all right here? I heard noises and looked out to see an ambulance parked out front."

I'd checked into Louis earlier, and I knew his room was one of the cheaper ones, without a lake view. To see the ambulance, he'd have to have left his room and gone to the windows on the third-floor landing.

I didn't bother to either point that out or to correct his use of my name. "Perfectly all right, thank you."

"I hope . . . I hope your mother is not alarmed. Noises in the night can be upsetting to a lady's delicate constitution. Obviously you're needed here. Shall I go and check on her?"

He gave me a sickly grin, and I thought of the unlocked door to our house. Maybe we needed to start locking it, particularly when Olivia was home alone. Just one more thing for me to worry about.

"No," I said.

"It's no bother."

"I said no." It was late, my feet were sore, we'd had a guest die on the premises. I was in no mood to be polite.

Randy came down the path, walking slowly. The night clerk and security guard were with him. I called to Bradley. "Please escort Mr. Frandenheim here to his room."

"That's not necessary," Louis said. "I can find my way, if you're sure I can't be of help."

I gave him my most unfriendly smile. The one I used in an attempt to keep new, young, inexperienced staff in line. "It's no bother. Off you go now."

I nodded to Bradley. He gave me a blank look. I jerked my head toward Louis, and finally comprehension dawned and he took a step forward. Louis headed for the staircase, and the night clerk followed.

I went outside, accompanied by Winston. "You okay?" I asked Randy.

His face was grim. "Yeah. Guy didn't make it."

"The ambulance drivers said they're calling the cops," the security guard said.

"The police? Why?"

"Guy was fully dressed, Elizabeth," Randy said. "And . . ." He glanced at the guard.

"And . . . ?" I asked.

"He'd been hit on the back of the head. The ambulance guys said that means he probably didn't slip and fall off the dock in the dark."

Velvet arrived in a flurry of pink, waving my keys. Her hair had come out of its clip and hung in wet strands around her face. Pink tulle, I decided, didn't fare well submerged in lake water. If any of our more imaginative guests saw her, they'd think they'd seen the Marsh Monster of Delayed Lake. Not that there is a marsh monster in Delayed Lake, but it doesn't take much to get legends started.

"Sorry I took so long," she said. "Olivia was up, demanding to know what's going on."

"You two need to get to your cabins and get changed," I said.

"So do you," Velvet said.

"I'm drying off." I suppressed a shiver. I should have asked Velvet to grab a sweater for me along with the keys. "Take Winston to Aunt Tatiana's first, please. Do you think the police will be coming tonight?" I asked the security guard.

"Probably," he said. "They'll want to have a look at the scene."

"Wait here for them. I'm going into the office for a minute. If the police arrive while I'm still here, come and get me. If they arrive after I've gone home, phone up to the house."

The security guard glanced at Randy. Randy shrugged.

"You're new here," I said.

"Yeah. Started last week."

"What's your name?"

"Edward Smith. Folks call me Eddie."

"Ex-army or ex-police?"

"I was in the army. Served in Europe."

"Well, Eddie, let me tell you something. My mother owns Haggerman's, and I run it for her. That means we pay your salary. Are you okay with that?"

"Huh?"

"What I mean is, if you're going to take money from us, the deal is you do what I say. Got it?"

"Huh?"

"You don't ask the lifeguard for permission."

Behind his back Velvet's eyes opened wide and a slow grin spread across her face. Randy cocked one eyebrow at her.

Finally, comprehension dawned, and Eddie said, "Yeah, I got it. Ma'am."

I didn't often have to assert my authority, but when there seemed to be any doubt about who was in charge around here, I'd soon learned I had to ensure there were no misunderstandings and do it quickly. Unlike most other businesses, in most other places, it's common in the Catskills for women to be in positions of authority. The hotels are family businesses, sometimes generations deep. Mothers, wives, daughters run the hotels and the departments, usually with iron fists, which means they boss the workers.

Occasionally we get men from the army, the police, or businesses in the city forgetting that.

The matter settled, hopefully, I went inside, conscious of my sore feet, trying not to limp too obviously. Winston followed, despite Velvet's attempts to call him to come. I shut the door firmly in the dog's face.

Bradley had returned from his errand and was back at his post. I crossed the empty lobby, dim and silent, and slipped into the hallway and then into the outer office. Moonlight streamed through the windows, so I didn't need to turn on the light. Desks were tidied, ashtrays and coffee mugs emptied, silent phones resting in their cradles, drawers closed, cloths thrown over typewriters. I found the key to my office, unlocked the door, and switched on the light. It flickered, as though trying to decide if it wanted to work at this time of night, and then it came on. I opened the largest of the metal filing cabinets and flipped quickly through the papers inside. The registration ledger kept at the front desk was filled out when guests arrived and it recorded only their name, number of people in their party, room number, and dates they'd be with us. When the reservation had been made, either by the guests themselves or through a booking agency, we would have asked for more information, such as a name and phone number or address to contact in case of an emergency. Being found floating in the lake unresponsive counted as an emergency. I quickly found the page I was looking for. Harold Westenham from Newburgh, New York, had given Jim Westenham, with a New York City phone number, as his contact.

It was coming up to two A.M. Late to be calling anyone. But if this Jim was Harold's son, as was likely, he'd want to know his father had had an accident. But first . . . I sat in my chair, lifted my right foot, rested it in my lap, and studied it. I brushed gravel, dead pine needles, and bits of grass off it. The small cut in my big toe had stopped bleeding. I then examined the left foot: much the same, but for a bigger cut across the heel. I'd live, I decided. I put on the black-and-white sneakers I keep under the desk in case of a sudden need to run somewhere, and then I picked up the receiver and pressed a button.

"Yes, Mrs. Grady?" Bradley said.

"I want to place a call to New York." I rattled off the number on the booking form, and the phone clanked and whirled as it did whatever phones did. Then it began to ring at the other end. I crossed my fingers hoping someone would answer. Otherwise, I'd be up all night trying to deliver my message.

I let it ring ten times, and I was about to hang up when the ringing stopped midnote and a man growled, "Who are you, and what the heck do you want at this time of night?"

"I'm sorry to bother you. Are you Mr. Jim Westenham?"

"You're not bothering me. I never mind being woken up by a lady." His voice was deep, sounding of late nights in smoke-filled jazz bars. "Yeah, that's me. Who are you?"

"My name's Elizabeth Grady, and I'm the manager of Haggerman's Catskills Resort."

The deep voice turned wary. "My uncle Harold's staying there."

"I'm sorry to have to tell you this, but Mr. Westenham had an accident a short while ago. He's been taken by ambulance to Summervale General Hospital. You were listed on his registration card as his emergency contact."

"An accident? What sort of accident? Is he okay?"

"He was found in the lake. I . . . I don't know any more than that."

"Sure you do. You know a lot more. I can hear it. What are you not telling me?"

"I'm sorry. That's all I can say. Summervale General Hospital. That's in the town of Summervale. Good night."

"I'll grab a pool car and drive up tonight. After I've seen him, I'll want to come to your hotel and have a look around. My uncle didn't swim."

"Good night," I said again as I put down the receiver.

A pool car? What did that mean? Who did he work for

that had pool cars available at this time of night? As for knowing I wasn't telling him the whole story—I don't have much experience in lying outright, but as a holiday resort manager I can prevaricate with the best of them. I closed my eyes. Had that last comment—Harold Westenham didn't swim—been meant as a threat? Was even now Jim Westenham thinking up reasons to sue us?

Cold settled over me, and again I realized I was shivering. I needed to get home, into a hot bath and warm pajamas before I froze to death at my own desk.

Chapter 7

BATH AND PAJAMAS WOULD HAVE TO WAIT. I WAS STILL
mulling over that phone conversation when a light came on
in the outer office and Eddie the security guard called,
"Mrs. Grady! Cops are here."

I stood up quickly, wincing as the rough inner soles of
the tennis shoes scraped the sore places on the bottoms of
my feet. I switched off the light and locked the office door
behind me. I had no place to put my keys, so I stuffed them
into my bra. I caught a glimpse of myself in the mirror one
of the clerks kept on her desk. The keys were a big bunch,
and I looked dangerously lopsided. Oh well, couldn't be
helped. My legs were bare, my shoelaces dragging behind
me, my beautiful new dress drying into a mass of wrinkles,
my neat poodle cut ruined, the curls sticking out in all directions, my lipstick smeared.

Maybe I shouldn't have been so quick to remind Eddie

who was in charge here. I couldn't blame him for thinking it wasn't me.

A black-and-white Pontiac with a red light mounted on the roof and the town's emblem painted on the door was parked in the circle, two men standing beside it talking to Eddie. Both men's tan uniforms had the town of Summervale's crest on the shoulder, and the younger one had a camera around his neck. Randy and Velvet had joined them. They'd changed into warmer (and drier) clothes. Velvet had even had time to tie her hair into a sweeping fold with a sparkling clip and apply a touch of pale pink lipstick.

"I'm Elizabeth Grady, the manager here," I said to the older of the men in uniform.

"Norm Monahan, chief of police." Monahan, the same name as our awkward dishwasher. I didn't bother to mention that. Everyone in the Catskills is related to everyone else, and most of them work in the hotels. The chief was well into his fifties and not going smoothly into his sixties. Overweight, watery-eyed, red-faced, nose with as many lines of rosacea as there were lines on a map of Europe. His uniform jacket and pants were crumpled, his tie askew, and his boots badly worn. He looked as though he'd just risen from his bed and grabbed his clothes off the floor, and I reminded myself that that was, probably, the case. He shifted his gun belt and looked at me. He appeared to be as impressed with me as I was with him. I shouldn't have had to explain, but I did.

"My coworkers"—I indicated Velvet and Randy—"and I jumped into the lake to retrieve the . . . uh . . . gentleman. I haven't had time to change."

"Around what time was this?" Monahan asked.

"The entertainment in the ballroom ended at midnight," I said. "My friends and I went for a walk along the lake. Maybe quarter after twelve?"

"About then," Randy said.

"Let's see where this happened," Chief Monahan said to Randy. "You can show us. We don't need to bother the ladies. You girls can run along to bed."

"It's no bother," Velvet and I chorused.

Despite the seriousness of the situation, my friend and I exchanged a secret grin. In school, the other girls had called us the Bobbsey Twins. We looked nothing at all alike, but we'd been inseparable and we sometimes said the same thing at the same time.

To put a stop to any potential argument, I turned and marched down the path. It was two o'clock in the morning, but a handful of lights were on in guests' rooms.

"Is everything all right out there?" a man called from a cabin porch.

"Perfectly fine, Mr. Reid," Randy shouted.

In the neighboring cabin a light came on in the front bedroom.

"Shush," I said to Randy.

"Too late now," Randy said as the cabin door creaked open and people came out to watch our little procession pass.

"Chief Monahan," I said. "The . . . the man is named Harold Westenham, and he is . . . was a guest here. I contacted Mr. Westenham's nephew in New York City, and he'll be on his way shortly."

Monahan grunted. We reached the end of the path, and everyone stopped. I pointed. "Through there."

"Give us a light, Dave," Monahan said to the younger officer, who took the flashlight off his belt and turned it on. He never had been introduced. He must have also risen from his bed at the call, but his uniform was clean and pressed, his hair combed, his face shaven. He shone the light through the trees, and the light bounced off water bubbling in the creek and the trunks of the trees. Small dark eyes, low to the ground, stared back at us, and something small scurried though the undergrowth.

"There's traces of blood there," the deputy said. "On that rock."

"Sorry," I said. "That was probably me. I ran in my bare feet and got some cuts and scratches." I pointed to a big scratch running up the outside of my right calf. "See?"

Chief Monahan gave me a filthy look.

"Sorry," I repeated.

"You two stay here," he said to Velvet and me. "You"— to Randy—"show us."

The men stepped into the trees. We heard Monahan grunt and then a splash as he attempted, and failed, to jump over the creek. The light wavered, bouncing off solid trunks and stirring branches.

"Jerk," Velvet said under her breath.

"He doesn't have to be personable," I said. "Just get the job done. Do you really think that man was murdered?"

She let out a puff of air. "It's possible he fell off the dock and hit his head going down. Unlikely he killed himself, not with the blow to the back of his head."

"Elizabeth?" A low voice came out of the dark forest.

My heart jumped, and Velvet let out a squeal of surprise, before we realized it was Olivia.

"Here," I said.

My mother stepped into the circle of light cast by an overhead lamp. She wore a peach satin nightgown under a matching wrap and had mules trimmed with peach fur on her feet. The thick braid she wears to bed was swept up and secured to the back of her head. Her face was clear of makeup, and the light from the lamp above her cast long, deep shadows under her eyes.

"Is everything all right? Velvet said a man has died."

"The police are here now. He fell into the lake."

"Do you know who?"

"His name's Harold Westenham, and he was staying in cabin nineteen."

Her face fell. "Oh, dear. That must be the man I briefly chatted to earlier this afternoon. He was in cabin nineteen, and he told me his name was Harold. I thought he was nice. A true gentleman. I told you about that."

"I remember."

"I don't like to say, Elizabeth, but you do not want the guests to see you like that. It's not good for our image."

"You're in your nightwear, Olivia," I pointed out.

"I don't intend to be seen. The police are here?"

"Yes. The chief and his deputy. Randy's showing them where the man was found. They don't want too many people milling around."

"I don't suppose they sent a *young* policeman?"

Velvet barked out a laugh.

"If they did," I said, "I won't be asking him to come to our house for tea to meet my mother. Go back to bed, Olivia. I'll handle this."

She slipped away, as quietly as she'd come.

"Mothers," Velvet said. "They do know how to focus on the important things, don't they?"

Leaves rustled, water splashed, twigs snapped, and the light from a flashlight shone in our faces as Monahan burst out of the woods. A twig was stuck to the side of his hat, and his scuffed and heavily worn boots were thick with mud.

"I'd like to search the man's room," he said. "Do you have a key?"

"I do." The master key to all the cabins was part of the bunch I had on me.

"Let's go, then. We don't need you anymore, honey," he said to Velvet.

"I don't mind," she said.

"I do. When they told me someone had died at a hotel, I knew it would be a mess. Always a mess with all these city folks poking around."

"Get a lot of sudden deaths in Summervale, do you?" Velvet asked cheerfully.

He scowled at her.

"This way," I said.

We walked back the way we'd come but turned off the main path before we reached the tennis courts. This path skirted the boundary of the public areas. Cabins and lawns and flower beds on one side, the thick woods leading up the steep hillside on the other. Monahan started puffing almost immediately. Velvet was in front, and she increased her pace so she was almost trotting.

"Almost there," she called over her shoulder. "Tell me if you need me to go slower."

As tempting as it was to make the man run, I slowed to match his pace. It wouldn't help matters if he had a heart attack.

The main section of this path ended at cabin nineteen and a sign that read STAFF ONLY PAST THIS POINT. Velvet gave us a wave over her shoulder and carried on toward the staff dormitories. Monahan and I climbed the steps, and I pushed open the door to the cabin's small screened-in porch. I unlocked the main door, and we went inside.

The place was immaculate. I'd expect nothing less from any chambermaid who worked under Aunt Tatiana, but in the afternoon and evening guests did start strewing their things about. That hadn't happened here. One pair of brown shoes, gleaming with polish, was dead center on the mat by the door. A recent copy of the *New Yorker* magazine lay on the coffee table, next to an empty ashtray. The brown cushions on the orange-and-brown-striped couch were fluffed and properly placed as the chambermaids would have left them. There had been no towels or bathing suits outside, left to dry over the porch railings, no sandals or water shoes kicked off by the door.

The windows were closed, the drapes drawn, and the air was thick. The lingering trace of tobacco smoke hung over everything. Monahan walked across the main room. This cabin had two bedrooms and one bathroom. All the doors were closed. He opened the first. The bed was made, the pillows undented. A book with a lurid green cover sat on the night table: *Foundation and Empire* by Isaac Asimov. A long red ribbon that was probably the bookmark was about three-quarters of the way in. The ashtray by the bed was also empty.

"Tidy guy," Chief Monahan said. "Do the maids come in at night?"

"No."

He opened the closet. A suit, the one I'd seen Mr. Westenham wearing earlier in the day, hung on a hanger, next to a sports jacket and two pairs of trousers. The cuffs of his two white shirts had some fraying around the edges. They'd been starched and carefully ironed, but they showed creases left by their confinement in his suitcase. A man who cared for his clothes but didn't spend a lot of money on them, and either didn't want to bother the housekeeping staff to iron his shirts or didn't want to pay the charge. His hat lay on the top shelf. Monahan opened the drawers. The top drawer held neatly folded handkerchiefs, underwear, and socks.

None of it was new, all of it clean. The other drawers were empty.

No bathing suit, no golf or tennis clothes. Not even a pair of shorts or something to wear to go boating.

The bathroom was between the two bedrooms. We went in there next. Toothbrush and toothpaste stood at attention in a mug, next to an empty water glass. The man's shaving things and a single black comb were neatly lined up next to the sink. The trash can contained cigarette butts and ash. A lot of cigarette butts.

We went into the second bedroom.

We stopped dead in the doorway, and I might have let out a gasp of surprise. The room was strewn with papers. Stacks of papers piled on the table, papers scattered across the bed like giant snowflakes, papers thrown on the floor. A typewriter, a solid Underwood, was on the table with a sheet of paper rolled into it and a chair pulled up to it. An ashtray, jammed full of gray ash and ground cigarette butts sat on top of a stack of papers covered in close type beside the typewriter. Two books rested on a sheaf of blank paper.

The picture of a Catskills mountain scene in winter that hung over the second-bedroom table in all our cabins was on the floor, propped up against the knotty pine wall. Two large maps had been pinned in its place.

"Goodness," I said. "It looks as though he was working on something in here."

Monahan crossed the room. He picked up the top book and sucked in a breath as his eyes opened wide. He showed it to me. *The Communist Manifesto.*

I looked at the maps on the wall. The layout of streets on the bigger one looked familiar, but I could tell right away it wasn't New York City. A wide river ran through the bottom half of the second map. "That looks like London," I said. "In England. The other's Washington, I think."

"I need to use your phone, Mrs. Grady," Monahan said.

"Okay," I said. "Who are you going to call?"

"This is a case for the FBI. It's obvious that what you have here is a communist cell."

Chapter 8

"HE KEPT HIMSELF TO HIMSELF," AUNT TATIANA SAID. "WE had instructions to clean the room every second day only, between ten and ten thirty. If the girls could not come at that time, they were not to enter his cabin at all. They tell me he appeared to be some sort of a writer. A typewriter is on the table in the smaller bedroom, and piles of papers are scattered around. He instructed the chambermaids not to touch the table or move any of his papers."

"We were told not to clean in the small bedroom at all." A woman gestured with her arms. "Papers. Everywhere!"

The circle of women nodded. "He never came to the dining room for his meals," one of the chambermaids said. "Everything was taken to his cabin on a tray even though that costs extra. You can ask the busboys, they didn't go inside. He opened the door, took the tray from them, and shut the door. If he didn't answer, they had instructions to leave the tray on the table on the porch."

"He was a big tipper," another said. "He always tipped the busboys."

"Never us, though," a third woman grumbled. "On the days we didn't clean the cabin, he left the trays out on the porch to be collected."

It was eight A.M., the morning after the death of Harold Westenham. I hadn't been to bed, but I had had time to wash myself in the sink, give my feet a good scrubbing, attempt to refashion my hair, and slip into clean clothes. I'd called Aunt Tatiana as soon as I thought she'd be up and told her I needed to speak to the chambermaids before they headed off on their rounds.

They'd been waiting in the laundry building at the back corner of the property near the maintenance shed when I arrived. Sheets, pillowcases, table linens were hung to dry, but the day's wash hadn't started yet, so the room wasn't too stiflingly hot. They were all older women, locals, with stout frames, rough red hands, tired faces, and seen-it-all eyes.

"Did he ever have any visitors?" I asked.

The women exchanged glances and shrugged.

"Did he talk to you at all? Tell you what he was doing?"

"I never spoke to him, Mrs. Grady. I've never even seen him."

"I saw him once. He was heading down the path as I came up at ten o'clock. He was never in the cabin when we arrived to clean."

"Because he knew what time you'd be there," I said. "Thank you, ladies, carry on with your day."

"Can we clean that cabin?" Aunt Tatiana asked.

"Stay away for now," I said. "The police told me we can't use it until they've finished searching it. The guest paid in advance, and the booking was until the end of July, so I don't need to be in a hurry to rent it out."

"Save on food costs," my ever-practical aunt said.

Chief Monahan had ordered Deputy Dave—whose last name I never did catch—to cordon off cabin nineteen. When I'd checked it this morning on my way to meet with Tatiana and her chambermaids, I'd found a flock of guests standing around outside looking at nothing. As nothing was happening. The deputy—early thirties, tall and as thin as one of the saplings growing up against the cabin, with sunken cheeks, a small chin, an excessively large nose, and thick eyeglasses—sat on the porch "guarding the scene," and looking mighty bored. Monahan had gone home and back to his bed, after being sure I—who hadn't even been to bed—understood what a hard job policing was. Before leaving, I'd taken him into the business office to use the phone, and he'd called the FBI night line. They'd promised to have an agent here first thing in the morning.

"Can I have a word, please?" I asked my aunt now.

We left the laundry as the chambermaids burst into excited chatter.

"Chief Monahan thinks Mr. Westenham was engaged in communist activity," I said.

My aunt shrugged.

"Have you ever . . . uh . . . heard about anything like that around here?"

"Why are you asking me, *lastachka*?"

"Because you know everything that goes on here, of course."

Her round red cheeks got even redder as she flushed with pleasure. "Mr. Westenham left a note for me when he checked in, letting me know of his requirements. He said he was a writer and he was here to write a book and he needed his privacy. That is all. If communists are here, they did not tell my ladies."

"Admittedly, that's unlikely to be a point of casual conversation." I thought about the man I'd spoken to so briefly. Polite, perfectly dressed and groomed, soft-spoken, wanting only to be left alone.

Did he look like a communist?

I didn't know what a communist looked like, but I didn't think they dressed or spoke so well.

"Mrs. Grady to reception. Reception for Mrs. Grady." All day long loudspeakers boomed out over the property. Summoning guests to the phone, announcing meals and activities, reporting lost or found children. Sometimes lost or found husbands.

"I'll let you know if I hear anything more about the unfortunate gentleman," Aunt Tatiana said.

I thanked her and headed down the path at a trot. I hoped I'd get a break so I could go home for a nap later, but my chances of doing that were not good. I didn't have to be on hand tonight for the entertainment, so I should be able to quit work when the office closed at five.

The bellhop opened the door for me with a nod, and I ran into the lobby. A man was sitting in one of the comfortable armchairs by a side window, smoking and watching the activity. He stood up as I came in and crossed the room in quick strides. He wasn't dressed for a day of Catskills fun, but in a loose-fitting suit of light brown with a white shirt and darker brown tie and highly polished black shoes. He held his hat in his hand. He was about my age—late twenties—with thick black hair long enough to have the slightest hint of a curl, cheekbones prominent in a pale face, and attractive blue eyes. His fingers were stained yellow with nicotine and blue with ink.

"Miss Grady?"

"Yes."

He passed his cigarette to his left hand and thrust out the right. "Jim Westenham."

His hand was dry, his grip firm but not hard enough to be an attempt at a display of dominance.

"Mr. Westenham. I'm . . . I . . ." I wasn't sure if I should say "I'm sorry for your loss." No one had called us to officially say Harold Westenham had died.

"Thank you." Jim crushed his cigarette in the nearest ashtray. "And thank you for taking the trouble to phone me last night. I got to the hospital too late to say goodbye to Uncle Harold, but I was glad to be there in any event."

"Were you and your uncle close?"

"We were at one time. We saw less of each other than I would have liked since the war, but when I was a child he was an important part of my life."

"I'm sorry," I said.

He smiled at me, and then he looked around the lobby. Guests were coming and going, filing into the dining room for breakfast or heading out to get a start on the day. The weather forecast for the next few days was for continued sun and heat, and I was glad of it. Nothing worse at a holiday resort than days of rain.

"Nice place you have here. The girl at reception tells me your mother owns it."

"That's right."

"I'm not going back to the city right away. The doctor I spoke to at the hospital said the local police have some questions about my uncle's death and thus they won't be releasing the body right away."

He waited for me to say something. I didn't.

"No one's spoken to me yet, so I'm planning to head back to town soon and drop into the police station. Find out what's going on. My uncle's room here's paid for. Any chance I can take it for a couple of days?"

That, I had to answer. "I'm sorry, but not today, and I don't know when it will be free. The police have ordered it sealed."

"That tells me a lot, Miss Grady."

"Elizabeth," I said.

He grinned at me. "I'm Jim. If not my uncle's, any chance of another room for a hard-done-by guy? I was woken up in the early hours this morning and drove all the way up here." He studied my face and grinned again. "Although I'd say you didn't get any more sleep than I did, as you're the one who called me."

I thought quickly. The hotel was satisfyingly full, but we did have a couple of small, dark rooms in one of the original buildings. They'd been guest rooms in the earliest days of Haggerman's but were now mostly used for storage of things no one had used since the 1920s but would probably want again. One day. One day soon.

"I can have a room made ready for you," I said. "But I have to warn you that, although it's a guest room, it's not a particularly nice one. It's in an older building we use these days mostly as storage, so there might be some noise during the day as staff come and go. It has a shared bathroom at the end of the hall, but considering none of the other guest rooms are occupied, that qualifies as a private bath."

"Elizabeth," he said with a chuckle, "if you're going to make it in the hotel business, you need to work on your sales pitch some more. I'll take it. I'm not here for a vacation."

"I won't charge you for the room, and I'll give you a discounted rate if you take your meals in the dining room."

"Definitely not going to make it in the hotel business."

His tone was light, teasing. He was very charming, and despite my attempts to be all business, I felt myself responding. I smiled back at him.

Finally, I stopped smiling. "It'll be at least an hour before the room can be made up. Breakfast is underway while you're waiting."

"Would you like to join me?"

"No, thank you," I said. I never eat in the dining room. "Check with reception in an hour. I'll have the head of housekeeping let them know when the room's ready."

I turned to go, ready to send a page with a message for Aunt Tatiana. The lobby doors opened, and two men walked in. Cheap suits, crew cuts, serious faces. I knew right away they weren't checking in.

"Now, that's interesting," Jim Westenham muttered. "Very interesting."

The men headed straight for the reception counter. Assuming they were here to speak to me, I cut them off. "Gentlemen, I'm Mrs. Grady. Hotel manager. Can I help you?"

"You in charge?" the older one said. He didn't look as though he believed me.

"I'm the manager. Like I said. My mother owns Haggerman's, and I run *everything*."

Jim Westenham had put his hat back on his head, stuffed his hands in his pockets, and followed me.

"You the guy in charge?" the new arrival asked him.

"I just told you I am!" I said. "This gentleman is a hotel guest."

"More than a guest," Jim said. "Agent . . . ? I didn't get your name."

"Jones." He jerked his head to his younger, shorter, rounder, uglier companion. "This is Agent Smith."

Smith said nothing.

"And I'm the Easter Bunny. Pleased to meet you. When I'm not handing out chocolate to deserving kids, my name's Jim Westenham. You're here about the death of my uncle Harold."

"We've got some questions," Jones said.

"You got here mighty quickly."

"We can move quickly, when it's important."

"Jim Westenham," Smith said slowly. "You're not—"

"Guilty as charged," Jim said. "I see my reputation has preceded me. Glad to hear it."

I was beginning to feel like chopped liver here. "Excuse me. As the person in charge of this establishment, can one of you gentlemen tell me what's going on?"

Guests were walking past our group, keeping a wary eye open. No one actually stopped to listen, but I did see a couple of older men casually flipping through the hotel's brochure, or spending a lot of time studying the day's activity chart tacked to the notice board next to the dining room doors.

"Jim Westenham," Smith said to Jones. Or was it Jones said to Smith? I'd already forgotten which was which. "*New York Times*."

That would explain the ink stains on Jim's fingers. Probably the tobacco stains as well.

"Right," Jim said. "I work the crime beat, but I'm not here in that capacity but to deal with my uncle's death."

"Muckraking journalist of the worse sort," Jones (*Smith?*) said.

"I take offense to that," Jim said. "I prefer 'muckraking journalist of the best sort.'"

Jones growled.

"I assume," I said before things could get out of hand. "You're here to see Mr. Westenham's rooms. I'll show you the way."

"Yeah," Jones said.

"You might as well tell me your real names," Jim said. "I've told you mine, the lady told you hers. It's impolite to lie to a lady."

The men hesitated.

"Whether I'm here officially or not," Jim said. "I'm not exactly without the resources necessary to find out. One phone call should do it."

"Agent O'Reilly," grunted the older one. "This is Kowalski. Before we see the room, *Jim*, were you aware your uncle was a communist?"

Jim's jaw dropped. He gaped at the FBI agents, and then he let out a roar of laughter. "I don't think this is a time for jokes."

"We never joke," Kowalski said. "Maybe you were more than aware. Are you a fellow red?"

He hadn't kept his voice down, and a buzz began to spread through the lobby. *Communist. Reds.*

"Why don't we find a private place to talk?" I said.

Kowalski checked his watch. "We're supposed to be meeting the chief of police here at eight thirty. It's twenty to nine now. Small-town cops. Waste of breath the lot of them."

"I'm not going to hang around all day waiting," O'Reilly said. "Show us the way to the dead guy's room."

As if summoned by some sort of underground telegraph, more guests were arriving. They stood back, watching us, whispering among themselves.

"They arrested a commie last night," one old man said to another.

"Are we safe here, honey?" a woman asked her husband.

I headed for the exit, hoping the FBI would follow. They did. Jim followed them. The wide-eyed bellhop opened the door for us. O'Reilly stopped on the front steps. "You don't need to come, Jim-boy."

"I think I do," Jim said. "My uncle's things will be in his room, and I need to ensure nothing goes missing. Accidentally, of course."

O'Reilly looked as though he was about to refuse, but at that moment the Summervale police car pulled up in a spray of gravel and a burst of exhaust. Chief Monahan leapt out. He bounded up the steps, as much as he was capable of bounding, and stuck out his hand. Introductions were made all around. Jim introduced himself as next of kin of the deceased, and Monahan mumbled, "Condolences." Today's uniform was slightly less rumpled than the one he'd had on last night.

"Yup, guy was murdered," he said to the FBI with what I thought a considerable lack of tact. "No doubt about it whatsoever. Bashed over the back of the head with a rock and rolled into the lake. The rock's probably at the bottom of the lake now."

"Has the autopsy been done?" Kowalski asked.

"No, but it's obvious to me what happened."

"It is, is it?" O'Reilly said.

"Yup. Been on the force a long time. I've seen it all. I was a cop in towns around here for a lot of years. Soon as the war ended I came back to Summervale, my hometown, so my dad could retire. He was the chief here before me." Monahan beamed at the FBI agents, expecting them to be impressed.

They weren't.

"Let's see these papers you said you found," O'Reilly said. "Uh, ma'am." This to a tiny wizened woman who'd placed herself directly in front of him. "If you would excuse us."

"What's this talk about communists?" She scowled at me. "What sort of hotel are you running here?"

"Me? Us? This has nothing to do with us."

"My daughter said we should go to Grossinger's this year, but they're getting too big for their britches over there and they put the rates up. Besides, your food's better."

"Ma'am," Chief Monahan said, "please don't concern yourself. I'm here to ensure that nothing spoils your vacation in our beautiful mountains. You run along and enjoy your day."

She harrumphed, but stepped aside.

I led the way down the path to the woods, followed by the chief of police, the FBI, a *New York Times* reporter, and about a hundred sets of eyes. The sun was rising, the heat building, and guests were emerging from their cabins and rooms. Bathing-suit-clad children ran for the pool, while towel-bearing mothers or hotel-provided nannies told them not to run; paddleboats were heading out; canoes and rowboats were leaving the dock. On the dock itself, Velvet's exercise class was going through their morning stretches. Out in the lake, Randy was getting ready for his first class of the day, teaching preteens to dive off the floating platform. A busboy passed me carrying a tray bearing the remains of a room-service breakfast.

Velvet noticed me and my little group and stopped to stare, her hips bent to one side, her arms forming a circle over her head. I gave her a shrug.

"Aaaaand the other side," she called to her class.

As we turned onto the side path, O'Reilly stopped, put his hands on his hips, and looked around. "Where does this trail lead?"

"To cabin nineteen, Mr. Westenham's," I said. "It's the last of the guest cabins. Beyond that to various equipment sheds and a side path leading to senior staff accommodations."

"Remote. Quiet."

"Yes. People request cabin nineteen specifically because remote and quiet is what they want."

O'Reilly and Kowalski exchanged a meaningful look.

"What?" I said.

"Good place to meet up with a contact if you don't want to be overheard."

"Anyone who wants to meet in secret without being overheard shouldn't have come to the Catskills in the first place," Jim said.

I stifled a laugh. He wasn't wrong.

Deputy Dave leapt to his feet when he saw us approaching. His Brownie camera was on the table in front of him.

"Have any trouble?" Monahan asked.

The deputy shook his head. "A few people wandered by and asked what was going on. No one tried to get inside, though." He attempted to stifle a yawn. His tie was crooked, his hair tousled, his eyes red, and stubble growing on his chin. He'd had a long, boring night. "Did you remember to call June? Tell her I wouldn't be home?"

"Yeah." Monahan's eyes slid to one side. He saw me watching him and flushed. Presumably June was Mrs. Deputy Dave, and Monahan either had forgotten to call her or couldn't be bothered. "I radioed the county dispatcher," he mumbled. "He knows where you are if June calls."

I unlocked the door to cabin nineteen, and we went inside. The deputy remained on the porch. The air was stale and stuffy, the scent of tobacco heavy. "It's going to get hot soon," I said. "Can I open a window?"

"No," O'Reilly said.

"Through there." Monahan pointed to the second bedroom. "I left everything as I found it and stationed my deputy outside to make sure no one broke in to remove evidence."

Jim and I hung back as the men went into the bedroom, and we stood in the doorway, watching.

O'Reilly let out a low whistle. "That's Washington, that map."

"Yeah," Monahan said. "Recognize the other one?"

"No," Kowalski said.

"The girl said it's London, England," Monahan told them.

"Place looks like it's been tossed," O'Reilly said. "Someone was searching for something. Wonder if they found it."

"No," Jim said. "This is normal."

"What?"

"My uncle was a tidy, well-organized man in most of his life, but when it came to his work . . . Let's say he was organized in a way other people wouldn't recognize. His office at the college and his study at his house always looked like this." He waved his hand to indicate the snowstorm of papers. "I'm not saying nothing's missing, I'm only saying don't read anything into the state of things."

O'Reilly flicked through the papers on the table, while Kowalski examined the ones on the bed. O'Reilly picked up the topmost book. He held it up. "This is the sort of thing your uncle read, is it?"

Jim crossed the floor. "My uncle was an intelligent, well-read man. Before the war he was a professor of history."

O'Reilly nodded knowingly. "Where'd he teach?"

"University at Albany, when it was called the College for Teachers. He didn't go back after the war. He didn't do a lot of things after the war." A note of sadness crept into his voice. Then it was gone as quickly as it had come.

"He has a copy of *The Communist Manifesto*, what of it? He was obviously doing research." Jim picked up the other book. "This one's *The Hinge of Fate*, volume 4 of *The Second World War*. Written by Winston Churchill. My uncle wasn't an English parliamentarian, either."

"That book's a cover," Monahan said. "In case one of the chambermaids got too much of an interest in what he was up to. Those maps are the cincher. What was he planning?"

Jim grabbed a piece of paper covered with type and began to read. *"He gazed into her warm blue eyes. 'Someday,' he said, 'someday.' 'Yes, mon chéri,' she breathed as her chest heaved, 'someday.'"* He threw the paper to one side. "He was writing a book. Okay, I'll admit it doesn't sound like a very good book, but it's still a dratted book. Sorry, Elizabeth. Pardon me."

"He needed a cover story for being here," Monahan said. "How many men do you get staying at this hotel, Mrs. Grady? Men by themselves, I mean."

"None. Mr. Westenham's the first."

"Exactly!" Monahan said. "Obviously he was up to something fishy."

Jim threw up his hands. "You're not listening to this rubbish, are you?" he said to the FBI agents.

"How long was he planning to stay?" Monahan asked me.

"Five weeks."

"Five weeks. Enough time to meet his confederates and make their plans."

"Plans?" I said.

The police chief pointed to the maps. "An attack on Washington, obviously."

Jim swore. He didn't bother to apologize this time.

"You hear any communist talk around here?" Kowalski asked me.

I didn't bother to mention the two old men arguing about Senator McCarthy over a chess game. "Of course not. Our guests are too busy trying to decide if they're going to have the orange juice or the tomato cocktail at dinner. If I'm asked, I always recommend the tomato cocktail. The orange juice is watery. Don't tell anyone I said that." Four men stared at me. I clamped my lips tightly together.

"I think you're onto something, Chief," O'Reilly said. "We'll take all these papers. See if there's any names or other details mentioned."

"You've reached a conclusion and now you'll do everything you can to prove it." Jim grabbed another piece of paper. *"The street was dark, and he couldn't see a thing. Thick clouds covered the moon, and the blackout curtains hid all light inside the houses."*

"They're planning a night attack," Monahan said. "You'd better warn the folks in Washington."

Jim threw the paper to the floor. "My uncle was writing a book! Not making plans for the overthrow of the United States government."

"That's enough from you," Kowalski said. "I let you in here as a courtesy, but you've seen enough." He turned to me. "I'm sealing this cabin. Got it?"

"Yes," I said.

"You can run along now, honey. And you"—he turned back to Jim—"can get lost."

"Where do we start?" Monahan said. "What do you want me to do?"

"You?" O'Reilly said. "I want you to go back to issuing jaywalking tickets. Think you can do that?"

"The autopsy's scheduled for later today. I'll have a chat with the doc and get back to you on that."

"Good idea," O'Reilly said. "Now get lost and take these

two with you. Oh . . . and, Westenham, if I see a word of this in the New York papers, I'll know where to start looking."

"When I have a story," Jim said, "I'll write it, and my editor will print it. A reclusive man trying his hand at writing a novel isn't a story."

I clamped my lips tightly together and forced myself not to speak. This was my mother's property; the safety and well-being of everyone here, not to mention the livelihood of the staff, was my responsibility, and I was being patted on the head and told to leave everything up to the men. I knew better than to argue. If they got it in their heads that I was obstructing them, they might well accuse me of being in cahoots with Mr. Westenham and his phantom communist cell.

I left the cabin. Jim's footsteps were heavy on the porch steps behind me. The chief of police followed us.

"Look," Jim said to Monahan. "They're FBI and national security's their job. I get that. Your job's finding out who killed my uncle. What's next?"

Monahan peered at him through narrowed eyes. "We have this under control. I don't need your advice."

"You have absolutely nothing under control. You should be questioning the other guests and the staff. Did they see my uncle talking to anyone? Did anyone come to his cabin? Who did he have his meals with? Who—?"

"The head housekeeper's name's Tatiana Rostov," I said. "She knows pretty much everything that goes on around here. I'll ask her to speak with you, Chief Monahan. If you need a room in which to interview the guests in privacy, I can—"

"Good idea," Monahan said. "Those old Russian ladies sure do love to gossip."

"It's not gossip," I said. "It's keeping track of the guests' needs."

"Same thing. I'll talk to her and some of your staff, but there's no need to disturb your guests."

"Why not? Maybe someone—"

"Folks come here, to the Catskills, to Summervale, to your pretty little hotel, for a relaxing holiday. Men need a break from work in the city, and you ladies love to be pampered. I don't want anyone disturbing that."

The deputy stood in the shadows, camera around his neck, saying nothing, just watching.

"But—" I said.

"You're new here, Mrs. Grady," Monahan interrupted. "You might not understand how much towns like Summervale and all the rest need these people. They spend fifty weeks a year in a hot, stinking, crowded New York apartment, going out every day to do a job they hate. They save every penny they can all year long, because the only thing that gives them any pleasure in life is looking forward to their annual vacation in the mountains."

"I know that."

"Glad to hear it. Towns like Summervale, the only thing that keeps us going all year is the money these city folks spend over the eight short weeks of summer."

"I know that, too."

"You wouldn't want folks thinking Haggerman's here isn't a safe place to come for this vacation, would you? Get them scared and they might decide to head back to the city early. They lose. The town loses. You lose."

"But—"

"I don't intend to lose. Dave, you head up to the hotel and ask them to find this Mrs. Romanoff."

"Rostov," I said.

"Yeah, her. I have to get back to town soon. We have more than one crime to deal with at a time, you know. The summer's our busiest time of year. I'm glad to have the outside help."

He glanced back toward cabin nineteen, and seeing that the FBI weren't in desperate need of his expertise at the moment, he wheezed off down the path. Deputy Dave trotted silently behind, having carefully avoided looking at either Jim or me.

I let out a long breath. "That was . . . interesting. I didn't get around to asking housekeeping to do up your room. Sorry."

"I'm in no hurry," Jim said. "In a situation like this one, sometimes I'd worry that some poor schmuck of a busboy was going to be railroaded."

"Why?"

"Cop like Monahan wants nothing but the easy way out. He pretty much came out and told you he doesn't care who killed Uncle Harold as long as it wasn't one of your guests. Who, presumably, wouldn't be spending any more money in Summervale if he was under arrest. Can't upset your guests by asking them any difficult questions, either. Even though most of them would like nothing more than to be the object of police interest. As long as things don't go too far, that is. If people start checking out of the hotel because of what happened and head back to the city, Monahan will be raked over the coals by the town council for not finding someone to blame and not having it all swept under the rug."

"I can't see this being swept under the rug." I jerked my head toward cabin nineteen, from which I could hear drawers being opened and papers tossed. "Not with the FBI here."

"Which is why I'm not too worried about your busboys. I would be worried about anyone who's ever said a thing that might be seen as favorable to communism, though. You know anyone like that?"

"You think I have time to discuss politics in a Catskill summer?"

"No." His face was dark. "My uncle was no communist, but that useless clown show has decided he was, and they'll hear nothing to contradict that. There's a reason those two FBI agents are stationed here, in your mountain paradise, and not in the cities where things are happening."

We walked slowly down the hill. Ahead of us Delayed Lake sparkled in the sun. Orange paddleboats skimmed across the water, and the laughter of teenage girls on the diving platform echoed off the surrounding hills. A doubles tennis match was underway on the main court, and the old men were bent over their chess game. Two women passed us, fresh from the beauty parlor, their hair not giving an inch to the breeze and the scent of hair spray wafting after them.

"It is a mountain paradise," I said. "Too bad I never get a chance to enjoy it. Tell me about your uncle."

Jim stopped walking and stared out over the lake, twisting the brim of his hat in his hands. I closed my eyes, enjoying the feel of the hot sun washing over me, and said nothing, letting him take his time.

"As I said earlier, we were close when I was a kid. He wasn't married, didn't have any children of his own, so he came to our place in White Plains for Christmases, Thanksgivings, his summer holidays. He was a college professor, not much of one to throw the ball around for his nephews but fun in other ways: full of interesting facts. He encouraged me to always be curious, about everything, and I got my interest in journalism from asking him questions. He never considered a question to be stupid, and if he didn't know the answer, he helped me find it. He joined the army soon as America got into the war, went to England in forty-two. He was in France and Germany in forty-four and forty-five, right in the thick of things, moving with the front lines. He was one of the first into some of the camps."

As though a cloud had moved over the sun and a snowstorm threatened in the distance, I was suddenly cold. I wrapped my arms around myself.

"He never talked about what he saw there, but when he came home, Uncle Harold wasn't the same. He'd always been a quiet man, but now he was morose. He'd always been a loner, but now he was a recluse. He didn't try to go back to teaching, just sort of drifted around. He'd never married, so he had no family to worry about. He did some writing, historical stuff for dry academic publications. Six months or so ago he called me, said he was in the city doing research, and he suggested we have lunch. He was looking well, and I was pleased to see it. He'd started a book, he told me, which is what the research was for. It was going to be fiction, a novel. About a group of crack OAS agents who parachute into Germany in 1943 with the mission to assassinate Hitler and put an end to the war."

"That must be what you read. The stuff about the blackout."

"Not to mention the breathless French woman." Jim chuckled. "He was excited about the book, and it was good to see some of the life coming back to him. I'm no psychiatrist, but I figured he was doing what he could to try to rewrite history. Two weeks ago he called me at the paper. I wasn't at my desk, so he left a message with the switchboard, saying he'd rented a place in the Catskills, and he hoped to get his book finished by the end of July. He said he'd let me read it when it was done. And that was that."

"The maps on the wall. He needed those for his research. He probably has scenes set in Washington and London. The same with the books. I can see him needing to refer to Churchill's history, but why *The Communist Manifesto*?"

"You gotta have conflict among the group to make an exciting story, so it's likely one of the characters in his fictional OAS team had communist leanings. Being Uncle Harold, the most pedantic person I've ever met, he'd want to know what would attract an intelligent man to that stuff."

We stood together, looking out over the water.

Velvet was at the edge of the beach, watching Randy, up to his knees in the shallow lake water, chatting to two bathing-suit-clad women well into their ninth decade. She spotted me and trotted down the path toward us, very cute in her daring two-piece black suit and black cap. She pulled her bathing cap off and shook out her unfashionably long golden hair. Late June and she already had the start of an impressive tan.

I introduced her to Jim. When she heard his last name, her eyes flicked toward me, but she didn't say anything other than "Pleased to meet you."

"Having a good morning?" I asked.

"So far. Can't have better weather for getting in the water, so Randy and I expect to be at it all day. Although"— she gestured to the women in the lake—"some of these ladies know perfectly well how to swim. And doesn't he know it."

Jim chuckled.

She fell into step beside us as we continued on our way. "Rumor has it the FBI are here investigating a communist cell operating out of Haggerman's. My ladies are all atwit-ter at the very idea."

"Nip that one in the bud mighty fast." I made a mental note to get word to the staff that if anyone was discovered gossiping to the guests or within hearing distance of the guests about Westenham's death, they'd be on the next bus bouncing down Route 17.

"As my room's not ready," Jim said, "I'm going to head into town. Regardless of what's happening with the police investigation, I have to start making some arrangements. I called my dad earlier, he and my mom live in Florida now, but no answer. I have to keep trying."

"You can use the telephone in my office," I said. "If you need one another time, there are phones for the use of guests in the writing room and the games room."

"Thanks, but no. I need to call the paper, too, find out what's happening with the stories I was working on. Does the library in town have a public phone?"

I glanced at Velvet. She shrugged.

"There's a phone booth outside the grocery store," I said.

"Here comes the clown show," Jim said. "Those two wouldn't look more out of place if they were wearing snow-suits."

I turned my head to see Agents O'Reilly and Kowalski heading our way. City suits, shirts buttoned to the neck, ties, hats, polished shoes, arms stacked high with papers. The guests—bathing suits, sundresses, shorts, capris, bare heads—stopped whatever they were doing to gape.

"That's not going to do much to stop the gossip," Velvet said. "Mrs. Windermere is already checking out the younger one as to his eligibility as a prospective husband for her one remaining unmarried daughter. That the daughter seems not the least bit concerned about her lack of marital prospects is of no interest to the mother. A word of advice, Jim: be on guard. Mrs. Windermere has come to the Catskills this year with one goal only."

Velvet, Jim, and I stepped aside to let the FBI agents pass. Kowalski's eyes flicked toward me, but otherwise they didn't acknowledge us.

Excited whispers followed in their wake.

"You can check in when you get back," I said to Jim. "I'll tell the desk what we've arranged."

"Thanks." Looking about as out of place as the FBI agents, he followed them.

"My goodness," Velvet said once he was out of earshot. "A newspaperman and a handsome one to boot. Good job, Elizabeth."

"Mrs. Windermere," I said, "appears not to be the only one with eligibility on her mind. I did absolutely nothing except miss an hour's work, which no one will have taken care of in my absence."

Chapter 9

I HEADED BACK TO MY OFFICE TO GET STUCK INTO THE day's labors, but I wasn't fast enough. As I was leaving instructions at reception to have a room prepared for Jim Westenham, Chief Monahan bustled in, all red-faced, puffing, stuffed with importance. His silent deputy trailed along behind him.

"Mrs. Grady!" Monahan bellowed across the lobby. Our lobby isn't that big, but clearly the chief liked to put on a display. "A word!"

I pasted a smile on my face. The few guests still inside at this time of day stopped all pretext of doing something and stared.

"Chief Monahan," I said. "How can I help you?"

"Let's talk in your office. No need to disturb all these nice folks." He turned to his deputy. "Poke around the staff quarters. Ask them if they saw anyone sneaking into Westenham's cabin or talking to him as though they didn't want to be overheard. Don't bother the guests, though."

The deputy turned and walked away.

Did he talk? I wondered. I led the way through the door placed discreetly under the main staircase, down the dimly lit hallway, and into the outer business office. Phones were ringing, clerks talking, typewriters clanging. Smoke filled the air, and fans circulated. Every eye followed us into my office. I shut the door and went around the desk to sit in my chair. Monahan plopped himself into the room's sole visitor's chair.

"I've spoken to Mrs. Rostov," he said. "She tells me Westenham asked for his privacy and said he didn't want to be disturbed. He didn't come to the dining room for his meals or join in any of the organized activities. Does that seem strange to you?"

"It might be considered so," I said. "At a place like this, which is a family resort. On the other hand, if the man liked the Catskills and he wanted to be left alone to write his book, it's not a bad place to do that. Particularly in cabin nineteen. I had a look at his booking when I was searching for his contact information last night. He specifically requested a remote and private room. Cabin nineteen isn't one of the most expensive, as it doesn't have a lake view."

Monahan nodded. "As I suspected. Mrs. Rostov says she never met him. Did you?"

"Yes, I did. Twice. He was down by the lake yesterday afternoon, by himself, having a smoke. We said no more than two sentences to each other. I could tell he wanted to be alone, so I left him to it."

"The second time?"

"He came to the ballroom for the evening's entertainment last night. We didn't talk, but I saw him. That was . . ."

not long before he died. Again, he was on his own. He came in late, in time to catch the last act. I don't think he even sat down. He stood at the back of the room and watched. He had a drink, but he didn't talk to anyone. Not that I saw."

"What was the act?"

"We have a comedian from the city here for a couple of nights. His first night was yesterday."

"What's this comedian's name?"

"Charlie Simmonds."

Monahan's face looked blank. "Never heard of him. Westenham came to see his show, but nothing else?"

"The rest of the evening consisted of dancing to our house orchestra. If he was as much a recluse as would appear, he wouldn't have been interested in dancing. Maybe he was a comedy fan. I didn't see him leave."

"A comedian from New York, eh? We know about them."

"We do?"

"Where's this Simmonds now?"

"I have no idea. He's free all day to do as he likes. His first show's at nine, the second at eleven. We put the entertainers up in staff quarters."

Monahan pushed his chair back and stood up. "Let's go see him."

"Now? I don't know where he is. He might not even be on the property. I don't know if he came on the bus or has his own car."

"If he's a comedian, he's probably still in bed." Monahan stared at me. "Come along, Mrs. Grady. I need you to show me where he's staying."

"I'll get one of the bellhops to take you."

"You," he said.

I indicated the stack of papers on my desk. The mountain of pink message slips by my phone. "But, but . . ."

"Let's go."

"Why don't I send a runner to get him? If he's not in, we've wasted our time."

"Do you have keys for the staff rooms?"

"Yes, but—"

"Get them. If he's not in, all the better. We might find the letters he's been getting from Westenham."

I slowly got to my feet. I did not want to have anything to do with this, but it seemed that I would be involved whether I wanted to be or not. Monahan had been dismissed, quite rudely, by the FBI. Clearly he was trying to compensate by ordering me around. I grabbed the giant bunch of keys and clipped them to my belt. Long ago, I'd seen an illustration in a history book of the chatelaine of a medieval castle with her key ring attached to her belt, and I'd adapted the style rather than have to carry a purse around all day.

All eyes were on us as we once again crossed the outer office. "Carry on with what you're doing," I said.

No one even pretended to do so. Instead of going back through the lobby, I continued down the small dark hallway that ends at the kitchen deliveries door. From the kitchen itself came the sounds of someone threatening to kill someone else, men's laughter, a woman shouting, "Have some respect," and a pot hitting the floor.

"Busy place," Monahan said.

"It never stops." And it didn't. We served nine full meals a day: to adult guests in the main dining room, children in the children's, and staff in theirs. By anyone's standards the meals were huge and elaborate. Then there was tea with sandwiches and cake on the veranda in the afternoon, a cocktail reception before dinner, and a late-night dessert buffet. Plus room service anytime between six A.M. and one A.M. It's said many people come to the Catskills mainly to eat. When Rosemary presented me with the week's grocery bills, I believed it.

The path up the hill to the staff accommodations was rough, worn flat by generations of passing feet, unmaintained, edged by struggling saplings and heavy undergrowth. We wasted no money on grounds' maintenance here. I walked slowly, pretending not to notice Chief Monahan—his uniform shirt already soaked with sweat, his face red and forehead dripping—huffing and puffing with every step. Staff passed us, coming or going, and every one of them nodded respectfully to me or said, "Mrs. Grady," and glanced warily at Monahan as they gave us as wide a berth as possible on the trail.

When Olivia and I first arrived here two years ago, the staff quarters were barely decent enough for wildlife to live in. I'd done what I could, with what little money we could spare and what time we had, to improve things a bit. No one in the Catskills indulged their employees—room and board was part of staff wages—but at least we'd been able to get the bathtub water in the female entertainment staff building running again, move the family of raccoons out of the lifeguards' ceiling, and rip out the black mold growing on the walls of the bellhops' rooms. Some of our workers lived locally, but most of our summer staff were college kids from the city. Some of them, I knew, didn't spend all that much time in their bunks anyway. I'd been told that some of the hotels encouraged (or didn't discourage) the better-looking male staff to "make friends" with the married women who spent the entire summer in the mountains with their children while their husbands stayed behind in the city and came up occasionally to join their families for the weekend. The husbands were supposedly working, but I had no doubt some of them had special "summer friends" also.

Charlie Simmonds might be an up-and-coming comedy star, but he wasn't a headliner yet, and so he didn't get the better accommodations we kept for the real stars, if we were lucky enough to be able to book them.

Monahan and I emerged from the line of trees protecting guests from views of the shabby structures that make our hotel work. A double line of wood-framed buildings with torn shutters, forest-debris-covered roofs, sagging porches, and leaky gutters.

"Number five," I said to Monahan.

We climbed the steps, creaking dangerously beneath our feet, and I opened the screen door. We stepped into a small, dark foyer, leading into a damp, gloomy hallway with doors both open and closed running off it.

"Good morning," I called. "Mrs. Grady here."

At the end of the corridor a door slammed. Another door opened, and the tousled head of the trombone player popped out.

"Hi," he said cheerily. Behind him, I caught a glimpse of what might have been one of the dance instructors scurrying across the room.

"Hi," I said. "I'm looking for Mr. Simmonds. The guest comedian. Do you know what room he's in?"

"Seven," he said. "Hi, Chief Monahan. Nice to see you. It's been a while."

"Let's keep it that way, Lenny," the chief said.

Wondering what on earth that meant, I walked down the hall and knocked on the door of number seven.

"What?" came a voice from inside. I was glad of it. I did not want to have to enter the man's room if he wasn't there.

"It's Mrs. Grady, resort manager. I need to speak to you for a moment. I'm with the police."

The door flew open. I was pleased to see that we had not woken him up. Charlie Simmonds was dressed for a day in the mountains in orange-and-brown-checked Bermuda shorts held up by a wide black belt, an open-necked gray shirt, and knee-high white socks in brown sandals. He might have used half a bottle of oil to slick back his dark hair, and he'd so recently trimmed the edges of his thin mustache that tiny bits of hair were stuck to his upper lip.

"Sorry to bother you," I said.

"Is there a problem?" he asked Chief Monahan.

"Mind if we come in?" Monahan asked.

Charlie glanced at me. I tried to smile as I studied his face, not sure what I was looking for. Guilt? Fear? Wariness? I read nothing but mild disinterest. The room contained a single bed, a small dresser, and a window looking directly into an overgrown patch of sumac, but as a guest entertainer, he'd had a private room written into his contract. He still had to share the bathroom down the hall, though.

Charlie shrugged and stepped back. Monahan turned to face me. "Thank you for your time, Mrs. Grady. I won't be needing your help any longer."

"I—"

He went into Charlie's room, and slammed the door in my face.

I debated what to do next. Aside from my normal workload, I needed to be a visible, calm, comforting presence, reassuring staff and guests alike that I had everything under control. I went outside to the rickety porch and sat on the rickety railing and waited.

At this time of day it was quiet enough I could hear birds
calling to one another from the trees and the distant sound
of guests enjoying themselves in the pool or the lake. I
closed my eyes and took deep breaths of the fresh forest air,
heavy with the scent of pine needles and leaf mulch. As
well as the contents of the overflowing ashtray on the porch
table. It was nice to take a quiet moment out of the day, but
I'd be paying for my idleness later.

I didn't have long to enjoy my solitude before Monahan
emerged from the building, slapping his hat onto his head.
He didn't see me, sitting quietly in the shadows, and thumped
down the steps and up the path. I watched him go and then
slid off the railing. When I turned, Charlie Simmonds was
watching me.

"All okay?" I asked.

"I didn't murder one of your guests," he said.

"Glad to hear it. Did you have anything to tell the chief?"

He dug in the pocket of his shirt and pulled out a pack
of cigarettes and a gold lighter. He tapped out a single cigarette, offered it to me, which I refused, and then he put it in
his mouth, flicked the lighter, held the flame to the cigarette, and took a deep breath. As he exhaled he snapped the
lighter shut and said, "I'm to go into town at one this afternoon. To the hospital to see the body."

"You knew Mr. Westenham?"

He picked a piece of tobacco off his lip. "I knew a man
named Harold Westenham. Sounds like it might be the
right guy. Right age anyway, so the chief wants me to have
a look. I didn't see him last night, and no one came to talk
to me after my show, except a couple of smart-aleck kids
who want me to introduce them to my agent. If it is the
same guy, I knew him in the army. He was an infantry
major, and I was with JAG."

"JAG? You mean military justice? What did you do there?"

The corners of his mouth turned up. "In my former life I was a lawyer. Gave it up for the glamour of comedy." He held his arms out to take in the silent woods, the crumbling, leaky accommodations. "And, yeah, before you ask, I like this life better. I was a lousy lawyer."

"What did that have to do with Mr.—then Major—Westenham? Was he in trouble with the law?"

"No, nothing like that. Our paths crossed, as so many did in the chaos of the war. It was France, I think. We were stuck in the same miserable town for a while, that's about all. Got to chatting now and again. He'd been a history professor in his past life, and he knew all sorts of interesting things about the area we were in. I remember one day when we drove through a town where the old cathedral had been just about completely bombed out. I thought he was going to cry. Come to think of it, he did cry."

"The Mr. Westenham who was staying here was a college professor."

"Doesn't mean it was the same guy, but sounds like it. We moved on, went separate ways, and I never thought about him again. Westenham, if it was the guy I knew, was one of those really serious types. Never laughed, never shared a joke. He worked. And then he worked some more. Not a lot to laugh about, in France and Germany at the end of the war, but even in the worst of times people need to laugh, maybe even more in the worst of times. That's probably why I went into comedy, if I stop to analyze it. Which I don't."

"Thanks for telling me." I started to leave. "I'd better get back to the hotel."

"I don't care to be called a communist, though."

I stopped. "Chief Monahan said that?"

"He seems to think Westenham was up here, at your pleasant little hotel, plotting the overthrow of the US government, and he came right out and asked if I was conspiring with Westenham. Guy's not all that bright. If I was a coconspirator, I'd be unlikely to admit it, wouldn't I?"

"Indeed."

"I didn't know Westenham well. We weren't friends, and I haven't seen him for eight or nine years. He was a serious guy, and he took his job seriously. He never talked politics, not to me anyway. I told your chief that."

"He's not my chief."

Behind Charlie, the door creaked open and a dancer came out. Her hair hung loosely around her face, but otherwise she was dressed as she would have been last night—one-inch heels, low-cut dress, crinoline-stuffed skirt. She ducked her head and slipped past Charlie.

"This is the men's accommodation," I said. "Do you have reason to be here?"

"Yes, Mrs. Grady, yes, I do." She lifted her head and looked intently into my eyes. Her own eyes were red and the bags beneath them deep. "My friend wasn't feeling too good, so he asked the kitchen to make some chicken soup. I brought it up to him." She laughed nervously. Her breath was terrible. "Nothing like chicken soup, is there?"

"No," I agreed.

She ran lightly down the stairs and disappeared into the woods.

"They don't tiptoe back to their rooms and slip quietly into bed with a mug of hot cocoa and a letter from home intent on getting a good night's sleep as soon as the evening entertainment ends, you know," Charlie said.

"I know that perfectly well. I don't care what any of

them get up to in their own time, as long as it doesn't disturb the guests. It's to make sure they don't disturb the guests that I have to pretend I'm keeping a stern eye out."

"No need to keep a stern eye on me," Charlie said. "I'm not much of a party guy. I like to think I'm a ball of laughs onstage, but offstage I prefer my own company. I came straight here when I was finished last night, and I didn't go out again. I was, in case you're wondering, alone. I told your chief that. I didn't see Westenham, if it was him. The walls in this building are mighty thin, and the place was buzzing all night. Someone had died they said, and the cops were here. I figured one of your guests had a heart attack. Half of them are heading that way."

"Did Chief Monahan believe you?"

Charlie's face twisted. "No. He thinks I followed Westenham out of the ballroom after my act finished, down to the lake, and bashed him over the head because we'd had a falling-out. As we communists, according to him, do. He says I can expect a visit from the FBI."

"Is that a problem?"

He threw up his hands. "It most certainly is a problem, Mrs. Grady. I don't need a reputation as a red. My career's finally getting off the ground. My agent's working at getting me into the Concord and he says we have a good shot at it. Word gets around I'm a possible commie, and my bookings will dry up overnight. Goodbye, Concord. I hope you don't have anyone moving into my room later this week?"

"Why do you say that? We have a magician starting on Saturday and he'll take the room."

"Chief Monahan told me I'm not to leave. Not until he, and the FBI, have completed their investigation."

I sputtered.

"Yeah," he said. "Typical Charlie Simmonds luck. A guy

I didn't talk to, didn't even see, came to catch my show and winds up dead, and I'm under suspicion. My name's not all that unusual, but you had my picture displayed in the lobby, right?"

"Of course. We always inform the guests who's appearing that night."

"Westenham, if it was the guy I knew from the army, must have seen it. Recognized me, and wondered what I was up to these days. Monahan says he didn't take part in the dancing or even take a seat. He came in, caught my act, and left. Didn't try to find me to say hi. Maybe he expected I'd hang around for a drink at the end of the night. I didn't."

"He might have been planning to talk to you tomorrow. Meaning today. At a better time."

Charlie shrugged. "Doesn't matter now, does it? I'm under suspicion for being not only a communist but a murderer. And you have an unexpected guest for a few more days. Now, if you'll excuse me, I'm going back to my room to change. I intend to take advantage of staying here, and I'm going to check out the pool."

"WHAT SORT OF PLACE ARE YOU RUNNING HERE, ELIZA-beth Grady?"

Instead of sneaking to my office the back way after my talk with Charlie Simmonds, I'd foolishly come into the lobby to check on how the day was going.

It was not going well.

Mrs. Brownville and her circle of cronies were sitting in a solid line on a sofa, backs straight, feet planted firmly on the floor, hands folded tightly over their purses. A row of vultures waiting to pounce. I sighed, smiled, and crossed the lobby.

"Good morning, ladies. It's going to be another beautiful Catskills day."

Mrs. Brownville clutched her massive handbag to her chest. "Not if we're all murdered in our beds."

Passersby stopped to stare.

"No one's going to be murdered in their beds or elsewhere, Mrs. Brownville."

"That man was. That . . . that communist."

Her friends nodded in unison. They even dressed alike: pastel shirtwaist dresses, pearl necklaces, heavy belts, stockings, closed shoes, rigid purses, hair wound into tight rolls.

"A guest died, yes," I said. "Most unfortunate. That he was murdered has not been determined."

"That's not what I heard." A man wearing a particularly florid shirt pushed his way through the crowd of onlookers. "He was shot and dumped into the lake, but the cement overshoes weren't attached properly, so he floated to the surface."

"That's ridiculous," I said.

"I heard knifed," Mrs. Brownville said, "but that doesn't matter. He was a communist, here to plot with other communists. And I want to know what you"—a finger stabbed in my direction—"knew about it."

"I knew absolutely nothing about it. Not that there's anything to know. The man, our guest, was a US Army veteran, here on vacation."

"Why did I never see him around? Can you tell me that?" Mrs. Brownville demanded.

"We have almost four hundred guests staying here this week. You can't say you noticed everyone."

"I certainly can. I keep myself attentive to my surroundings at all times."

She was probably right about that. She would have been searching for fault in every one of them.

"He was here to write a book. He wanted his privacy, and we honored that."

"Ha!" Mrs. Brownville crowed to her circle. "A writer. I knew it!"

The crowd was building. Guests wandered in from outside to see what was going on. Staff members were coming out of the offices or the dining room. The bellhops gathered at the entrance, wondering if they should be doing something.

"The police were at the staff cabins just now," a man said. "I saw them poking around. Asking questions. No smoke without fire I always say. Are you aware your staff harbors communists?"

"I . . . I . . ." I floundered for words. None came.

"What were the police looking for?" another guest asked.

"Did they arrest anyone? Maybe we should think about leaving if there's a killer on the loose."

"I . . ."

"That comedian has something to do with it," Mrs. Brownville snapped. "Mark my words."

"I . . ."

"If they aren't communists, then why are the FBI here?" the flowered-shirt man said. "Those guys don't come out for any common murder."

"Mabel," a man said. "We're checking out. Now."

"But we've paid for another week," Mabel protested.

"We'll ask for our money back."

"You can ask, but you won't get it," I said. "Ladies and gentlemen, please. There's nothing to be concerned about. Go back to what you were doing and continue to enjoy your day. The police were only doing . . . what police do."

A loud voice broke through the hubbub. "Is it raining out?"

Everyone, including me, turned to see Olivia posed in the doorway. She was dressed in white capris and a short-sleeved pink-and-white-striped shirt with the collar turned up to frame her face. Her hair was arranged into a French twist, and large square pink earrings were clipped to her ears. Her lipstick matched the shirt and the earrings, and round sunglasses covered her face. She was the very picture of Hollywood glamour on vacation. Velvet stood behind her among a cluster of nervous bellhops.

"Everyone inside on such a lovely day? How very odd." Olivia took off her sunglasses, dangled them in her long fingers, and floated across the room as though she were in Fred Astaire's arms, her eyes resting briefly on every face she passed. "Yes, it's true that a member of our Haggerman's family passed away last night." She shook her head sadly. "A tragedy, and I know you'll all join me in mourning his passing."

Olivia put a perfectly manicured hand lightly on florid-shirt man's arm. Blood rushed into his face.

"It's vitally important we do all we can to help the police, don't you agree, sir?"

He swallowed and nodded.

Olivia cocked her head to one side and smiled shyly at Mabel's husband. "The authorities might be suspicious of people who leave unexpectedly."

Everyone glared at Mabel's husband.

"I didn't mean—" he began.

Mrs. Brownville was not to be distracted. She stood up. "What about the communists? What about that comedian fellow?"

"Communists? In *my* hotel!" Olivia exclaimed. "Never.

Wouldn't be allowed. Mr. Simmonds was doing his duty in talking to the police when asked." Her eyes swept the room again, before ending up back at Mrs. Brownville. "As should we all, I'm sure you'll agree."

People muttered their agreement.

"A toast to all of us in the Haggerman's family would be a lovely way to honor our dear friend who left us so prematurely."

Olivia raised her right arm and snapped her fingers. Every one of the bellhops, the office and kitchen staff crowding the doorways, and the clerks behind the reception desk leapt to attention.

"You." Olivia pointed to a receptionist. All the color drained out of the young man's face, and he looked as though he might faint. "Instruct the bartenders to open up in the ballroom a mite early today." Olivia checked her watch. "Shall we say in ten minutes? And, because we are honoring a member of the Haggerman's family, tell them to forgo asking for room numbers until the dining room opens for lunch at noon."

Free booze for an hour! The rush was on. I stifled a groan as I saw dollar bills flying out the windows, but I couldn't be too concerned about losing money on drinks. It would be a lot worse if guests stampeded to check out and new ones didn't check in because word got around that we were a hotbed of communist activity.

Everyone headed for the stairs, wanting to be first in line in case Olivia changed her mind. Or the booze ran out. Olivia took one step forward and grabbed Mrs. Brownville's arm. Her grip was so firm it made dents in the skin. She smiled sweetly into the other woman's face. Mrs. Brownville's friends had abandoned her in their rush to get to the front of the line.

"Thank you so much, *dear*," Olivia said, "for bringing your concerns to management. Why don't you join me for a drink? I do believe there's a bottle of my special champagne on ice in the ballroom."

Mrs. Brownville's mouth opened. It shut again.

"Excellent." Olivia guided her guest toward the grand staircase. The crowd separated to let them through.

"Nicely done," Velvet said to me in a low voice.

"I cannot begin to imagine how much this is going to cost us."

"Less than if you had a riot on your hands and people demanding to check out. I suspected there was going to be trouble when I saw Mrs. Brownville and her pack heading this way, so I left my volleyball game in midthrow and ran for Olivia."

"That wasn't necessary. I could have handled it," I said weakly.

"No, you couldn't, Elizabeth. Olivia's the star. She's got the charm and the grace and the style. Not to mention the iron will. You don't, but that's okay. You have other good qualities."

"I'll ask another time what those qualities might be."

Word had spread, as it did, and people came running from all directions. Some were still in their bathing suits, which was not normally permitted in the main rooms of the hotel. I wondered if Olivia would make an exception this time only.

"Chief Monahan didn't want to question the guests because he doesn't want anyone getting upset and leaving early," I said. "Instead of simply talking to people and telling them a sanitized version of what's going on, he has the FBI marching out of here carrying stacks of documents, the police car parked in front of the hotel all morning, and his deputy sneaking around in the shrubbery waylaying the staff. Are they still here?"

"The police car's gone," Velvet said.

"I'm going to my office. I need to calm down."

"And I need to get back to my volleyball game. If there is a game still going on and they all haven't deserted it for the pleasure of an open bar. Before I go, I forgot to ask: How are your feet doing today?"

I glanced down. "My feet? What about them?"

"You got some cuts last night."

"Oh. Right. With all that's going on, I forgot about them. I guess that means they're fine. Look, Velvet, we have to talk this over. All of us. Meet me at the house at two. I'll get Aunt Tatiana and Rosemary to come as well."

Chapter 10

EVERYONE CROWDED INTO OUR LIVING ROOM AT TWO
o'clock. I wasn't used to being at home in the middle of the
day and decided it was rather nice. The sun streamed in
through the open windows, the big leafy trees draped the
house in cool shade, and the inner door was open to let a
soft breeze cut through the sticky heat.

Aunt Tatiana and Rosemary had come, as invited, and
uninvited Randy had trailed along after Velvet. Winston
wandered in from somewhere and dropped down on the rug
in the center of the living room. We stepped over him to
take our seats.

I'd not invited all the department heads to this meeting.
That might be necessary later, but I wanted to talk recent
developments over with my family and personal friends
first.

"Before we begin," I said, "how much booze do you
think we went through this morning, Olivia?"

My mother waved her hand in the air. "That doesn't matter."

"It matters to me," Rosemary said. "I have to put in a rush order to restock."

"It matters to me," I said, "as I have to pay for it."

"Better than guests running for the exits," Randy said.

I muttered something in agreement.

"This is not good," Aunt Tatiana said around a freshly lit cigarette. "My chambermaids have been questioned about the man in cabin nineteen. They're mostly adult women with families, local people, worked here or in other hotels for many years. They aren't going to quit, but—"

"But," Velvet said, "two of the college girls who look after the children asked me if it's safe to stay here."

I snorted.

"I told them that, sadly, when you have hundreds, thousands, of people staying at a place, as we do, then it's possible, likely even, some are going to fall ill if not die. Particularly considering how many elderly guests we have. I kind of implied that's what happened in this case, and the police were called as a matter of routine."

"We have more than nervous girls away from home for the first time to worry about," Rosemary said. "I overheard a couple of the waiters saying the police had asked them to keep an eye out for any talk of communism. They sounded as though they were mighty anxious to find it. You know what these college boys are like. Hotheads the lot of them. Out to prove something. To themselves if no one else."

"Elizabeth," Olivia said. "Tell our employees they are not spies."

"I can, and I will, send a memo around, reminding the staff they are not to gossip about, or with, our guests," I said.

"I can't instruct them not to cooperate with the police, as much as I might like to."

"A memo against gossiping," Velvet said. "You might as well send a memo to the creek ordering it to flow up the mountain."

"Charlie Simmonds has been ordered not to leave Haggerman's," I said. "Monahan practically accused him of being in cahoots with the late Mr. Westenham."

"Who is Charlie Simmonds?" Olivia asked.

"The comedian who was onstage last night. You recommended him, Olivia."

My mother shrugged. "I forget names."

"He was good," Velvet said. "Everyone thought so. I saw Mrs. Brownville suppressing a laugh at one point. I thought she might explode under the pressure. What does he have to do with any of this?"

I quickly explained about Charlie's nebulous connection to Harold Westenham and why that aroused Chief Monahan's suspicions.

"Why is that your problem, Elizabeth?" Olivia asked.

"We have that magician coming for the weekend, and he was supposed to go into the room Charlie's in on Saturday. I've had to ask Aunt Tatiana to open yet another room in the old staff quarters, so we can put the magician up in there."

"Is no trouble," Tatiana said.

"Perhaps not, but we're not in the business of giving away free accommodation."

"Yet another room?" Olivia asked.

"Harold Westenham's nephew Jim needs a place to stay."

"Oh yes, Jim," Velvet said. "The handsome newspaperman without a wedding ring, around our age, who's taken a shine to Elizabeth."

"He has?" Olivia said.

"He has not," I said.

"I didn't think he was that handsome," Randy said.

"Elizabeth's right," Rosemary said.

"You think he's handsome, too?" Randy asked.

"Elizabeth is right that we can't keep giving away free rooms. Why not tell this comedian he has to work for it? The guests won't mind an extra element added to the nightly show."

"Good idea," I said. "When we're finished here, I'll let him know if he stays past the end of his contract, he has to perform in exchange for his room. As for the aforementioned Jim Westenham, who's Harold's nephew, he's come up from the city to make his uncle's arrangements. The police have roped off cabin nineteen until further notice, and we're almost full, so I put Jim up in the old staff accommodations."

"The mice might not like sharing," Velvet said.

"They're going to have to. I gave him the room for free, but he has to pay for his meals."

"Why?" Olivia asked. "I mean, why does he need a room? Has he decided to make a vacation out of his uncle's death?"

"The police are holding the body, pending the results of their investigation. Jim wants to stay until things get sorted out. He says any idea his uncle was some sort of communist agent is ridiculous."

"If he was a spy," Randy pointed out, "he wouldn't have gone around telling everyone."

"True," I said. "But Jim and his uncle were close, and he would have noticed, you'd think, if Harold had those leanings."

Jim had told me he and his uncle hadn't had much contact over the last few years. A lot can happen in a few years. I decided not to mention that. "Jim dropped into my office just before I came here to tell me that word of this mess has spread beyond our property."

"That's bound to happen," Velvet said. "We can't stop people from talking about it."

"Talking is one thing, but spreading rumors and panic is entirely another," I said. "People are talking about us in town. Specifically, they're saying that Haggerman's Catskills Resort is a nest of communist activity and the army is preparing to raid us at any minute."

Everyone stared at me, openmouthed.

"That's what Jim said, anyway."

My mother was rarely at a loss for words. Finally she said, "Well, I never—"

Winston growled and rolled over.

"That might not be as much of a problem as it appears," Randy said. "Few, if any, of our guests ever go into town."

"Why would they?" Olivia said. "When we meet every need they have right here. Isn't that what you tell them, Elizabeth?"

"It says so in our advertising, so it must be true. But we don't live in a complete bubble out here. The staff go into town. Some of the teenage guests do."

"Your newspaper friend—" Olivia said.

"He's not my friend," I said.

"So you keep saying. If he's hearing talk in town, we need to ask where this talk's coming from. The unfortunate death of our guest happened late last night. Almost all the staff who live at home would have left by then, and they wouldn't be finished with their work today yet. They wouldn't have had time to start spreading these rumors."

"The FBI might have been asking questions," Randy said. "And people leapt to conclusions."

"I doubt they're usually so chatty," Rosemary said.

"It must be coming from Chief Monahan and his barely verbal deputy," I said. "Jim told me the local newspaper, the *Summervale Gazette*, was quick to jump on the story. He said the reporter from the paper isn't simply asking questions but dropping highly suggestive implications into those questions."

"What does that mean?" Randy asked.

"Questions like, were you aware that Haggerman's might be a front for a communist cell?"

This time it was Olivia's turn to snort.

The inner door had been left open so the air could circulate, and out on the porch a squirrel jumped onto the railing. I thought Winston was sound asleep, but he leapt to his feet with a startled yelp and ran for the screen door, barking furiously. Aunt Tatiana patted her chest.

"I was thinking about that as I walked over here," I said. "As Olivia pointed out, this is all happening very quickly. Monahan might have told someone who then rushed out and spread the news far and wide, or it might have originated at another source."

"Don't ty to be so mysterious," Olivia said. "What are you talking about?"

"Richard Kennelwood was here last night. He came to the dance and the comedy show. He stayed until the end."

Olivia's eyebrows rose.

"From Kennelwood Hotel?" Randy asked. "What of it?"

"Jerome Kennelwood was ill over the winter, and his son has taken control of the hotel," Olivia said. "You think he had something to do with this?"

"Not necessarily with the murder, but he was here. Maybe he hadn't left when we found the body and called the police. Even if he had, the Kennelwoods have been in Summervale for a lot of years, and Jerome's an important man in these parts. Did Jerome or his son make a quiet, friendly call to the chief of police to ask what's happening?"

"And then," Velvet said, "they took advantage of what happened here to try to blackball Haggerman's."

"The nerve!" Aunt Tatiana crushed out her cigarette in a Niagara Falls souvenir ashtray and immediately lit another.

"I'm not saying that's what happened," I said. "Only that it's a possibility."

"I will ask Irena," Aunt Tatiana said. Irena was her friend, the head housekeeper at Kennelwood.

"They're not going to tell her if they're up to no good," Olivia said.

Aunt Tatiana raised her eyebrows and cocked her head toward her sister. "Tell her? No. They won't *tell* her."

"We're getting off course," Randy said. "I was there, remember, when the ambulance drivers checked Westenham out. They had no doubt the guy was murdered. So the big question has to be—who killed him?"

"I am sorry for not asking earlier," Aunt Tatiana said. "Randy, are you okay? That must have been a traumatic experience for you."

He gave her a brave smile. "Thanks, Mrs. Rostov, but I'm fine. It was unpleasant, but I can deal with it."

Velvet rolled her eyes to the heavens.

"Randy's question's important," Rosemary said. "If this Mr. Westenham was murdered, deliberately, do we want to ask who did such a thing?"

We looked at each other. Squirrel seen to, Winston settled down at Tatiana's feet and resumed his nap. The only sounds coming from outside were birds calling to one another and the gentle movement of the wind in the trees. So peaceful and quiet; such a contrast to the dark mood that had settled over this room.

"That's not our business," I said. "People bring their troubles with them, whether they want to or not."

"It might become our business," Rosemary said, "if the police keep at the communist angle. Never mind now the FBI's involved."

"Do they have any suspects?" Olivia asked. "Other than these mythical communists taking their vacation at my hotel."

"I don't know," I said. "Chief Monahan isn't sharing information with me. I can't see a Haggerman's guest killing Mr. Westenham. The man kept to himself. He didn't speak to anyone; he didn't take his meals in the dining room. He stayed in his cabin and wrote his book and took a stroll in the afternoons by the lake. Even when he came to the ballroom, he kept to himself, had a drink, and then left without having said a word to anyone. Who would have killed him? Why would someone have killed him?"

"You said it yourself," Velvet said. "People bring their troubles with them. Did a guest recognize him and remember an old grievance? Did someone follow him from the city specifically intending to, as they say, bump him off?"

"I bet that's it," Randy said. "Easier to bump someone off when they're on vacation, not paying attention to their surroundings, and then slip back to the city, leaving the local cops with no suspects."

"Ask Jim about that, Elizabeth," Velvet said.

"Why me?"

"I'll go with you if you want," Randy said. "In case he tries something. He got here awfully fast, if you ask me."

"You'll protect Elizabeth, will you?" Velvet said. "I think she can take care of herself."

"I'm not asking anyone anything," I said. "I have a hotel to run. I'll point out, if I have to, that you all have jobs around here, too. All except you, Olivia. Maybe you should be the one to ask the questions."

I didn't mean to put an edge into my question, but that's how it came out. My mother raised one sculpted eyebrow. "I do believe I did my job rather well this morning. No one checked out, did they?"

"She's got you there," Velvet said.

I had to admit, she did. Whenever I felt myself getting resentful at the amount of work Olivia had put on my shoulders, I tried to remind myself that when she did step up to the plate, she did it in spectacular fashion.

Olivia continued, "This newspaper friend of yours—yes, Elizabeth, you keep saying he's not your friend—told you these rumors originated with the local press. I have, I need not remind you, a good deal of experience with news-papermen. One cannot always believe what they say."

"What do you mean?" Velvet asked.

"When I was in Hollywood, preparing for my role in that movie with Cary Grant—you all remember the one I'm sure—I comforted a dear friend when his wife—"

"Velvet means," I said, "what are you implying about what's happening here? Now. She's not asking about you and your *dear friend*."

"I'll tell you the story later," Olivia said to Velvet. Velvet hid a fond smile. She'd heard all of Olivia's stories of when she was rich and famous, many times. "Newspapers have been known to embellish facts on occasion. All you know, Elizabeth, is what this man told you. Perhaps he's the one asking these questions, spreading these rumors. And then coming back here and trying his charms on you."

"He's not trying to charm me or anyone else. He doesn't want to see his uncle's reputation besmirched."

Olivia peered at me through wide eyes. "So he told you.

That might not be true. I wonder if there's any inheritance involved."

"Good question," Randy said.

"May I remind you all that I spoke to Jim last night less than an hour after his uncle died? He was in New York City."

"Maybe he hired a contract killer," Randy said.

"Don't complicate things any more than they are," I said. "I'll admit that Olivia's right—"

"As I always am," my mother said.

"Don't press your luck," I replied. "I shouldn't automatically believe what he's telling me."

Velvet stood up. "As much fun as this has been . . . It's almost two thirty. Randy has a swimming lesson for preschool kids in the pool. Normally, I'd suggest finding someone else to teach the class, but we can't disappoint the mothers, can we? And I have the tennis round robin to referee."

"I left the chef threatening to chop off the saladman's index finger," Rosemary said, "and give it back to him to use as decoration on the Jell-O salads. Hopefully it's safe to venture once again into the kitchen."

"As Elizabeth has decided to open two unused rooms," Aunt Tatiana said, "I should check if any more will be able to be made habitable, if needed."

"They won't be needed," I said.

"You never know," she said.

My mother yawned. "That champagne I had earlier is making me sleepy. I think a nap is called for. I'll put in an appearance at dinner this evening and attend the entertainment later. Rosemary, tell the maître d' to have a head table prepared and suitable guests invited to join me. My calming, comfortable presence might be needed once again. Elizabeth, find out what they are saying about us in town."

The screen door slammed as Randy, Rosemary, Aunt Tatiana, Velvet, and Winston made their escape.

"*What?*" I said to the sound of rapidly departing footsteps—and paws. "I'm not going into town, and I'm not finding out anything about anything. I have a hotel to run. I've already lost almost the entire day with this foolishness."

Steel settled behind my mother's eyes. She got to her feet swiftly and crossed the room to the telephone table. She opened the top drawer and took out the keys to my car. "If these rumors continue to spread, if the person who killed one of our guests in cold blood is not found, and quickly, we might not have a hotel for you to run much longer. I do not trust the Summervale police. I do not trust this newspaperman. I most certainly do not trust Jerome Kennelwood or his son, and I don't trust many of our employees not to turn on us if it suits them to do so. I trust you, Elizabeth." She handed me the keys.

I took a deep breath. My mother trusted me with the only thing she had left in the world: Haggerman's Catskills Resort. She could have hired someone with hotel experience to run it for her, but she hadn't hesitated to ask me. She could have left the police to fumble around with this investigation. But she was asking me.

I accepted the keys. "Okay."

Chapter 11

I LEFT MY MOTHER HEADING FOR HER NAP AND SKIPPED lightly down the stairs. As my foot hit the path, I heard a branch crack from inside the woods edging close to our house, and a grunt of pain coming from my left. I stopped dead. "Who's there?"

I held my breath and listened. Twigs snapped and leaves rustled. A squirrel ran up the trunk of a scraggly white pine.

Someone was out there, watching me, but I wasn't frightened. It was the middle of the afternoon on a bright sunny summer's day. Hundreds of people were within the sound of my voice if I yelled for help.

"This section of the property is out-of-bounds to guests. If you're not a guest, then you're trespassing."

Leaves rustled and a figure stepped out from behind the pine tree.

I muffled a groan and didn't bother to be polite. "What are you doing here, sneaking around my house?"

"I'm not sneaking, Miss Peters," Louis said. "I have to say, I don't care for your tone. I'm enjoying a walk in the woods, and I got lost." His eyes flicked toward the house. The house where my mother was having a nap. With all that had been going on, I'd forgotten to tell her we needed to start locking the door. Blood was leaking from a deep scratch on Louis's right cheek, and dried needles were caught on the fabric of his jacket. He'd clearly been battling with the forest.

"I want you to stay away from my mother," I said.

He attempted to look offended. "If your mother would enjoy my company, who are you to refuse it?" He waved his cane at me.

"Thing is, Louis, my mother doesn't want your company." I tried to soften my voice. "My mother's a private person. She guards that privacy carefully. I'm sure you understand. I'm going up to the hotel now. Why don't we walk together?"

He hesitated, giving the house one last longing glance, and then he followed me. He leaned heavily on his cane, and I didn't think that was a pretext.

Despite her bad leg, or perhaps because of it, Olivia exercised regularly. She was still dancer-quick and agile. I didn't worry that Louis would physically harm her, but he had no business being a pest. And he certainly had no business trying to peek into our windows.

We walked slowly along the lakefront, his cane tapping the path. "Are you visiting with your wife?" I asked him.

"Oh, no. I never had the good fortune to marry. I'm with my sister and her family. Twenty years, we've being going to the Concord, but I managed to persuade her that a smaller, more intimate hotel would be nice for a change."

A hotel that just happens to be owned by Olivia Peters.

"What's your sister's name?"

"Edith Lowman. We're a big group. Edith and her husband, their son and daughter with their spouses, and six grandchildren."

Thirteen guests. Maybe it wouldn't be a good idea to kick Louis out, not if he left taking his entire family with him. We reached the steps to the hotel.

"Please don't go near my mother's house again," I said to him. "If you promise not to, I might be able to persuade her to stop by your table at dinner one night and meet your family."

The cloudy eyes shone in the wrinkled face. "That would be marvelous. I'm a great admirer of hers. I'll never forget seeing her live on Broadway back in forty-six. Or was it forty-seven? Perhaps it was both. How time flies. Do you think she'd do that?"

"If I ask her to."

He bustled off, happy.

I was not so happy. I tossed the car keys from one hand to the other. I had a full hotel. It was the start of the season. And now I had to go into Summervale and attempt to salvage Haggerman's reputation, which shouldn't need salvaging. I told the reception clerks I was going out and went into the office to tell the women there the same.

"That big group of wedding guests booked to stay here for the last week in July just canceled," one of the clerks called to me. "The wedding's off."

The woman at the desk next to her laughed through a cloud of smoke. "Do tell. Who got cold feet? Him or her?"

"How many people?" I asked.

"Twenty-five guests. Ten rooms. Four of the families are coming anyway. Probably glad to have the vacation and not have to bother about having to dress up and go to a family wedding." She chuckled.

"We'll keep their deposit, and shouldn't have trouble renting out the rooms. Let the booking agencies know we have rooms available for that time."

"Chef Leonardo wants to speak to you," another clerk called. "He came in here demanding to talk to you as soon as you got in. He says he can't take any more of the unprofessionalism of your saladman and he's quitting."

"Ignore him. As usual," I said. I went into my office for my purse. I grabbed it, trying not to look at the stack of pink message slips piled beside my phone. I'd been out of the office for less than an hour and I'd swear that pile had doubled, if not tripled, since I'd seen it last. I unsnapped my bunch of keys off my belt and threw them into my purse. I locked the door to my office and snuck out the back way, heading for the delivery and staff parking areas at the top of the hill. I hadn't taken the car out for a couple of weeks, and my 1946 Chevrolet, a two-door coupe with a baby-blue body, white roof, and silver trim, was covered in a light layer of dust. Weeds were peeking through the cracks in the pavement underneath the car. I'd never owned a car before, but I decided I'd need one living in the Catskills. Delivery trucks arrive and depart our property throughout the day, and the bus into town runs regularly in the summer season but less often in the winter. Olivia balked at the expense of the car, but I didn't like the idea of being trapped up here on our mountain.

I opened the door, slipped behind the wheel, and turned the key. The car struggled mightily to start, and just as I was afraid I'd have to call a mechanic for help, it roared to life.

I threw it into gear and started down the hill toward Route 17. About halfway down, I spotted a lone figure climbing up, fanning himself with his hat, hair oil glistening in the sun, and I pulled to a halt. Charlie Simmonds waved his hat at me and crossed the road. The bus from town stops at the bottom of our road, and I assumed he'd gotten off there.

"Did you get to the hospital?" I asked. "Was it the man you expected?"

He leaned against the car and spoke to me through the window. He'd dressed in his worn brown suit and a tie for his trip to the hospital, and he was red-faced and dripping with sweat. "Harold Westenham, my old army buddy. Yeah, it was him. I'd say he hadn't changed a bit, but hard to tell considering the circumstances."

"I'm sorry you had to go through that."

"See him, you mean. Don't worry. I've seen worse. Rarely been accused of worse, though."

"What does that mean?" Once the car stopped moving, and air was no longer flowing through the windows, the heat began building in the car. I wiped away beads of sweat dripping down my forehead.

"Your police chief was there. Once I'd confirmed it was Harold Westenham, the man I knew, he asked if we'd arranged to meet at Haggerman's in general, and after my show in particular. I said I had no idea Harold was even here, but I don't think he heard me, he was too busy talking. Started asking me about my communist connections and what Harold and I had been planning and who else was in on it. He thought he was being clever, I think, by hinting that I might be able to get out of trouble by fingering our coconspirators for the murder. But, as we were not conspiring with anyone to do anything, I couldn't exactly throw suspicion on anyone else." He wiped sweat off his forehead, leaving a streak of road dust behind. "Man's a single-minded fool, and his deputy's no better. He just stands there nodding."

"Were the FBI there?"

He put his hat on his head. "Didn't see them. If you'll pardon me, it's too darn hot to stand here on the road."

"I'm going into town, but I can turn around and give you a lift to the top of the hill."

"Don't bother. Despite the heat, I like being in these woods. Makes a real change for a boy from the Bronx."

"I thought you were from Monticello?"

He grinned at me. "You caught me. That's the act. Apart from when I was in the army, I'd never been outside of the five boroughs until the first time I stepped onstage in the Catskills. I had an army pal from Monticello. He talked nonstop about the hotels, the bungalow colonies, the people—staff and guests. *Mountain rats*, he called people like him. I took his stories and turned them into my act." He shrugged. "What can I say? People love it."

I smiled. "You're not afraid your friend from Monticello will sue you?"

Charlie shrugged. "He died. Catch you later, Elizabeth." He turned to go and then swung back around. "Oh, the chief repeated that I was not to leave Summervale until he gives me permission. I guess you're stuck with me."

"In exchange for which we'd like you to appear each night. Two shows. Our scheduled act over the weekend is a magician, so your act shouldn't clash with his."

"You drive a hard bargain, Mrs. Grady. Asking a comedian to perform." He walked away, and I watched him go in the rearview mirror.

Chief Monahan was, as Charlie had said, single-minded.

But that didn't mean he was wrong. Jim was adamant his uncle was not a communist, and I had to agree with him that one copy of *The Communist Manifesto* doesn't mean anything. Was it possible someone else thought Harold Westenham was a communist and killed him because of it?

No, I couldn't see that. All this person would have had to do would be to report Westenham to the authorities, and they would've taken it from there. No need to kill him.

If I didn't get moving, and get some air into this car, I was going to roast. I threw the Chevrolet into gear and continued down the mountain.

Y

SUMMERVALE IS INDISTINGUISHABLE FROM MANY CATS-kill towns. A small, bustling community in the summertime, largely deserted the rest of the year. Olivia had remained in her castle over the winter, as aloof as ever, but I'd wanted to get to know our neighbors and ventured into the community and had made some friends. I'd enjoyed being part of the small year-round Summervale community, but as soon as the snow melted and buds began appearing on the trees, we all swung into action at our own properties, promising to meet again after Labor Day.

I drove slowly down Main Street, not sure of what I was doing here or what I hoped to accomplish. I couldn't go up and down the street telling people Haggerman's was a safe place to work and stay, as though I were some sort of carnival barker. The best I could do would be to try to find out if it was true people were gossiping about what had happened at Haggerman's. I believed Jim, but I had to admit to myself that I had no reason to. He was a newspaperman, and regardless of the death of his uncle, he'd have his own agenda.

I had absolutely no idea how to go about asking if we were the subject of town gossip. If I said, "Are you talking about us?" people would then start talking about us.

I drove past the newspaper office, a large impressive red-brick building in the center of Main Street. I might pop in there later, maybe under pretext of inquiring about taking out some advertising. The Red Spot Diner, owned by the McGreevy family, was next door to the paper. The diner was a popular spot with tourists and area residents alike. I'd met Lucinda McGreevy over the winter, and we'd become friends. Lucinda told me staff from Haggerman's and other area hotels hung out at the Red Spot on their days and evenings off.

The town's small police station was situated on the other side of the diner. I briefly considered going in and asking if they'd come across anything I should know, but I dismissed the idea almost immediately. It was unlikely they'd tell me if they had, and Chief Monahan, if he was in, would just start barking out questions and making accusations.

Main Street was lined with vehicles, but I found a place outside the hardware store. I parked the car and trotted down the sidewalk to the diner. The sidewalks were busy with casually dressed, sun-soaked families in town to enjoy an ice cream treat or to shop for groceries. At Haggerman's and the other hotels, we supply everything our guests could possibly need for their vacation (apart from their clothes and other personal items), but this area is full of bungalow colonies. Basically a cluster of cabins for rent, around a lake or swimming pool, at which guests fend for themselves. As well as families, several groups of young people crowded the sidewalk: staff from the hotels on a rare day off or waiters sneaking into town between serving meals and clearing up after.

The bell over the door of the Red Spot Diner tinkled as I opened it, and I was hit by the scent of greasy fried food, strong coffee, and fresh baking. My hair blew in the wind created by the big fans mounted on high shelves. In the middle of the afternoon, the popular diner wasn't completely full. Waitresses in red dresses and white aprons adorned with huge red polka dots carried laden trays to the tables or whisked away used dishes.

The tiles on the floor were black and white, the walls painted a fresh bright white, and the curtains a cheerful red. Matching red vinyl covered the seats of the stools lined up at the counter. Pictures of fun-loving people enjoying all the Catskills have to offer hung on the walls.

"On your own, hon?" a short, round middle-aged woman asked me. Her thick black hair was tied behind her head in a tight bun, the bags beneath her eyes were a tired purple, and the lines on her face were deep. She wore a white blouse with a giant red bow at her throat and a full red skirt. This was Mrs. McGreevy, Lucinda's mom. Clearly she didn't recognize me.

"Yes, I am." I nodded to an empty stool at the counter. "That'll be fine."

"Help yourself," she said.

I crossed the room and hopped onto the high chair. The man on the stool next to me put two-dollar bills onto the counter, slapped his hat on his head, and left. At the end of the counter, near the kitchen door, a selection of pies and cakes were arranged under glass domes, looking absolutely delicious. I plucked a menu out of its stand and opened it. My intention in coming here had been to have a cup of coffee. The moment I walked through the door, I realized I was starving. Meals were usually hit-and-miss in my life these days. More miss than hit sometimes.

"Coffee, hon?" asked the smiling waitress gripping the full pot. "Or you can have a soda or shake if you'd rather, and we do a killer egg cream."

"An egg cream would be great. I haven't had one of those since I left New York."

"Best in the Catskills, right here. You wanting lunch?"

"Yes, I will. Let me have a look at the menu. I was hoping to have a chance to say hi to Lucinda. Lucinda McGreevy. Is she in?"

"I'll get her. Be right back with that egg cream." She bustled off, yelling, "Egg cream, and make it snappy. Lady don't have all day here. Lucinda, you're wanted!"

I had time for no more than a quick glance at the menu before the kitchen door swung open and Lucinda came out, wiping a handkerchief across her brow. The waitress jerked her head in my direction, and Lucinda broke into a grin. "Hi there, stranger. Didn't think I'd see you until September."

"I came into town on an errand and couldn't pass up the chance for an egg cream."

"Best in the Catskills."

"So I've been told." I nodded to the vacant stool next to me. "Do you have a minute?"

"No, but when did that ever matter?" She came around the counter and hopped onto the seat with a satisfied sigh. "That feels good. Dare I hope you're looking for a job? One of the line cooks up and quit yesterday. He got a better offer."

"Lucinda, what are you doing? We have customers."

"It's okay, Mom. I need to sit down sometime."

"You can·sit in September," her mother said.

The door opened, the chimes tinkled, and Mrs. McGreevy gave her daughter a disapproving frown before turning to greet the new customers. Mrs. McGreevy's English was excellent, but despite her Scots-Irish married name, the accent was full of memories of her home city of Naples. Lucinda had taken directly after her mother and was a true Mediterranean beauty, with smooth olive skin, huge dark eyes, and thick black hair cut in a stylish bob.

"One egg cream." The waitress put a tall triangular-shaped glass in front of me, with a long-handled silver spoon as well as a pink straw next to it. Chocolate syrup dripped down one side of the glass and the milk foam threatened to spill over the rim. "Whatcha havin', hon?"

"A hot turkey sandwich with a side of fries would be great," I said.

"Comin' up."

"I heard someone was murdered at your place," Lucinda said. "That's awful. Did you know him? Was he really murdered, or was it an accident?"

"No, I didn't know him, not personally. He was just a guest. I mean, he was a guest. Not someone I knew. As for murdered, that would seem to be the case, and that's why I'm here." I dipped the spoon into the glass and scooped up the chocolaty liquid and a topping of milk foam off the top and tasted it. As good as I expected. Maybe even better. I popped the straw into the glass and took a long delicious sip.

When I could talk again, I said, "Tell me what you heard and from who. From whom?"

"Whom." Lucinda pointed to herself. She was wearing the diner's waitress uniform but had pulled a gray cook's apron over it. "I was waiting tables at breakfast while at the same time trying to help the single remaining cook in the kitchen. Dave Dawson and Chief Monahan came in around ten thirty, eleven. Dave said they'd been up all night investigating a murder at Haggerman's. Dave might have been up all night, but I doubt the chief had."

"Is Dave Dawson the deputy?"

"Yes."

"He talks?"

She grinned. "I know what you mean. Dave's a good guy, but he doesn't say much when the chief's around. He's not allowed to. Chief Monahan likes to be the one doing all the talking."

Her tone was not teasing. Lucinda did not like Norm Monahan. "What did they say about that?" I asked. "About us?"

"He, the chief I mean, not Dave, said the dead man had been a communist."

"He told you that?"

"Not me. I'm a waitress. He wouldn't talk to me. Bunch of road workers were here. Regular guys, local. They start work early and then come in for a late breakfast, so they're often here when Monahan is. They take that booth in the middle of the room." She half turned on her stool and pointed toward it with her chin. "Talk loud, eat lots. Tip well. Monahan, on the other hand, talks loud, eats lots, and does not tip well. Dave Dawson doesn't talk loud, never eats much, and always tips well. His wife, June, works at the paper in the advertising department."

The business of the diner swirled around us. People left, people arrived. Food and drinks were served, used dishes taken away. Mrs. McGreevy cleared tables and glared at her daughter every time she passed.

"Monahan told the road crew communists are in the area, so they'd better be on the lookout. Those guys are generally pretty sensible. One of them said he didn't think communists ever took vacations, and they all laughed. And so Monahan had to put the guy in his place, and he told them he'd found evidence that the dead man at Haggerman's was a communist. The FBI were on the case, and they'd be relying on him, Monahan personally, to help them out, seeing as he knows everything that goes on around here. Not a lot of people put much stock in anything Norm Monahan says, but mention of the FBI shut the naysayers up fast enough. The place was full, Elizabeth. I don't know why, but the breakfast rush was late today. Thirty people must have heard what Monahan said. Might as well have put it on a billboard outside of town."

I groaned. The waitress put a loaded plate in front of me. The hot sandwich was piled high with turkey, the top slice of white bread thoroughly smothered by dark gravy, the thickly cut potatoes brown and crisp.

"So yeah," Lucinda said, "half the town's checking under their beds for reds."

"Tell me about Chief Monahan." I grabbed the bottle of ketchup from the metal container the waitress had put in front of me and drenched my fries. "Not hard to tell you don't like him much. Why?" I stuffed a forkful of white turkey meat, gravy-soaked bread, and delicious gravy in my mouth. I closed my eyes and chewed happily.

"Good?" Lucinda asked.

"Oh yeah."

"Monahan's dad, Norman Sr., was the chief here for a lot of years. He was a popular guy. Tough but fair, they always said. I remember Chief Monahan Sr. dragging one or another of my brothers home by the ear plenty of times." She chuckled.

Lucinda was the only girl in her family of six children. Her parents had started the diner when they were first married, and all the kids grew up working in it. Her dad died a few years ago, some of the brothers moved away, some started their own tourist-related businesses. Only Lucinda and her mom still worked here regularly.

"His son, Norm Jr., not so much. Neither tough nor fair. Everything I know, Elizabeth, is secondhand, understand? My brothers are all respectable family men now, most of them anyway, so we don't need any more ear-pulling. We have to call the police now and again when we get a bunch of drunken college kids in here who won't leave, but Dave usually takes those sorts of calls."

I dragged a ketchup-laden french fry through gravy and popped it into my mouth. "What do you mean by not fair? Is Monahan on the take?"

Lucinda glanced around. No one was close enough to us to overhear, but she dropped her voice, not taking any chances. The counter waitress had disappeared into the back. "You hear a lot of gossip in this place. I've found over the years that when folks are sitting in a booth with their friends, having a cup of coffee or a glass of iced tea, they sometimes forget they're out in public. I've heard he can be bribed, and the big hotel owners know how to get on his good side."

"By good side, you mean pay him off, I presume. About what?"

"Keep scandals at the hotels out of the papers. Run troublesome workers, or those who just want a fair shake, out of town. Did he suggest that if you helped him out, he'd hush up that death you had?"

I thought back to last night. "Not at all. The opposite, if anything. He's the one who called in the FBI, almost right away. Hard to keep that under wraps. He said he wasn't going to bother the guests, but he wasn't subtle about questioning the staff." I had a sudden thought. Could it be possible Monahan was attempting to make Haggerman's look bad for the benefit of another hotel or hotels? As a favor to a friend? I filed that thought away.

"The smaller-business people," Lucinda said, "people with shops in town or managers of the cheaper hotels or the bungalow-colony owners, think Monahan's lazy, always looking for the easy way out. Dave does his best, but it's hard to get the police in this town to pay much attention to a shoplifting of a candy bar at a concession stand or a broken window on Main Street. From what I've seen when Monahan's here, and he comes in several times a week, it's not necessarily that the big hotel owners are bribing him, although that's possible, but that he wants to be their pal. He wants to be the big man in town, like his father was. His father worked for our respect. Norm doesn't want to go to any trouble. Did he speak to your mother when he was at your place?"

"No. My mother doesn't have much to do with the actual running of our hotel. Why do you ask?"

"I would have thought he'd want to meet her. Maybe have the photographer from the paper take a picture of him with her. Something to splash across the front page."

"You mean with a headline like 'Broadway and Film Star Olivia Peters and Chief Monahan Smile at Location of Vicious Murder'?"

"You laugh, Elizabeth, but that's exactly what I mean. The publicity's the point. Our chief doesn't get nuance."

"I'll warn Olivia to be on the lookout for him." I scraped the last of the gravy off my plate; the fries and egg cream had disappeared long ago. Now that Lucinda had mentioned my mother, I realized that no one had bothered to ask her about her brief conversation with Westenham the afternoon before he died. If he'd said something significant, she would have told me. But the police didn't know that. Other than poking around our staff quarters, the cops weren't doing much at all. Was Monahan as lazy as Lu-

cinda believed he was, or was he confident the FBI were on
it? The FBI hadn't been back to question anyone, least of all
my mother. They must be directing their investigation elsewhere. If so, that was good news for the resort.

"Pie?" Lucinda asked.

I patted my belly. "That was so good, but I can always
find space for pie. Is that lemon meringue I see?"

"It is. My mom and a friend of hers make all the desserts
and pastries themselves." Lucinda lifted her hand and beck-
oned the waitress. "Two slices of lemon pie, please."

"Nothing like mom-made pie," I said. "Not that I'd
know. A kitchen is as foreign an environment to my mother
as the Sahara, and Aunt Tatiana never made American-
style pie. We had plenty of cakes, though. Her Russian
honey cake, rum balls, and *syrniki* are what childhood
memories are made of."

"What's *syrniki*?"

"A bite-sized cheesy fried cake much like a round
pancake. Aunt Tatiana always served them with a straw-
berry jam-like sauce to dip them in. You should consider
serving them here. Lots of eastern Europeans come to the
Catskills."

Lucinda glanced at her mother and smiled softly, her
eyes full of love. "As far as my mother's concerned, if it's
not Italian it's not worth making. Or eating. We serve
American food here, because the diner was started by her
and Dad, and Dad knew what visitors want in a diner.
When they got married, she begrudgingly learned to make
hamburgers and tuna casseroles and things like that, because she loved my dad, and my dad had good old American working-class tastes. Mealtimes were interesting in our
house. For Thanksgiving we always had turkey *and* la-
sagna."

Once the pie was delivered along with fresh forks we both dug in.

When I came up for air, I said, "Back to the subject at hand. We have a dishwasher named Francis Monahan working at Haggerman's. Might he be a relative of the chief?"

"Skinny guy, average height, early thirties?"

"Yes."

"That's Norm's oldest son. He has another son who's with the police in the city."

"Francis is a dishwasher. Not a particularly prestigious job for the chief's son."

"Francis is on the slow side, Elizabeth, and he speaks with a slight stutter when he's nervous. Which is most of the time. He's older than me, but he's the same age as my oldest brother, so he came to our house sometimes. Francis had a tough time in school. The other boys bullied him mercilessly. He's slow, he's awkward, he can't express himself very well, and he cries easily. Makes an attractive target for a pack of schoolboys."

I thought of the smooth college-student waiters slapping each other on the back and laughing when Francis had dropped a tray in the kitchen, and others jeering at him after he'd delivered my supper.

"Francis was the absolute apple of his late mother's eye," Lucinda said. "People say a lot of negative things about Norm Monahan, but no one ever says he didn't adore Kathy, his wife, or he wasn't a good father to his two boys. So, yeah, Francis works as a dishwasher. He couldn't get a better job, even if he was capable of holding one. Not with a dishonorable discharge from the army."

"Really? What was that for?"

She shrugged. "No one knows for sure. Lots of rumors

floating around. Theft's the most believable. He did some time in military jail in Europe at the end of the war, I heard."

I finished my pie. It had tasted as good as it looked. "Let's change the subject. What's Tony doing this year?"

Antonio Baracaldo was Lucinda's fiancé.

"He's working at an employment agency, but he's not happy with it. He wants to learn how to manage a business, but so far most of his job consists of picking up staff at the bus or train stations and dropping them off at the hotels. And sometimes taking them back again. My mother's getting tired of asking when we're going to make wedding plans. I'm not getting any younger, you know." Lucinda was the ripe old age of twenty-four. "We're hoping we can make some decent money this summer, enough to get us out of here. Neither of us want to stay in Summervale." She lowered her voice and peeked guiltily over her shoulder. "Don't tell my mom. Other than a murder, how's things going up on your mountain?"

"Good, I guess. We're full, which is what we want, right?"

The waitress ripped a piece of paper off her pad and began to pass it to me. Lucinda intercepted it. "This is on me. One night when I can get some time off, if ever that happens, ha ha, I'll come up to Haggerman's to catch a show. Maybe I can snag Tony and we can go dancing."

"You'd be very welcome." In season, the diner's open from seven A.M. to midnight, seven days a week. Like everyone in the Catskills, Lucinda and her mom had not much more than eight or nine precious weeks to earn most of a year's income. "One more thing before I go. The newspaper office is next door. Do the paper's reporters ever come in here?"

"Sure. Best egg cream in the Catskills."

"So I've been told. They'll be writing up the death at Haggerman's, particularly if they can add the suspected communist angle. Anything I should know about them?"

"It's a family-owned paper, and the editor in chief's the son and grandson of past editors. The paper's been around a hundred years or more. I wouldn't expect any trouble from them, Elizabeth. The paper's pro-Summervale, as you'd expect. They won't report on anything that makes the town look bad, particularly not at the beginning of the season. Although, I have to add, they are a newspaper, and selling papers is what keeps them in business." She shrugged. "If they have to balance the interests of the town with reporting a viable story, I can't say which way they'll lean."

I hadn't thought to ask Jim for the name of the reporter who was dealing with our story.

"They have a new junior reporter this year," Lucinda said as though she'd read my mind. "Junior as in low ranking, not age."

"Do you know his name?"

"Sorry, no. Like so many people around here, they come, they go. Other than the family members themselves, the turnover of reporters and photographers is pretty high. They're all aiming for a bigger and better paper, and the *Summervale Gazette* is nothing but a stopgap far as they're concerned." Lucinda looked around the Red Spot Diner, and I could tell by the longing look on her face that she was also dreaming of the bigger and better.

I hopped off my stool. Or rather I tried to hop. I was so full of egg cream, hot turkey sandwich with gravy and fries, and lemon meringue pie, I more like toppled off. "Thanks for this. The news and the lunch."

"Anytime," Lucinda said. "I'll admit I used you for my

own nefarious ends. I got to sit down for twenty whole minutes."

"Lucinda!" her mother called. "Table nine is waiting for their fried chicken."

I left her to it and went outside. I dug my sunglasses out of my purse as the sticky heat soaked into my pores. My stomach rolled over, and I resisted the urge to loosen my belt. That lunch had been sooooo good. And I was soooo going to regret it.

The police station was to my right, the newspaper office to my left. Cars and trucks drove slowly down Main Street, and the sidewalks were full of families out for the day or people heading to and from work. I turned right and peered into the dusty window of the small police station. The blinds were up, and I could see a woman sitting at a desk facing the door. The wall behind her was covered in posters, some of them turning yellow with age. Her gray hair was pulled tightly back, and black-framed glasses perched on her beak of a nose. Her head was turned toward the papers on the desk as she pounded the keys of a typewriter. As I watched, the phone rang, and she picked it up. When she lifted her head she saw me peering at her, and her eyes narrowed.

Anger, or maybe just indigestion, clutched at my chest. If Monahan was trying to get Haggerman's in trouble, at the behest of some of the other hotel owners, he was playing a dangerous game. He should have some loyalty to Summervale. Did he not realize the town itself would suffer if the reputation of one of the largest hotels came under suspicion? Plenty of other Catskills resort towns around, all of them eager to take visitors' money.

I told myself to relax as I reminded myself that I simply didn't know enough to get angry at anyone or anything. Not yet. Except for the person who had killed Mr. Westenham. That person, I could be angry at.

I scurried away.

Far more impressive than the clapboard police station, the newspaper office was a sturdy brick structure, three stories tall, with a large sign prominently displaying the paper's name hanging above the double-doored entrance. The big red newspaper box by the door held copies of the day's paper, with a sheet of the front page displayed behind glass. I glanced at it but saw nothing about the death at Haggerman's, which was to be expected as the paper would have been printed overnight for delivery first thing this morning. I peered in the window but couldn't see much because of the half-closed blinds. The door opened, and I heard typewriters clattering and men shouting. A man hurried out, short and thin, pale-faced, small chin, cheap suit, stuffing his hat onto the top of his head. He glanced at me, gave me a quick up and down, and clearly not terribly impressed, he pushed past me. I turned to see him going into the diner.

I decided there was nothing I could achieve in the newspaper offices. I couldn't ask them not to report on the death at Haggerman's: that would make them suspect I was covering something up. I'd have to trust Lucinda's belief that the paper would protect the reputation of the town.

I went back to my car and drove to my mountain.

Chapter 12

THAT HAD BEEN A MISTAKE.

When I finally got into my office and dropped into my chair, I leaned back and closed my eyes. I would have loved absolutely nothing more than to grab a quick nap, but the pile of message slips threatened to bury my desk beneath a pink snowstorm. I sighed, opened my eyes, plucked a pencil out of the holder, and picked up the pages. I was about to flip the stack, to start with the earliest, when the name on the topmost caught my eye.

Lucinda McGreedy. Never mind the spelling error, my friend had called half an hour ago. That would have been only minutes after I left the diner. I picked up my phone and read the number off the paper to the hotel switchboard operator.

"Red Spot Diner. What do you want?" Mrs. McGreevy snarled.

"May I speak to Lucinda, please?"

"Lucinda's working."

"It's very important. I won't take much of her time."

Mrs. McGreevy's martyred sigh poured down the line. "I'll see if she's not busy."

I crossed my fingers, hoping for the best. Lucinda was never not busy.

"Hello?"

"Lucinda, hi. It's Elizabeth. Did you call me?"

"I'm glad you got my message. I was afraid you'd have so many messages you wouldn't see mine for days." In the background I heard a man screaming at someone. Something about hot water, not boiling water. "Only moments after you left, that newspaper reporter, the new one, came in."

"It must have been him I saw on the street. Drat. I'm sorry I missed him."

"Too bad you didn't see who joined him."

"Who?"

"None other than our beloved chief of police, Norman Monahan Jr., who came in about five minutes later. They huddled together in a back booth, just the two of them. I tried to get close enough to hear, but all they ordered were two coffees, plus a blueberry pie for the chief, and Janie brought it to them before I could intercept."

"Did you hear anything they said?"

"Not a single word. Sorry. They were keeping their voices down, and when Janie brought their bill they stopped talking altogether. That must mean they weren't exchanging baseball scores."

"No."

"One thing I should have told you earlier. The chief's a rabid anti-communist. Nothing wrong with that, except that he's accused people of being reds who flatly deny it. The big hotel owners like that about him. He ran off a couple of guys from the city who were trying to organize the grounds-keepers at one of the hotels to argue for better pay."

"Wanting better pay doesn't make you a communist," I said.

"No, but it does give the bosses a good excuse to get rid of troublemakers. All of which might not have anything to do with your murder, Elizabeth, but it's been said that the chief sees reds where none exist. Partly because of genuine political conviction, but partly because it's a way to get himself noticed in the wider world of law enforcement."

"Like calling in the FBI for an ordinary murder. If there is such a thing as an ordinary murder."

"Exactly."

More background screaming. "Gotta go," Lucinda said. "I'll let you know if I hear anything more."

"Thanks. If you can get away, you and Tony come to the hotel one night. Dinner and drinks and dancing, all on us."

"I'd like that." She hung up.

I picked up the next pink slip.

I PUT MY HEAD DOWN AND TRIED TO WORK, BUT I HAD A great deal of trouble concentrating. I had no reason to believe Chief Monahan and the newspaperman had been discussing events at Haggerman's over their coffee and blueberry pie. They might have been exchanging news about another story. People were flooding to our small towns by the hundreds, by the thousands. Plenty was happening in this area. My phone rang, and I glanced at my watch as I answered. Almost five o'clock. The clerks would extinguish their cigarettes, rinse out their coffee mugs, cover their typewriters, collect their purses, and go home, and the switchboard would stop putting outside business calls through to me.

I didn't even have enough time to finish saying hello before my caller got straight to the point. "This is Ralph McIntosh from the booking agency. What's this I hear about communist activity at your hotel?"

I sat up straight. I sputtered. "That's absolute nonsense. Where did you hear that?"

"Look, Mrs. Grady, Haggerman's is almost full for most of July, but you've got vacancies in August. If you're going to be shut down, I need to know before I book my clients in."

"*Shut down?* Where did you hear this?"

"I'm not at liberty to say."

"Kennelwood probably. It was Jerome Kennelwood, wasn't it?"

"Mrs. Grady."

"There is no communist activity at Haggerman's. Absolutely none."

"The FBI are investigating. They don't get called in for a common murder."

"The FBI are doing their jobs, and good for them. They were asked by the local police to assist, but they haven't returned. That means nothing was found that concerns us, right?" I'd checked with the reception desk when I got in, and the clerks said the deputy'd been back, poking around the scene of Westenham's death and his cabin, but no one had seen the FBI agents since this morning.

"Okay," Ralph said. "I believe you, but you'd better nip these rumors in the bud and fast. You've got a good hotel there, Mrs. Grady, and Miss Peters's name's attracting well-heeled guests. But there are plenty of other good hotels, and celebrity is fleeting. Mark my words: you don't want trouble. Now, put me through to your reservations clerk. I have a family booking for the two weeks before Labor Day."

"Thank you." I pushed the appropriate buttons.

I put the receiver down and groaned. There's nothing on earth harder to stop than a rumor. The only thing that would have been worse would be if our suspected communist had been found in flagrante delicto with a movie star. Or my mother.

I leaned back in my chair and thought. Might it be true that Harold Westenham was a communist? His nephew was adamant he wasn't.

Did it even matter?

Other than in Monahan's fevered imagination, nothing indicated that anyone had been meeting with the man to plot a communist takeover or anything else—at least, as far as I knew, and I had to admit to myself that the police and the FBI weren't sharing their findings with me. Whoever killed Harold Westenham might have done it for other, more personal reasons. What might those have been? I tried to think like a killer. How did a killer think? I had no idea.

I then tried to think like a detective, but I didn't have much luck at that, either. One thing detectives do, which I know from reading books and going to the movies in the off-season, is decide who the prime suspects are. On the one hand, I had no prime suspects, and on the other hand, I had a hotel full of potential prime suspects. I thought it unlikely the killer had come from outside. If someone had walked up the road from the bus stop, or driven onto the property at that hour of night, they would have risked being seen by the security guards, and remembered.

Then again, they could have parked on an adjacent road and walked in through the woods, or caught a lift with one of the staff who had his own car. The police were questioning the staff, much to the delight of gossip-loving guests. Surely if one of them had given a lift to a stranger, they would tell the police so. Unless they had their own reasons for keeping mum. The same logic applied to our guests. Many of them went to other hotels for an evening's entertainment, and guests at other hotels came to ours. Monahan had ordered his deputy not to question the guests, but surely if one of them had seen something they'd report it. Wouldn't they?

Not if they'd been involved.

About the only person I could be confident hadn't killed Harold Westenham was his nephew Jim. I'd called Jim in New York City shortly after finding the body, and he'd answered the phone.

I swiveled my chair and looked out the small window at the overgrown bushes scratching at the office walls. If Westenham had been killed by a person I didn't know, for reasons unknown, I had no chance of figuring out who that person was. I could concentrate on people I'd recently encountered who'd been behaving suspiciously. Whatever "suspiciously" meant in a Catskills summer.

One name came to mind.

"Hi!"

I leapt out of my skin and spun my chair around.

"You're jumpy," Velvet said.

"Sorry. I didn't hear you come in. I'm thinking about the murder."

"Don't dwell on it. Nothing you can do about it."

"There might be, Velvet."

"Hold that thought, first I bring good news." She gave me a big bright smile. She'd pulled a short, cheerful yellow summer dress over her bathing suit, her golden hair was pulled into a high bouncy ponytail, and the tip of her nose was turning red from the sun. She looked, I thought, like summer itself.

"They've caught the killer?"

The smile faded. "Not that good. Sorry. Mrs. Berkowitz and her preschool twins are staying here for a month. Mr. Berkowitz intends to come up on weekends from the city. Mr. Berkowitz is a bank manager, by the way. They have loads of money. They're in cabin two, one of the best, and the girls who look after the children say the kids are absolute horrors. Spoiled rotten."

"Get on with it, Velvet."

"A good story"—she crossed her arms and leaned comfortably against the wall—"deserves to be told properly. A good story cannot be rushed, Elizabeth."

I made *Hurry it up* gestures in the air, and she grinned.

"Okay. No more teasing. Mr. Berkowitz decided to get an early start on his weekend, give his family a nice surprise, and he arrived this afternoon. He gave his wife a surprise all right, although not a particularly nice one."

"Velvet, if you are not telling me he found her engaging in communist activity or burying evidence in the woods proving she killed Harold Westenham, I do not care."

"Yeah, okay, what happened is totally predictable. He found his wife enjoying the comforts of the main bedroom of cabin two in the company of a waiter named Luke, who I've been told is a first-year law student at Columbia. Cabin two, as you well know, is situated in a prime location near the beach between the pool and the courts. Mr. Berkowitz and Mrs. Berkowitz did not bother to keep their voices down, and to ensure that things were even more memorable, Luke made his escape without worrying about first finding his clothes. To the delight of the bridge club ladies gathering for a refreshing dip in the lake and the teen girls in my afternoon calisthenics class. I personally, Elizabeth, am here to tell you that if one were looking for a romp in the hay, a girl could do worse than the aforementioned Luke. Not that I wanted to look, of course. I was trying to protect my girls."

I chucked. "Okay, I'll admit that story was worth hearing. Shall I let the booking agencies know one of our best private cabins has come unexpectedly available?"

"I don't know about that. But my point is no one is talking about the death of Mr. Westenham. Fortunately, the two Berkowitz daughters are too young to understand what everyone's saying. Because *everyone* is talking about it. Absolutely everyone. Anyone who's not heard about it, soon will."

"Do you think it will stay that way?"

"Oh yes. As you know, the main bedroom in cabin two is located at the front of the building, meaning next to the path. The window was open as befits such a hot day. Mrs. B. had some things to say about what Mr. B. and his secretary get up to when she's away, and he had a few things to say about a man needing to satisfy his needs when they are not being fulfilled at home because his wife never gets off the blasted phone complaining to her shrew of a mother. Plenty of fodder for gossip for a good long time. I wonder if they'll come in to dinner. They might have been so caught up in their own little drama they aren't aware everyone and their dog heard them. I might have even seen Winston edging closer to listen in. My point is, Elizabeth, no one saw what happened to Harold Westenham. The few people who were up at that time saw the police and the ambulance, but that's about it. They weren't personally involved. People, lots and lots of people, were witness to the Berkowitz imbroglio. I'll take a guess that Luke himself won't be doing anything to help the talk die down, either. The other lonely ladies will be lining up to find out what all the fuss is about."

"Thank heavens for marital strife."

"What are you planning to do?"

"Do? About the Berkowitzes or Luke? Nothing."

"No, I mean about the murder. When I came in you said there was something you could do."

"Meet me in the lobby at eight tonight," I said.

"Why?"

"Just be there. Please. I need your help with something." I waved my pencil at her. "Do you want to go over this budget for me? I can't balance it."

Her face was a picture of horror, and she threw up her hands. "I don't do numbers."

"Then leave me to it. Eight o'clock. Don't be late. Wear practical shoes."

▼

I ROLLED MY SHOULDERS AND STRETCHED MY ARMS OUT in front of me. The stack of pink message slips was down to a manageable pile. I picked up my phone. "Put me through to my house, please."

"Miss Peters speaking," Olivia said.

"It's me. Elizabeth. It's seven o'clock now. Are you still planning on having dinner in the hotel tonight?"

"Yes. I am the owner of this establishment, and I will do whatever I must to keep it running smoothly and efficiently and our guests as happy as little clams."

Too bad Olivia didn't consider balancing budget sheets or answering guest complaints part of what she must do.

"I'll also attend the dancing later," she said. "I might even have a dance or two with the guests. That will make them happy. I took tea on the veranda earlier this afternoon in another attempt to spread cheer. As I was finishing I heard some considerable hullabaloo down at the beach and a naked man ran past."

"So I heard."

"A lady who was in the process of pouring a cup of tea kept right on pouring into her friend's lap."

I chuckled at the image. "I have a special request for you at dinner tonight."

"What?" she asked suspiciously.

"Sit with Louis Frandenheim."

"Absolutely not. He's an irritating little man."

"You don't have to stay for the entire meal. Have the first course with them at least. He won't be on his own. He's here with his sister and her family."

"Why?"

"Did you know they've been going to the Concord for twenty years and came to Haggerman's this year only because you're here?"

"I did not. But I am not surprised. Isn't it part of your business plan to take advantage of my name and my fame?"

"Part of *our* business plan, Olivia."

Silence.

"Very well," she said at last. "If I must, I can do that for you. For *us*."

Y

OLIVIA ARRIVED AT QUARTER TO EIGHT, LOOKING EVERY inch the star in a lilac gown with a scalloped neckline, one shoulder strap, a tight bodice, a thin belt, and a draped floor-length skirt. Elbow-length white gloves, her good costume jewelry, and glittering silver dance shoes completed the outfit. Her dark hair was piled on top of her head, secured by a red clip the color of her lipstick. I was standing by the maître d' station when she sailed into the dining room. A handful of guests were still arriving, but most had settled at their tables. People chatted, glassware and cutlery tinkled, smart young waiters in their neat black suits circulated taking orders. I studied them all, wondering which was the well-endowed and newly famous Luke. I settled on the one who'd cheekily eyed me yesterday when Rosemary and I had been admiring the cocktail party food, and had then laughed at Francis's clumsiness. He wasn't particularly good-looking, but he had a certain air of arrogance about him. He went about his duties efficiently, but I could tell he was aware of the glances thrown his way. Aware of, and very pleased about.

It was also obvious who were the Berkowitzes, because everyone was either watching them or pretending not to. They sat at a table in the center of the room. She was round-faced and chubby with hair dyed an unnatural jet-black and sprayed into stiff curls, her back ramrod straight in her expensive dress. Her face was bright red, her angry eyes a sharp contest to the toothy smile with which she greeted their table companions. He, equally round-faced and equally chubby, with a few stands of hair and a thin black-and-silver mustache, leapt up and down like a jack-in-the-box, shaking hands, slapping backs, giving everyone the benefit of an enormous smile. They so pointedly ignored each other, they might have erected a wall of ice between them. He'd ordered a scotch and she had a Singapore sling. Both glasses were already almost empty.

Whispers spread through the room, and one by one everyone's attention turned from the Berkowitzes as they noticed Olivia. The maître d' escorted her into the dining room. He was an older man, chosen for his important job precisely because he was tall and distinguished and handsome in his black suit. The rest of the time, he fixed the plumbing and attended to other maintenance problems.

They stopped at the Frandenheim family table. I could hear Louis's gasp across the room. The maître d' asked if Olivia could have the honor of joining them. The woman next to Louis, who I assumed was his sister, turned pale. The maître d' snapped his fingers, and one waiter immediately appeared with an extra chair and another with a tray carrying a full place setting. I had, of course, told them ahead of time what we wanted.

The maître d' held the chair for Olivia, and she sat down in a flurry of lilac fabric. The waiter fluffed the napkin and spread it over her lap.

I slipped away. Ten to eight.

Velvet was waiting by the reception desk. She'd changed out of her yellow dress into dark, slim-legged trousers, shoes without heels, and a navy-blue blouse with elbow-length sleeves.

"You're early," I said.

"Bad habit. I'm anxious to hear what this mysterious errand you have for me is."

The guests had all gone in for dinner, the lobby was empty, except for the bellhop waiting by the door and the clerk behind the counter. Jim Westenham came in, dressed in a nice suit, rubbing his freshly shaven jaw. He gave Velvet and me a smile and came to join us. "I'm late for dinner. Will they still seat me?"

"Yes," I said.

"I took a nap and overslept. I guess I didn't realize how tired I was after the late-night drive up from the city. You two haven't gone in yet, would you care to join me?"

"I'm staff." Velvet pouted prettily. "I'd be thrown out of

the dining room on my ear. The owners run a tight ship here. Real slave drivers."

"Most amusing," I said.

"Would the owner care to join me, then?" he asked.

Velvet gave me a not-very-subtle elbow in the ribs.

I ignored her. "My mother's the owner here, not me. Aside from that, thank you but no. I have something I need to do."

"Another time perhaps," he said.

"Did you hear anything more from the police?" I asked.

"No. I called the police station before lying down, but neither the chief nor the deputy were in. They might have been in but not taking my calls. I didn't hear from the FBI, either."

"Do you know why your uncle came here? Specifically to Haggerman's I mean, rather than one of the other places."

Jim shook his head. "I've no idea. Probably no particular reason. You advertise in the city papers and on the radio, don't you?"

"Yes, and we're represented by the major booking agencies."

"You were able to offer the seclusion he wanted, that was probably good enough."

The reception clerk was edging ever closer to us, ears flapping. I gave him a stern look, and he ducked his head and pretended to be consulting the registration book.

I walked toward the stairs, and Velvet and Jim followed.

"I finally managed to get hold of my father," Jim said. "He told me he hasn't heard from Uncle Harold for several months. Like I said, he could be reclusive."

"It's none of my business," I said. "But do you mind me asking if your uncle had any enemies who might have followed him here?"

"He was found on your property, and the police are disrupting your business. I'd say that makes it your business, so go ahead and ask all the questions you want. The answer is no. Absolutely not. He was a former college professor, and I'm sure he rubbed some of his students the wrong way—he didn't suffer fools gladly—but that was a long time ago. College kids can be all sound and fury when they think they've been offended, but those grudges rarely last until the next morning, never mind more than a decade. These days, he was trying to write a book. The newspaper business can be highly competitive, if not out-and-out murderous, but such is not the case, as far as I know, in writing fiction."

"Someone from the army maybe?" I said.

We stood at the bottom of the stairs. From the floor above came the sound of the ballroom being set up for the evening's entertainment.

"The war ended eight years ago." Jim gestured to his surroundings: the beautifully decorated lobby, the attentive staff, the faint sounds of dinner conversation and laughter leaking through the closed dining room doors. "Ancient history, it feels like now."

"Were you in the army?" Velvet asked.

"Navy. I was stationed in San Diego for the entire duration. I had what they call an easy war, and I have no guilt about that. Uncle Harold had a hard war. Plenty had it a lot harder."

Velvet's eyes flicked toward me. I kept my face impassive, but a twitch in Jim's eyebrow told me he'd noticed.

"Some say we're in a new war now," he said. "A cold war. If that's the case, Uncle Harold was well out of it. I'm sorry, Elizabeth, but if you're asking me who killed my uncle, I simply can't help you."

I checked my watch. After eight. I had to be moving.

"About that, I have an idea. You can come with us, if you promise you can be trusted."

"That sounds mysterious. Trusted to do what?"

"What you're told." I started up the staircase. Behind me I heard Velvet say, "Don't look at me. She doesn't tell me anything, either."

The wide sweeping staircase ends at the entrance to the ballroom, but rather than take the elevator to the next floor, I led the way up the smaller set of stairs mainly used by the hotel staff.

The dimly lit third-floor corridor stretched out ahead of us. All was quiet, no one around. The chambermaids were finished for the day, the guests at dinner. I took my key ring off my belt.

"We're breaking into a guest's room," Velvet said. "Neat."

"Shush," I said. I stopped at room 319. "This man has been following my mother around. Hiding in the bushes, creeping through the woods, watching our house. He's obsessed with her. An obsession, I have to admit, I've recently encouraged by asking her to join him for dinner."

"Why'd you do that?" Velvet asked.

"So I'd be sure he stayed in his seat while I search his room."

"What does this have to do with my uncle?" Jim asked.

"Your uncle had little or no contact with anyone in the hotel, not even the staff, as far as we can tell. Since arriving here, he didn't have the time or opportunity to make an enemy out of anyone, but it's possible he did something completely innocent, which someone misinterpreted. My mother talked to him on one occasion. They had a pleasant chat on the porch of his cabin. She didn't go inside, and she didn't stay long. Did Louis see them together and get jealous? Did he decide he had to get rid of his rival?"

"You're taking this too far," Velvet said.

"Murder's too far. Louis is a frail older man. He walks with a cane, and I don't think that's a pretext. I'm sorry, Jim, but whoever killed your uncle didn't need a lot of strength or agility. Stop for a friendly chat, bash him over the head, and watch him roll down the slope into the lake."

I put my master key into the lock, and it turned. I edged the door open. "Velvet, you wait here. I'll keep the door partially open, and if you see an old man with a cane getting out of the elevator, warn me and then intercept him so we can slip away unseen."

"How am I supposed to do that?"

"Use your feminine wiles."

"I have feminine wiles?"

"Jim, you help me." I slipped into the room.

"What am I looking for?" he said. "He's not going to have— Oh."

"Oh, indeed."

We were looking at my mother. A wall of my mother. Photos clipped from newspapers and magazines covered one wall. Some were old—her in her dazzling youth— some more recent—taken at the grand reopening of the hotel last year.

"You're right," Jim said. "The man's obsessed."

The photos were attached to the wall with thumbtacks. For a moment all I could think was that I'd make sure the cost of replastering and repapering the room went on Louis's bill.

Jim opened drawers and began flicking through the contents. "Nothing in here but what you'd expect a man to bring on vacation." He moved to the wardrobe. "Same here." He crouched down. "Some dried mud on these shoes, but you said he'd been in the woods watching your mother's house."

All I could do was stare at the wall. "These publicity pictures are bad enough, although I know a star, which my mother was, should have little expectation of privacy. But, Jim, some of these are not publicity shots." Several of the pictures had been taken recently, and not by a professional photographer. They were grainy, shot from a distance, most of them badly focused. Olivia coming out of the door of our house, calling over her shoulder to whoever was inside. Olivia down by the lake, catching a (so she thought) private moment. Olivia near the tennis courts, talking to me. I could tell by her clothes the pictures had been taken this summer.

"There's a camera here, on the dresser," Jim said. "A Brownie Hawkeye. Not one of the best, but a good model. Is there a place to get photographs developed in town?"

"Yes," I said. "They promise fast turnaround so people don't have to wait until they get home to see their holiday pictures."

I felt Jim stand beside me. He pointed to one picture. Cabin nineteen, surrounded by woods. Olivia stood on the step, her sunglasses propped on the top of her head, nestled in her dark hair. Harold Westenham, slightly out of focus, caught in the act of standing up to greet his visitor.

"I think we have enough to take to the police," Jim said.

"I cannot imagine why the chambermaid in charge of this floor didn't tell me about this," I said.

"What's happening in there?" Velvet called.

"We're almost finished," I called back.

Jim reached out and plucked the picture of his uncle off the wall.

"Shouldn't you leave it in place?" I said. "To show the police?"

"Can't take the chance of him finding out we've been here and destroying it. There are plenty enough pictures to show the cops."

"Let's go. I can make the call from the reception desk."

We slipped out, and I locked the door behind me.

I PHONED THE POLICE WHILE A WIDE-EYED CLERK watched, and told them I needed an officer at Haggerman's immediately. Someone, the bored voice on the other end told me, would soon be there.

Velvet, Jim, and I took seats in the lobby and waited.

We waited some more.

The doors to the dining room opened, chatter filled the room, and guests began filing out. Some headed for the elevator, ready to retire, while others climbed the stairs to the ballroom, eager for the evening's entertainment to begin. The Berkowitzes were at the front of the throng, and I guessed they hadn't kissed and made up during dinner. He marched in front, his eyes fixed straight ahead, while she scurried behind, a storm cloud hanging over her head.

My mother was escorted out by an elderly couple. She looked relaxed and, dare I say it, happy. She bid them a good night and headed our way. Jim leapt to his feet, and I made the introductions.

"Did you have a nice dinner?" I asked her.

"I did. Once I was able to make my excuses and depart the table you insisted I join, Elizabeth. I won't say I don't like to hear praise of my performances on occasion, but even I get tired of it eventually. Particularly when it would seem as though my best days are long behind me."

I noticed Louis peeking out from behind a potted palm, his watery eyes wide with adoration as he stared at my mother. I gave him a stern look, but I don't think he even noticed. I handed my mother the picture. "What do you make of this?"

She studied it and gave it back. "I make nothing of it. I told you I had a brief chat with the late Mr. Westenham." She smiled at Jim. "He was a lovely man, charming and witty, but as protective of his privacy as I am. That's cabin nineteen, where he was staying, and I'm wearing the slacks I often wear in the early afternoon if I go out for a walk. Why do you have this?"

"A guest took it," I said.

Olivia shrugged.

I was about to explain when in marched Chief Monahan and his deputy. Their timing was not good, as just about every guest we had was at that moment crossing the lobby after dinner. I'd made a big mistake by waiting for them in such a public place. I ran across the lobby. "Thank you for coming, Chief. I've discovered something you need to know about the Westenham case."

"This better be important, Mrs. Grady," Monahan said. "I've had a long day."

"It might be vitally important." Conscious of all the curious eyes watching us, I added, "This is maybe not the best place to talk. We can use the clerical office." I led the way across the lobby, followed by Velvet, Jim, Olivia, and the two police officers. A wave of whispers followed us. I unlocked the door beneath the stairs and stood back to allow the others to enter.

Monahan took off his hat and eyed me suspiciously. "I don't care for civilians involving themselves in police business." He shifted his bulk and pulled up his belt.

I switched the hallway light on and handed him the photograph. The deputy peered over his shoulder. "You asked me to keep an eye out. I have been keeping an eye out. I found this in a guest's room."

Monahan examined the photo and then he lifted his head to study my mother's face. She stared at him. He looked at the photo again. Monahan nodded with satisfaction, and then he said, "How long have you been a communist, Miss Peters?"

Chapter 13

THAT HADN'T GONE AS WELL AS I'D EXPECTED.

Monahan accused my mother of being a communist and having killed Harold Westenham because of it. Jim Westenham insisted, one more time, that his uncle had not been a communist. Velvet told the chief he was being stubbornly single-minded. The chief threatened to arrest Olivia, whereupon Olivia treated the unpleasant situation in her usual fashion by simply turning around and marching out of the hallway. When the door had slammed shut behind her and Monahan had recovered his wits, he asked me if I'd known about my mother's political leanings and had I been aware she'd invited fellow communists to gather at Haggerman's. When Velvet objected to his tone, he accused her of being in on it with us and threatened to arrest her on the spot.

The deputy twisted his hat in his hands and said nothing. Jim put his fingers in his mouth and blew a whistle.

"That's enough. You're jumping to conclusions, Chief. If you can produce solid evidence my uncle was a communist, please do so. In the meantime, you have to agree there's nothing in the least bit suspicious about a hotel owner spending a few minutes chatting to a guest. I'd say that's part of the job. They're sitting on a porch on a pleasant day, for heaven's sake. Not huddling over maps or passing stolen secret government documents. What is unusual, and what Mrs. Grady is trying to tell you, is a guest following Miss Peters, spying on her, and papering his room with her photograph. Obsession can lead to jealousy, and jealousy to . . . who knows what."

"So you say, pal, but you're not out of the woods yourself. Any of you." He shoved the photo into the deputy's hand. "Dave, talk to this guy and find out what he knows. I have to call my contacts at the FBI and let them know about this."

"You can use the phone in my office," I said, in an attempt to be helpful.

He sneered at me. "I know what switchboard operators are like in places such as this."

I could have said they were far too busy to listen in to anyone's conversation, what with the department heads placing orders; calls from booking agencies, employment agencies, and entertainers' agents; businessmen needing to keep in touch with the office; weepy teenage girls complaining to their friends about how dreadfully bored they are; and wives grumbling that if they had to spend one more day with their mother-in-law they'd . . . Wisely, I hoped, I said nothing.

"I need a *secure* line," Monahan said. "I'll make the call from the station." He put his hat firmly on his head.

"Uh," Dave said. "How do I get back to town?"

"Hitch a lift. I don't know what sort of hotel you folks are running here, Mrs. Grady, but I wouldn't want to stay at any place where the staff search the rooms looking for something to gossip about to pass the time."

"Believe me, the last thing I'm ever looking for is ways of passing the time," I said as the door slammed once again.

Deputy Dave gave me a rueful grin. "Sorry about that. I'll have a talk with this guy. Where is he?"

"Last I saw him, he was hiding behind a plant watching Olivia."

We went back to the lobby, but Louis was nowhere to be seen. I asked a bellhop to check his room, and the man soon returned saying no one answered his knock. I then organized some of the waiters and bellhops into a search party. I went into the kitchen to ensure none of the knives or heavy pots had gone missing, and Velvet ran upstairs to check the ballroom. She reported that Louis's sister and her party had taken a table, but Louis was not with them and they hadn't seen him since dinner. Meanwhile, Deputy Dave surveilled the perimeter of the property.

It took a while, but one of the bellhops eventually found our fugitive at the bottom of the path that led to our house, pretending he was out for a walk but obviously hoping for a glimpse of Olivia.

He'd been escorted back to the hotel, protesting loudly and demanding to know what was going on. I showed Deputy Dave to the writing room, where he could speak to Louis in private. I'd been hoping to be allowed inside, but Dave politely said, "Thank you, Mrs. Grady," and shut the door in my face.

I waited outside, hoping to hear raised voices. In that, I

was to be highly disappointed. The interview didn't take long, and when they came out the deputy told me Louis was not under suspicion at this time. He'd simply taken a photograph of Olivia Peters chatting to a guest. Louis vehemently denied having spoken to Harold Westenham at any time or having had any contact with the man.

"You're taking his word for it?" I asked.

"Can't arrest a man for taking a picture. I've got his name and address. I'll be in touch with the police in New York, see if he has any record of trouble."

Louis smirked at me, but the smirk disappeared fast enough when I told him he was no longer welcome at Haggerman's and he was to pack his bags and be on his way. Tonight.

🍸

I STOOD ON THE VERANDA AND WATCHED THE CAB PULL away. A burst of applause from the ballroom told me Charlie Simmonds had finished his second set. Moments later, people began streaming out of the hotel. Some took seats on the veranda and ordered one last drink, some went for a stroll by the lake before turning in, and some headed to their cabins and bed. Above my head, the orchestra struck up the next dance number.

"Is it safe for me to come out?" Olivia called to me.

"Yes." The red lights of the cab turned into the road and disappeared. Louis Frandenheim was on his way to the bus station, where he'd spend an uncomfortable night before catching the first bus leaving for the city.

I'd been worried his entire family would storm out with him, but that turned out not to be a problem.

"I am so sorry," his sister said to Olivia and me as the lights of the taxi faded into the night. "My brother's harm-

less, really, but his obsessions do take control of him sometimes." She shook her head sadly. "Poor Elizabeth Taylor."

Olivia tucked the woman's arm into hers. "Mr. Simmonds and I are going for a late drink. Why don't you join
us and you can tell me all about it."

"Everything okay?" I asked Charlie Simmonds, who'd
followed Olivia onto the veranda.

"If you mean regarding the cops, I haven't heard another
thing. I keep expecting someone to break down my door,
but nothing. My agent's been on the phone. It didn't take
long for him to go from mildly concerned to panicking to
threatening to drop me if I miss an engagement."

"Agents can be so tedious." Olivia linked her other arm
through his. "I'll have a word with him, and let him know
I'm delighted you've agreed to stay on for a few more performances." To Louis's sister, she said, "As for Elizabeth
Taylor, I could tell you a story or two."

They went inside, and I headed home to bed. Charlie
said he hadn't heard from the police or the FBI again, and
Jim had reported the same. I dared to hope that was the end
of talk of communists at Haggerman's.

**RED CELL OPERATING OUT OF ONE OF
SUMMERVALE'S TOP LUXURY HOTELS?**

"Thought you might want to see this." George threw today's
edition of the *Summervale Gazette* onto my desk. "Hot off
the presses."

I groaned and buried my head in my hands. "I'll sue the
pants off them."

"My dad was in the newspaper business," George said.
"He liked working with words. I prefer machinery. It doesn't

bite back. You can't sue them, Mrs. Grady. See that question mark there? That's called covering their—"

"Yes, yes. I know. Don't put today's paper in the boxes."

One bushy eyebrow rose. "That would be censoring the press."

"So it would," I said.

"You're the boss lady." He shifted from one foot to the other, his big boots depositing clumps of mud all over my office floor. "Just so you know, Mrs. Grady. The old-timers here, guys like me, we're happy you're in charge. Until you got here, this hotel was going downhill and mighty fast. You're doing a good job. For a girl, I mean."

"Gee, thanks."

"What I'm saying"—a grease-and-dirt-encrusted, calloused, broken-nailed finger pointed at the paper—"is we like working here and we all know this for a pack of nonsense. No one knows more about what goes on in a hotel than the guys who unplug the sink or trim the bushes under the windows. Except maybe the chambermaids. Communists in my hotel? Nah."

"Did you tell the police or the FBI this?"

He lifted one shoulder. "No one asked me or any of my boys. I'll see that today's paper doesn't get put in the boxes. Anyone asks, they didn't have it ready for us when I did my pickup in town. Have a nice day, Mrs. Grady."

"You, too, George. And thank you."

Looking on the bright side, the paper had called us a "top luxury hotel." Once George had left, depositing a second trail of mud on the floor, I went into the outer office. The clerks collectively lifted their heads from their papers or typewriters and chirped,

"Good morning, Mrs. Grady."

"Good morning, ladies." I took the microphone connected to the hotel's loudspeakers off the wall. "Mr. Jim Westenham to Mrs. Grady's office."

I had barely enough time to read the short, scandalous article before Jim came through my door, a slice of toast in one hand and a glass of orange juice in the other.

"You're right," he said by way of greeting.

"I hope that's not an entirely rare situation, but what specifically am I right about today?"

"The orange juice is watery." His eyes fell on my desk. "Oh."

I turned the paper around and stabbed at the print. "Did you know about this? Why didn't you tell me last night this was coming?"

"Because I didn't know. Not for sure. The reporter I spoke to is named Martin McEnery."

"That's what the byline says."

"He's not young, not by a long shot, but he's still mighty hungry. His days of getting a chance at the brass ring are fast running out, and he knows it. He's got the whiff of a big story, something that'll attract attention in New York, and he's running with it as hard as he can. Can't say I blame him."

"Well, I do. My friend Lucinda told me the paper would protect the reputation of the town."

"Up to a point. But they seem to be a legitimate newspaper, although small, and they're not going to bury a valid story. Martin might have threatened to take the story to another paper in one of the other Catskill towns. They wouldn't want that to happen." He popped the last of his toast into his mouth, put down the orange juice, picked up the paper, and read quickly. I leaned back in my chair and studied his face. He was freshly shaven, his dark hair damp around the edges, and he was casually dressed in light-colored pants and an open-necked blue shirt. The corners of his mouth turned down as he read, and his eyes narrowed.

He finished reading. "Okay. Maybe I will blame him. This is a heck of a lot of innuendo disguised as facts. You and your mother, as the hotel owners, weren't asked for a comment. Were you?"

"No."

"The police are quoted but not named. He makes it sound as though there was an FBI raid in the dead of night, not two guys carrying away a box of papers while the little kids splashing in the pool watched. Uncle Harold never cared about public opinion or his reputation, but I do. This is verging on libelous, except that he disguises a lot of his statements as questions. I'll make a few calls, Elizabeth. Find out if this is spreading to the city papers, and if it is, I can tell them that, so far, it's a load of nonsense."

"I'd appreciate it. Thank you. Not many of our guests go into town, and they don't usually have any interest in the local news, but I do not need people checking out of my hotel because they're afraid they're going to be murdered in their beds. If they do that, they'll tell all their friends why they came home early, and the story will grow in the telling. I don't need cancellations, either."

He gave me a smile. "Do you ever relax, Elizabeth?"

"Sure, I relax. I have a couple of hours free every Tuesday between October and April."

"You'll relax tonight. I'm taking you out to dinner."

"I can't—"

"If you want to hear what I learn from my contacts in New York, you'll have to have dinner with me. Otherwise . . ." He pouted and shook his head slowly. "You'll be kept in the dark."

I felt a smile creep across my face. "Put like that, I have to agree."

"Seven o'clock in the lobby. I'll ask around, find a nice place."

"We can eat here."

"Absolutely not. I suspect that would be the opposite of relaxing for you. Seven o'clock."

He saluted me and left my office. He left his orange juice behind.

"A DATE!" OLIVIA SQUEALED. "DID YOU HEAR THAT, TATIana? Elizabeth has a date."

"But a newspaperman, O," my aunt said. "Not good."

I'd come home to dress for my dinner not-a-date and found my mother and her sister relaxing on our porch with a stack of sandwiches and glasses of icy vodka for their dinner.

"A man is a man," Olivia said. "Are you sure he's unmarried, Elizabeth? A lady can't be too careful."

"It is not a date," I said. "We're going out to . . . discuss the case."

"What case?" Aunt Tatiana said.

Winston sniffed my shoes.

"The death of his uncle, of course. That reminds me. Do you not instruct your chambermaids to be on the lookout for . . . shall we say odd things going on in the guests' rooms?"

Aunt Tatiana chuckled.

"I don't mean that sort of odd thing. If we scolded everyone in our hotel who's tiptoeing between rooms, we'd be out of business. As would every other place in the Catskills."

"I have no idea to what you are referring, Elizabeth," my mother said.

"Sure you do, and you don't need to pretend you don't. I am, that is *I was*, a married woman, Olivia."

"Rosemary tells me one of her waiters has suddenly become quite popular with some of the *temporarily* single ladies," Tatiana said.

Olivia wiggled her eyebrows.

"The chambermaids?" I prompted.

"If you're referring to the photographs in room three nineteen, the maids on that floor have been spoken to. They didn't seem to think it was a problem." Aunt Tatiana offered Winston a piece of cheese, and he snapped it up. As usual, Aunt Tatiana shared liberally with Winston. That is, she shared her sandwiches with Winston, not her vodka. Although nothing would surprise me.

"It should have been up to you to decide if it was a problem, not them," I said.

"About that, they have been corrected. No more needs to be said, Elizabeth."

"Thank you." I went to my room, had a quick bath, and attempted to rearrange my hair. I studied myself in the mirror, and as always I cursed the curly red locks my father had given me. My mother and Aunt Tatiana have thick wavy black hair that looks fabulous piled on top of their heads in a French twist or a chignon. Velvet's blessed with fine, sleek blond tresses that drape so elegantly over her shoulder. My mess of red curls curdle in the heat and humidity of a Catskills summer. Hair attended to, I decided it would be safe to wear the new green dress I'd worn Wednesday evening. It had been laundered since I'd jumped into the lake with it on and had turned out better than I'd dared hope. Jim hadn't seen me in it.

Rosemary had joined Olivia, Tatiana, and Winston on the porch. She'd brought a pitcher of martinis with her. The sandwiches were finished, and so was the vodka. Winston stood on the top steps, his blunt nose sniffing the soft evening air for any sign of intruding squirrels or chipmunks.

"Fancy!" Rosemary said when I came out.

"You think I've overdone it? It's just dinner."

"You haven't overdone it. You look nice. You've got a date with our handsome young newspaperman, Olivia tells me."

"It's not a date," I said.

"Sure looks like it," Rosemary said. "I stopped in at your office but you'd left, so I grabbed this"—she pointed to the tray containing the pitcher—"from a passing waiter, as I figured you could use a nice drink."

"Excellent plan," Olivia said. Rosemary had brought two martini glasses. Olivia sipped from one, Tatiana had the other, and Rosemary was drinking her martini from a water glass.

"Not tonight," I said. "He said seven and it's almost that now. If we're going to one of the hotels, we'll want to be there in time for seating."

"You've got a couple of minutes," Rosemary said. "You never want to be early. Makes you look too eager."

"As it's not a date, I don't need to worry about looking eager. I want to look punctual. Like the professional hotelier I am."

"If you say so, Elizabeth. I have something I need to talk to you about."

"Okay, if it's quick."

"Francis Monahan, one of the dishwashers."

"What about him?"

Rosemary let out a long breath. "I can't keep him on. He's just about the clumsiest guy I've ever met. At lunch today he knocked over a cart. Dishes and glasses went everywhere. Maybe twenty plates were broken, as well as glasses and cups and saucers. The kitchen looked like a disaster area, and I thought Chef Leonardo was going to have a heart attack."

Tatiana grunted. "Fool of a man threatens to have a heart attack if the milk turns. Why have you brought this to Elizabeth? You're responsible for the staff in your department, as are we all. Fire him."

Rosemary glanced at me.

"He's Chief Monahan's son," I said.

"Yup." Rosemary nodded. "I thought there might be political considerations."

"Did anyone see this accident happen?" I asked.

"I don't know. Does it matter? Francis was taking the cart to the sinks, and it's not the first time he's broken things or tripped over his own feet. A busy kitchen can be a dangerous place, Elizabeth, you know that."

I thought about what Lucinda had told me, the other boys making fun of Francis when they'd been in school, and what I'd seen and heard myself when the college-boy waiters had mocked and laughed at him.

"What are you thinking?" Olivia peered at me over the rim of her martini glass.

"I'm thinking you'll have to hold off, Rosemary. Regardless of what happened, this is not a good time to fire the son of the chief of police. I get the feeling Monahan's a man who knows how to carry a grudge."

"After a previous incident, I told Francis he had one more chance," Rosemary said.

"Maybe the kitchen is not the best place for him," Aunt Tatiana said.

"Mario told me he needs to hire a new gardener," I said. "He's lost a couple to Kennelwood. This heat's making the grass and the plants grow like weeds. It's making the weeds grow like weeds. Let's move Francis Monahan. Get him out of that crowded kitchen." And away from those college boys, not that the groundskeepers were likely to be any kinder. "Into the fresh air. The only damage he can do with a pair of garden shears is to the geraniums."

"Or to himself," Rosemary said.

"I wish all our problems could be settled so easily."

"I'm now short a dishwasher."

"Rosemary," I said. "I have complete and total trust in your ability to locate and hire a suitable replacement. I'm off now."

I skipped down the steps. "Don't wait up," I called to Olivia.

"She won't," Aunt Tatiana called after me, "but I will."

Winston barked his agreement.

Chapter 14

JIM WESTENHAM DROVE A PLYMOUTH CRANBROOK CLUB Coupe, with a blue body and white roof and trunk.

"Nice car," I said.

"Sadly not mine. It's the paper's pool car."

"Your paper must be doing good business."

"Good enough. Not good enough to let me keep it. They're demanding I bring it back."

"Can't you tell them you're after a story?"

"Chasing communists in the Catskills?"

"Maybe not that story," I said.

He held the passenger door open for me, and I slipped into my seat. He'd dressed for the occasion in a smart charcoal suit of a lightweight summer fabric and a white shirt, with a blue striped tie and matching pocket handkerchief. The white shirt could have used the touch of an iron, and I smiled to myself, thinking of him stuck in a quickly tidied-up storage room.

"Where are we going?" I said.

"I asked the bellhop to recommend someplace nice, and he suggested the neighboring hotel. Not too far to go, and he said the restaurant's the best in the entire area, so I called and made a reservation."

"The neighboring hotel? You don't mean Kennelwood? One of my employees said Kennelwood had the best restaurant in the entire area?"

"Is that a problem? We can try someplace else, if you'd rather."

"No. No problem. I should probably see what makes it the so-called best in the area."

Kennelwood Hotel is older, grander, flashier, and bigger than Haggerman's. It's the property next to ours, only a few minutes away by foot through the woods or by boat across the lake, but driving the winding roads takes twice the time.

The long sunset of a late June evening threw golden light through the trees lining the road as we drove up the hill. To my left I caught brief glimpses of the lake, blue and calm. We crested the hill and the complex came into view. Two buildings, each six stories tall, backed onto a pool about four times the size of ours. The lake spread out in front.

Jim drove up the sweeping driveway, lined with lampposts and trimmed bushes. A bellhop hurried to open my door while Jim tossed the keys to another. We walked up the grand staircase, and a third bellhop held the door for us with a slight bow.

"Fancy place," Jim said.

I harrumphed.

The lobby was so big it had a fountain in the middle, with a huge chandelier hanging from the second-floor ceiling above it. The drapes on the long windows were gold, tied back with gold ropes and tassels, the chairs and couches upholstered in golden fabric. Six-feet-tall imitation marble statues of graceful long-limbed women were mounted on pedestals on either side of the long mahogany reception counter, and the ashtray stands dotted around the room were covered in gold gilt. *Ornate* was the word that came to mind. Ornate and lavish. And, to my eye, stiff and formal and unfriendly. I found the décor intimidating, rather than welcoming. Haggerman's, I liked to think, was welcoming. Welcoming and friendly, offering our guests an extra touch of luxury, and a feeling of being cared for, that they wouldn't get at home.

"Fin de siècle European decadence, badly imitated," Jim mumbled to me.

I gave him a grin. "Precisely what I was thinking. At our place we want to give the feeling of an all-American home-coming. If your home's a bit fancier and nicer than it actually is. And you have servants catering to your every wish all day long."

"Don't we all have that at our homes?" Jim said.

I tried not to stare as we followed the signs to the dining room. The maître d' took Jim's name, made a swift tick on the sheet in front of him with a flourish, and escorted us to our table. We were stuck in a dark corner, near the kitchen, but I didn't mind, as it was a table for two. Most of the big hotels, including ours, had few if any small tables, and guests were expected to share if they weren't part of a large group. Once we were seated, I studied everything, full of professional interest. The room was huge; it would probably seat something like five hundred people. Gold and brown floor-to-ceiling drapes along one wall were pulled closed, and the room was lit by wall sconces and multipoint chandeliers. The linens were clean and starched, the cutlery polished, the pickle tray on our table full, the waiters smartly dressed and decently groomed.

"Nice place," Jim said.

I had to admit it was.

"But you don't like it," he said.

"I like it fine. The owner hasn't been all that welcoming to Olivia and me, that's all."

"His loss," Jim said.

A waiter put typewritten menus in front of us and filled our water glasses. "Can I get you a drink? The bar's open."

Jim asked for bourbon on the rocks, and on a whim I ordered a grasshopper. I was having a night out. I was supposed to be having fun.

Jim had also been looking around, taking it all in. "Older crowd here than at your place. I don't see a lot of young couples and not many teenagers. Plenty of grandparents, though."

"That might be good for us, long term," I said. "Families come back to the Catskills year after year, generation after generation, and they usually go to the same place out of habit. Many people still go to the hotels their great-grandparents went to back in the twenties, but some families are looking for a change. As the old people pass on or get too frail to make the trip, the younger ones try to find something new, something more suited to their age or their tastes. Hopefully, for some of them, that will be Haggerman's."

"It must be a hard life," he said, "running a hotel."

The waiter placed our drinks in front of us. "Ready to order?" he asked. He took our full order—juice to dessert— and wrote it carefully on his pad. All around us conversation buzzed, waiters shouted orders into the kitchen, glassware and cutlery tinkled, but I felt as though Jim and I were tucked into a little alcove all our own.

"I work a lot harder than I ever thought I would," I said. "Pretty much all the time, come to think of it. But that only lasts a few months of the year. On the bright side, I get to live in this marvelous place, although I don't get a lot of time to enjoy it in the spring and summer. I'd always lived in the city before coming here, Brooklyn first, then Manhattan after I was married. When Olivia inherited Haggerman's and asked me to come with her and run it, I was horrified at the very idea of leaving the city. But it didn't take long for me to fall in love with the mountains, the lakes, the woods. I've been here only two years, and I don't think I can go back to the city."

I took a sip of my drink, sweet and delicious, and realized Jim was smiling at me.

"I'm sorry," I said. "Am I talking about myself too much?"

"Not at all. I wouldn't have invited you to have dinner with me if I didn't want to hear what you have to say."

"Most men like to talk about themselves."

He roared with laughter. "Is that what women think? They're probably right. I'm a newspaperman. Asking questions is what I have to do. Asking questions of"—he lifted his glass in a toast—"beautiful women is what I like to do."

I dipped my head.

The waiter put our juices on the table. Orange juice for Jim and tomato cocktail for me.

"Looks watery to me," Jim said, and I laughed.

"You and your mother live here year round?" he asked.

"Yes, we do. Our house and the main building are winterized, and this year we're planning to keep the hotel open in the winter. We'll close all the cabins and the top floor of the hotel, and operate with reduced staff, of course. We're going to try to attract guests for Thanksgiving, Christmas, New Year's celebrations. Skiing and skating are becoming popular around here, so we're hoping to take advantage of the wooded winter wonderland surroundings of our property. That's the plan anyway."

"Sounds like a good one."

Our pickled beet salads arrived, along with bowls of clear consommé. Little noodles cut to look like letters of the alphabet floated in the soup.

I asked Jim about the newspaper business, and he talked about that with obvious pleasure. "Best job in the world for a curious guy like me," he said.

For our main courses I had the Italian spaghetti, and Jim had ham with scalloped potatoes. I didn't mention that the spaghetti served at Haggerman's was far better than this. I hadn't enjoyed my soup much either, and the bread roll had been slightly stale. The consommé was largely tasteless and, unlike here, my kitchen reserved alphabet noodles for the children's dining room.

"How's the ham?" I asked my companion.

"Good. Although I suppose I should say not as good as the ham at Haggerman's."

"Have you had the ham at Haggerman's?"

"No. But I'm sure it's good. You have an expressive face, Elizabeth. I see you studying your food, everything around us, making comparisons. Tell me about your late husband," he said suddenly. "I'd like to hear about him. If you want to talk about it. Was he killed in the war?"

Jim had ordered a bottle of wine to go with our dinner, and I grabbed for my glass. I took a breath. "I don't talk about it. About him."

"I'm sorry," Jim said. "The grief must still be fresh." He

bent his head over his plate and scooped up the last forkful of potatoes, to give me a moment's privacy.

I never talk about Ronald Grady. Not to Olivia. Not to Velvet. Not to Aunt Tatiana. Especially not to them.

I didn't tell anyone I wasn't grieving his death.

I was glad of it and consumed by guilt because I was glad.

I'd married too young and far too quickly. I'd been nineteen; Ron was twenty-five. I'd known him not much more than a month before our quick registry-office wedding. It was wartime, 1944, and all around us couples were rushing for the altar before the man was shipped out. Olivia didn't approve, and she told me so.

"Marry in haste, repent at leisure," she said as she helped me adjust the small veil on the beige hat I wore to be married in. Aunt Tatiana said nothing, but she watched me dressing for my wedding through her dark Russian eyes, and she did not smile. Velvet, in contrast, had thought it all sooooo romantic and called me the luckiest woman on earth. Ron was dreadfully handsome in his uniform, with bottomless brown eyes and a mustache like Clark Gable's.

Olivia and my father had married when they were both eighteen, also in a rush of young love. It hadn't lasted long. As she zoomed toward the big time on Broadway, his career as a jazz musician remained stranded in smoky clubs with below-street entrances. It hadn't been an angry or bitter divorce. They simply realized they were on different life paths and walked away from each other. I was handed over to Aunt Tatiana and Uncle Rudolph to raise, my mother hit the stage and the screen, and my father continued to be a regular presence in my life. Picnics at the zoo, trips to art galleries or museums or just the local park. Some months,

I saw more of him than of my mother. I'm still in touch with him, and I'm hoping he'll come for a visit in the off-season. I know Olivia would welcome him.

I hadn't feared a quick, impulsive marriage because I'd seen how, when love ended, my parents continued to be fond of each other, but I'd been wrong.

Ron Grady had been a charmer. He'd certainly charmed me, straight to bed and then to the altar when he got word that his unit would soon be needed in Europe. We'd had one month of married life. One month of him not coming home until the sun touched the horizon, of drunken rages, of smelling of cheap perfume with lipstick stains on his collar. One month of my own wages disappearing from my purse and him telling me I was too stupid to keep track of how much I was spending.

He'd never hit me, but he was quick to fly into a rage and throw things around, glassware, cutlery, a pretty little china statue my grandmother had given me on my twelfth birthday. The blows, I feared, were coming.

I said nothing to the women who loved me—Olivia, Tatiana, Velvet. I was too ashamed.

And then he was gone. Ten months later the telegram arrived. He'd died on the twelfth of May. The war in Europe had been over for five days. I'd gone out that night, and for the first time in my life—and hopefully the last—I'd gotten falling-down drunk.

Not because I was grieving but out of sheer relief that he wouldn't be coming home. Once his mother, a hollow-eyed, hard-faced, bitter woman, realized her son had not left me pregnant, I never heard from her again. I burned our wedding photograph and kept only his last name and my cheap wedding ring as a memento of what had been a dreadful mistake.

A few months later one of Ron's "buddies" paid a call to me. He brought his wife and clearly both of them had stopped at more than one bar on the way. The buddy told me Ron died in a bar brawl. He and another guy had gotten into a fight over a German woman, and Ron had fallen and hit his head. When his wife went to the bathroom, Ron's "buddy" told me if I needed a man to "support me," he'd be happy to help.

Wink.

"Elizabeth Grady!" A voice boomed above my shoulder, pulling me out of my memories. "Isn't this an unexpected pleasure." Jerome Kennelwood, nattily dressed in a single-breasted tuxedo with a narrow black bow tie and a thin line of pocket handkerchief.

Jim leapt to his feet.

"Bobby," Jerome said to the waiter who'd just brought our desserts. "Do you know who you're serving here?"

"No, sir. Mr. Kennelwood, sir. Should I?" Bobby peered at me. I tried to smile.

"None other than Liz Grady. The little girl who's trying to make a go of Haggerman's."

Bobby looked highly disappointed. He'd been expecting a movie star at the least.

"The lady who's doing a good job of it," Jim said.

"My name is Elizabeth," I said. Never, never, never Liz, or even worse, Lizzie. Ron had called me that. I didn't like it, even then, but Ron had never much cared what I thought.

"Bring Liz and her friend another bottle of wine, Bobby. Get something better than that plonk. And be quick about it."

"Yes, sir. Mr. Kennelwood, sir." The waiter scurried away. I noticed the other waiters suddenly giving our table a wide berth.

"Time will tell, eh?" Jerome said to Jim. He turned to me. His tuxedo might have been expensive, but he'd lost a lot of weight since buying it. His eyes were watery, his thin hair greasy, he'd missed a couple of patches when shaving, and the cuffs of his white shirt showed traces of ground-in dirt. He'd suffered a heart attack over the winter, I remembered.

His smile was as fake as his overly large teeth. "I heard you had an unfortunate accident at Haggerman's the other day. Although from what the police and the paper have to say, it might not have been an accident. Did you know the guy was a communist?"

"I—"

"Communist?" Jim said in a voice designed to carry. "You mean there are communists here? At this hotel?"

Jerome's eyes narrowed. He looked at Jim. "Enjoy your dinner." He walked away, and Jim dropped back into his chair.

"I see what you mean. Not nice." He nodded to the dish of rainbow sherbet in front of me. "Do you want to leave?"

"Be run out of town, you mean? No. I'll enjoy the rest of my meal. Although I don't think I want any more wine."

"I'll ask the waiter not to uncork the bottle. If Kennelwood's paying for it, we might as well take it with us. Provided it's a good bottle, that is. Not like the first one we got."

Over our desserts and coffee we chatted about life in the Catskills.

"Place is a gold mine," Jim said. "Every second person, maybe every person, in the five boroughs wants nothing but to get out of the city in the heat of the summer. And here you are a couple of hours away by car or train, with woods, lakes, and cooling mountain breezes. It can only go from strength to strength. The Catskills is the place to be, Elizabeth."

"My mother and I hope so." I'd be fine, although not happy, if Haggerman's failed and I had to go back to the city and find a bookkeeping job, but Olivia had nothing else to fall back on. I lifted my napkin off my lap, touched it to my lips, and excused myself. Jim stood politely.

The dining room was emptying out. I'd read the bulletin board when we came in to see that none other than the comedian Milton Berle would be performing tonight. Even Olivia's contacts weren't enough to get us Berle, and his fees were far out of our price range. Perhaps naively, I hoped that when people like Charlie Simmonds hit the big time, they'd remember the places that had given them their start.

Then again, probably all Charlie Simmonds would remember about Haggerman's was that he'd been told he couldn't leave as he was under suspicion for murdering a guest.

The ladies' room was full as diners tidied themselves up. I took my earrings off and gave my earlobes a nice rub. Those green glass earrings were lovely, but they were heavy and they pinched. Two gray-haired women at the mirrors next to me chatted.

"I tell you, Dorothy, I'm disappointed. Highly disappointed."

"What's happened now?"

"As you know, I like to get an early start on the day. First in the pool, every morning, even before I go into breakfast." She shook her head. "Standards around here are slipping, Dorothy. The pool hadn't been cleaned when I got there this morning. There were bugs—big nasty flies—floating on the surface of the water." She shuddered. "And glasses, dirty, empty glasses, still on the poolside tables. Tonight, my bread roll was completely stale. It wasn't fit to feed to a pack of starving birds."

I snapped my earrings back on and studied my lipstick.

"Betty, you know Jerome Kennelwood had a heart attack recently. He's doing his best and putting up a brave front, coming into the dining room every night, greeting the guests, but his color doesn't look good. He's lost a great deal of weight."

"I don't care one whit, dear. We're paying the same amount to stay here as we did last year, whether he's been ill or not, and I expect my bread roll to be fresh."

Earrings on, lipstick applied, I adjusted the bodice of my dress.

"His son's come up from the city to handle the day-to-day management of the hotel. Such a handsome young man. The way I heard it, the son and Jerome had a falling-out years ago, when Jerome refused to listen to his ideas for modernizing the place. And so the son, Richard I think his name is, left. Now he's back, because his father needs him, but they're clashing."

Earrings on, lipstick applied, bosom readjusted, I made sure my stockings were straight.

"All I have to say about that is they shouldn't be clashing over cleaning the swimming pool. Shall we join the others? I must say I'm looking forward to hearing Mr. Milton Berle later."

"Janet went to Haggerman's last night and she said the comedian they have there is excellent. A star in the making."

"Haggerman's? Where's that?" Dorothy said.

"Not far from here. Olivia Peters owns it. She knows all the top acts. They say she comes to dinner sometimes and sits with the guests."

Dorothy sucked in a breath. "No! I adored her in *Moonlight Dreams* on Broadway. I wonder if I could talk Fred into going to her place next year. I'd expect a famous dancer to have an eye for detail."

The door shut behind them.

Curiosity satisfied, I headed back to my table.

Dinner was slowly ending, and people were gathering together their things and rising from their seats. I was, I realized, enjoying the evening, and I was in no rush to go home. I'd ask Jim if he'd like to have another drink and perhaps we could stay for Milton Berle's show. Dodging people and chairs, I headed across the big room toward our table. Jim wasn't there, and I guessed he'd gone out for some air and a smoke.

Jerome Kennelwood occupied the center of the dining room, surrounded by a group of men with cigars clamped in their teeth and highball glasses gripped in their hands. At the nearby tables, the women had pushed their chairs closer and were leaning across the white tablecloths, chatting.

Jerome's back was to me, and I had to suck in my stomach and turn sideways to squeeze between him and a chair at an empty table. "Mark my words, gentleman, if you don't nip that sort of thing in the bud, it can only spread. We don't want that rubbish in the Catskills. Not good for business."

The men mumbled in agreement. "You're not implying that those women who took over Haggerman's are communists, are you, Jerome?"

I stopped dead.

"They don't have to be. You know how susceptible women are."

Full round bellies trembled as the men chuckled in agreement. A wave of cigar smoke rolled over my head.

"A long-past-her-prime Broadway *dancer* and her snip

of a daughter think they can run a big hotel to Catskill standards?" Jerome scoffed. "I've heard that staff over there are quitting in droves. So many have left, the kitchen can barely put together a tolerable dinner."

"Can't have that," one of the men said. He noticed me listening to them, and gave me a vacant smile, no doubt assuming I was the daughter or much younger wife of one of the others.

"The chief of police, Norm Monahan, great guy, is a personal friend of mine," Jerome said. "He agrees with me that sloppy management and unsupervised staff create ripe conditions for anti-American activity to take root."

The laughter stopped, and the men muttered among themselves. "My wife suggested we go to Haggerman's to-morrow for the evening show," one of them asked. "Do you think we shouldn't, Jerome?"

"Probably best to stay away. The police are keeping a sharp eye on the place. I've heard—"

"And I've heard that you have dead bugs in your swim-ming pool!" I snapped. Jerome Kennelwood turned around. Amusement danced behind his eyes, and I knew he'd been aware of me standing behind him all along. I tried to take a step back and bumped into a chair. "Your bread rolls are stale, and your chef puts children's noodles in the soup."

"Liz," Jerome said. "I didn't mean—"

"Of course you meant it. You meant every word. Please allow me to introduce myself," I said to the men. "I am Elizabeth Grady, and I am Olivia Peters's daughter. It is our intention to turn Haggerman's into the most popular hotel in this section of the mountains. If not the entire Catskills."

"That's nice, sweetheart. I like pretty girls with ambi-tion. How about it, Jerome, are you up to the competition?"

The men all laughed. Some of the women had turned in

their chairs when I spoke. I had not attempted to keep my voice down.

"Competition is one thing, but let's keep it fair," Jerome said. "I hate to see hardworking Catskills folk thrown out on their ear in the middle of the season when a place can't pay their wages."

"I have no intention of not paying anyone their wages."

"Maybe you don't, Liz. Not now. But you're in over your heads, you and your mother. How did she get that place anyway? Win it in a poker game?"

The men laughed heartily. The women were watching me carefully. Conversation all around us had died, and people were no longer heading for the doors.

"She inherited it honestly," I said. "We run an honest business. We don't go around bad-mouthing our neighbors to anyone who'll listen."

"If you're referring to me, I'm not bad-mouthing anyone. I'm telling my friends here—and at Kennelwood Hotel we consider all our guests to be our friends—the state of affairs. A man was murdered at your hotel. I consider it fair to ask how safe your place is."

People exchanged glances. The word *murdered* began to spread through the room.

Blood pounded in my ears. "A man died, yes, and that was highly unfortunate. Let me ask you, Mr. Kennelwood, in all fairness, what you had to do with it?"

"Now, see here."

"No, you see here." I stabbed my index finger in his direction. Lucky for him that the knives at the nearby tables had been cleared away. "Convenient for you, isn't it, with your failing hotel, buggy swimming pool, and stale dinner rolls, if the up-and-coming place next door gets into trouble. Did you kill him yourself, Mr. Kennelwood, or simply take advantage of an unfortunate man's death to spread nasty rumors about your competition? You were quick enough to try to turn the townspeople against us last summer. If there's any communist activity going on around here, I have to wonder how much of it is going on inside your own head. Or how much of it you're encouraging in an attempt to place the blame on your competition."

"How dare you!" A vein began to pulse in his forehead.

"Answer the lady, Jerome," an elderly woman at the nearby table said in a firm voice that carried considerable weight behind it. She pounded her cane on the floor. She was tiny and wizened; her hair was thin, her hands dotted with liver spots, and her fingers bent. Diamonds glittered in her ears and around her throat, the style of the jewelry and the signs of wear on them indicating long-held family heirlooms, probably from the previous century.

"Thank you so much for stopping by, Mrs. Grady." A strong hand grabbed my arm. "I hope you enjoyed your evening."

I shook the arm off and turned to face Richard Kennelwood. He smiled at me. I did not smile back.

"Can I walk you to your car?" he asked.

"No, you may not. I'm not finished here."

"I think you are," Jerome said. "Get off my property or I'll phone the police and have you removed."

"Have them in your pocket, do you?" I shouted. "Your *good friend* Norm?"

"Richard, get this woman out of here."

"I want to hear what she has to say," the woman said. "You always were a fool, Jerome, and your recent illness doesn't appear to have improved your disposition any. My

late husband was a friend of your father's, and for that reason alone I continue to come here. Shall I reconsider that
option?"

Jerome sputtered.

"Not at all, Mrs. Masterson," Richard said smoothly.
"Your friendship and support is invaluable to my family."

"As is my late husband's money, I'm sure. I might drop
into this Haggerman's resort tomorrow. See what the fuss
is about. I approve of women in business. I don't approve of
communists, though. Are you a communist, girl?" Her
small eyes were almost buried in folds of skin, but the
spark of intelligence shone within them.

"No, ma'am," I said. "I am not. Nor is my mother."

"Glad to hear it. Now, Edwin, you may escort me to the
theater. I'm anxious to hear Mr. Berle. And do get rid of
that ridiculous cigar. Mary, take my purse."

"Please," Richard Kennelwood said to me in a low voice.

"I've said my piece." I lifted my chin and marched away.
Despite the throb of anger in my chest, I was careful where
I placed my feet. The last thing I needed would be to trip
over a loose piece of carpet and fall flat on my face.

Although, if that did happen, I could sue them.

Richard Kennelwood muttered his apologies to his
guests and then ran after me. "My father didn't mean all
that about you and your mother."

I stopped and turned. He stood very close, and I had to
tilt my head back to look into his face. His eyes were thickly
lashed, the deep hazel flecked with traces of green and
gold. I realized my entire body was trembling, and I
gripped my hands together. Enough of admiring his eyes.

"He meant every word. He knew I was standing right
there the entire time. I hate to think what he says about us
when I'm not around. Actually, I know what he says about

us when I'm not around. He called the booking agencies today, didn't he? Telling them we would be out of business before the end of the season."

"I'll have a word with him. I don't want bad blood between us."

"Whether you want bad blood or not, you've got it." I headed for the doors, my heels tapping furiously on the tiled floor. More than a few people stood back, watching me, and I realized that I probably looked as incompetent as Jerome Kennelwood said I was. I slowed my pace and tried to wipe the fury off my face. I lowered my voice. "Do you want a lawsuit on your hands? You'll get one if you keep saying my mother and I are communists."

"I'm not saying that. I'm not even thinking it, but I assure you I don't want any legal trouble. Elizabeth, please. I'll have a word with my father. I can't promise you he'll pay any attention to me, but I will try."

I turned once again, and once again I stared up into his face. He was, I realized, a very handsome man. His well-tailored suit fit properly, his dark hair was cut short, and he was close-shaven. I mentally kicked myself for noticing.

"I don't believe you. You were at our place Wednesday night, the night Mr. Westenham died. You and I talked. You stayed for the last show; I saw you. I told the police that. After the show, did you follow Mr. Westenham down to the lake?"

Instead of getting angry, Richard grinned at me. "Why would I do that? I'd never met the man."

"Because your father told you to. He told you to cause trouble for Haggerman's. Cause enough trouble that we might be shut down. Or have to shut down if people stop coming. Same result."

"I don't do a great many things my father tells me, and

I certainly don't kill men I don't even know, no matter who might tell me to. Before you take the next step and accuse my father . . . He isn't a well man, Elizabeth. He puts on a pretext in the evenings of playing the host at dinner, but that's about all he's capable of these days. Wednesday night, like every night, he went to his room as soon as dinner ended. He wasn't driving around to Haggerman's looking for an opportunity to run you out of business."

"Why did you come?"

"I'd heard the comedian was a good one. I'd also heard the new management was an attractive woman, and I thought I'd check them both out."

"Oh, please, don't give me that."

He held up his hands, palms out. "I apologize." He gave me a soft slow smile. "Do you accept my apology?"

"No," I said. The bellhop opened the door, and I marched through it. Only once I was outside, standing on the steps, did I remember Jim. I wanted to drive away in a cloud of dust and righteous indignation, but I hadn't come in my own car.

Richard had followed me, and he read my indecision. "Can I offer you a lift back to Haggerman's?"

Fortunately, before I could tell Richard what to do with his lift, Jim broke out of the darkness, threw his cigarette to the ground in a shower of sparks, and ran up the steps.

"Elizabeth, what's going on? I'm so sorry. I came out for air and got chatting to some old guy who's been coming to Summervale every year since he was a baby. As long as I'm here, I'm thinking of putting together a story on the appeal of the Catskills to New York immigrant families. What can I say? I'm a newspaperman. Once the old guy got telling me his stories, I fell into it." He stopped talking and looked at Richard, standing on the step behind me. He thrust out his hand. "Jim Westenham."

The men shook. "Richard Kennelwood. Westenham? You must be—"

"Kennelwood? You must be—"

"My father owns this place."

"My uncle was Harold Westenham. I've come up to settle his affairs and try to find out what the heck happened, and this nice lady kindly found me a room at her inn."

"My condolences," Richard said.

"Thank you."

"I've heard good things about Haggerman's."

"It's a nice place."

I grabbed Jim's arm. "Let's go. Don't listen to him, he's trying to avoid being sued."

"Sued?" Jim said. "About what?"

"Get the keys and let's walk to the car. I don't want to hang around here any longer than I have to."

"Did something happen, Elizabeth? Richard? What's going on? Hold on, I have to go back inside. I haven't paid yet."

"It's on the house," Richard said. "Take her home. I'm new to running this hotel, but I'm trying my best. Thanks for the tip, Elizabeth. I'll make sure the rolls are fresh tomorrow."

I marched down the driveway, between rows of tall lamps around which clouds of moths had gathered.

"You might want to have a word with your pool attendant," I called over my shoulder. "The pool should be sparkling clean when the first swimmers come down. Have the glasses collected before daybreak."

Chapter 15

I DIDN'T SLEEP AT ALL WELL THAT NIGHT. I'D BEEN SURLY to Jim on the drive back to Haggerman's, and I'd rudely turned down his suggestion that we have a nightcap in the bar. I felt bad about that almost as soon as I walked away, but when I went back to apologize, I found him chatting to a group of men on the veranda and ordering himself a drink, so I'd slipped into the darkness.

Olivia had been up, flipping through a copy of *Vanity Fair* while listening to a radio play, with Winston curled at her feet. "You're home early, Elizabeth," she said when I stomped into the house. "Did you have a nice evening?"

"Yes!" I yelled as my bedroom door slammed behind me.

"I'm glad that went well," I heard her say to the dog.

I hadn't seriously considered that Jerome Kennelwood might have killed a Haggerman's guest in order to ruin us, but once the thought was in my head I couldn't get rid of it. Not that Jerome himself had done it, but had he put his son up to it?

Richard Kennelwood had been on our property at the time.

Richard was handsome, charming, making the attempt to be friendly. I didn't trust him one little bit. I'd learned the hard way about handsome, charming men. Jerome, on the other hand, was not handsome and was most definitely not charming, at least not to me, but otherwise, what did they say? Like father like son. Was Richard also out to ruin us, just not as obvious about it as his father?

I FINALLY FELL ASLEEP AS THE BIRDS WERE STARTING TO call good morning to one another. When I woke, the sun was streaming through my window, Olivia was humming to herself in what passes for our kitchen, and the scent of coffee was in the air. I stumbled out of bed.

My mother turned in a swirl of peach satin and fluff and held up the coffeepot. "Do you need one?" We had a small kitchen, but coffee was the only thing ever prepared in it. A bowl of sliced fruit and another of cereal on a room-service tray lay on the table.

"I'll have a cup, thanks."

"Did things not go well last night?"

I sighed. "If you mean dinner with Jim, it went well. I enjoyed his company, and we had a lovely evening. Unfortunately it didn't end as a great success when I had a confrontation with the Kennelwoods. Father and son. To cut a long story short, I was kicked out of the hotel, which didn't matter, as I was in the process of storming out anyway."

"Jim took you to Kennelwood? Perhaps not the wisest choice."

"In fairness, Olivia, he had no reason to know we don't get on with them."

I took my coffee and went back to my room to get ready for the day. I would be late arriving at the office, but considering I worked most nights long after everyone had gone, I decided I'm entitled to the occasional instance of tardiness. I phoned the switchboard to get the day's weather report. Midnineties, plenty of humidity, and no chance of rain. If I was going to be unprofessionally late for work, I'd dress unprofessionally, and I slipped into a pair of yellow pedal pushers, a short-sleeved white blouse with yellow stripes, and sandals. Last of all I tied a belt around my waist and fastened my key chain to it.

Olivia glanced up from her magazine when I came out. Perfectly sculpted eyebrows rose. "Surely that is not what you are wearing to work."

"It's time to let my inner rebel out. Did you go to the hotel last night?"

"I skipped dinner, but I went to the ballroom later. Mr. Simmonds was quite amusing, although verging on scandalous."

"Should I ask him to tone down his act?"

"Most definitely not. If people don't want to be scandalized, they shouldn't be attending a comedy show at eleven at night."

"Was there much talk about the death of Mr. Westenham?"

Olivia pursed her lips and thought. She shook her head. "Not that I heard. And I would have. As nothing more seems to be happening regarding that, talk has moved on, as it so easily does. I understand there's one waiter in particular who's making himself an object of gossip among the weekday widows. Mrs. Liebert's dramatic and overly dyed blond hair turned green in the swimming pool, and she refuses to come out of her room. Fortunately for the reputation of our stylists, the ladies said she refused to pay what she called the exorbitant fees at our beauty parlor and went to a place in town. Uninterested in the drama of ladies' hair, the gentlemen were in deep discussion of one Mr. Black, who lost so much at the casino at the Concord the night before last, he will be talking to you about leaving prematurely and getting a refund. It was generally agreed that Mr. Black is a fool."

"He is a fool if he thinks I'm going to give him his money back. Have a nice day." The screen door slammed behind me, and I skipped down the path that meandered near the woods. I was in a better frame of mind this morning. As my mother had said, our guests wanted nothing but the latest gossip, and the murder was getting stale without fresh developments. If the Kennelwoods had tried to frame us, I was on to them, and they knew I was on to them. They wouldn't try anything like that again.

I hoped.

Breakfast was over, and everyone was getting a start on their day. Games were underway on the handball and tennis courts. As I came down the path, a cluster of bathing-suit-clad toddlers swarmed around me, gripping their plastic pails and spades.

"Good morning, Mrs. Grady," the nannies called.

Two excessively thin women were relaxing on lounge chairs by the beach, cold drinks in hand and hats and sunglasses in place.

"Five thousand dollars!" one woman said to the other as
I passed. "Can you believe it! I heard she's threatening to
divorce him. He spent five thousand dollars for a car!"

"It must be a mighty nice car," her friend said.

"No car is that nice."

The loudspeaker crackled to life, and Randy's voice
echoed over the lake and the hills. "Don't forget, folks!
The Miss Haggerman's pageant is at four o'clock on the
dock. This is for girls eighteen to twenty-nine, so you men
won't want to miss it! And, girls, get those Haggerman's
smiles on!"

I actually laughed out loud. If there was one thing I did
not have on last night at Kennelwood, it was a Haggerman's
smile.

Charlie Simmonds was heading to the beach, but he
changed direction when he spotted me. He had a loose robe
thrown over his bathing suit, a threadbare towel over his
arm, and a short glass containing a couple of inches of
brown liquid in one hand. I couldn't help but notice he had
exceptionally thin legs and knobby knees. "You're in a
good mood this morning," he said.

"I guess I am," I said. "Why would I not be? It's a lovely
day."

"Going to be a hot one."

"I was away from the hotel last night. How did your
evening go?"

"Good. I think it went real good. The audience seemed
to think so, too. Look, as long as I have you . . . My scheduled gig ended here last night. My agent canceled tonight
and tomorrow's shows, but I have got to be on my way if
I'm going to save any more appearances before my reputation is completely ruined. I haven't heard another thing

from the cops since I saw them on Thursday. Do you know what's going on?"

"No, I don't. They've been quiet."

"I'm thinking if I just up and leave, they won't even notice." He fell into step beside me, and we carried on toward the main building.

"Up to you," I said, "but I wouldn't chance it. Why don't you give them a call? Or better still, drop into the police station. If you don't want to take the bus, I can get one of the guys to take you into town next time they go."

"That'd be great, thanks. It's the not knowing that's so bad, right? My agent says we can't take the chance on canceling any other shows and then me being told I can be on my way." His face settled into serious lines. "You don't think they're planning a raid, do you?"

"Who? The police? A raid? Good heavens, I hope not. Why?"

"I don't know much about how small-town cops operate, but I did have some experience of criminal investigations in my lawyer days. The first forty-eight hours after a murder's the critical time for finding evidence. I'd expect them to be crawling all over the place, asking questions, trying to figure out who killed that guy and why. Instead, nothing. I'm thinking maybe they hope to take the killer by surprise."

"Surely not." Raging gun battles echoing across Delayed Lake, accompanied by the screams of guests (not to mention the screams of Olivia and me), between the police and a gang of outlaws would definitely not be good for Haggerman's reputation.

"The police must have plenty of other cases to deal with," I said. "It's a busy time of the year around here."

Perhaps Mr. Westenham's killer had followed him to the Catskills after all and returned to the city once the deed was done. The Summervale police might have handed the case over to the city detectives and forgot to let us know.

"Speak of the devil," Charlie said. "And he arrives."

A police car was pulling into the circle. Chief Monahan had come alone, and he climbed out from behind the wheel. He glanced around, saw me heading his way at a rapid trot, and remained by his car, waiting. Charlie came with me.

"Good morning, Chief," I said, trying to sound cheerful and not at all worried about what he might be here to tell me. "What can we do for you today?"

"I need a word, Mrs. Grady." Monahan, on the other hand, did not attempt to be cheerful. His round face was tight with anger.

"Certainly. Would you like to come into my office? How about a coffee?"

"No. This won't take long." He stepped toward me. I could smell the coffee and cigarettes he'd had for breakfast, and the smoke on his stained and dusty uniform. I took an involuntary step back.

"You fired my boy." His voice was low and menacing. "That wasn't nice."

"Your boy? You mean—" I was about to say "Deputy Dave," but then I remembered. "Oh, Francis. Your son. There was an accident in the kitchen and—"

"He's a good boy. A good man. He's a hard worker. He was involved in an incident in the army that got blown up all out of proportion, it went on his record, and now he can't land a decent job. And you—"

"Please, Chief. Let me finish. I did not fire Francis. What did he tell you?"

"He told me nothing. He spent last night at my sister's place, like he does sometimes. He told her he'd been ordered to leave the kitchen and not come back, and she called me this morning to tell me."

"That's not the entire story. His supervisor and I decided the kitchen wasn't the right place for Francis, so we transferred him to grounds maintenance. We move staff around all the time."

His eyes narrowed. "Is that so?"

"If you want, you're welcome to go to the shed where we keep the maintenance equipment and ask if Francis reported there for work this morning. Although"—I cleared my throat—"you need to realize that the hiring—and firing—of staff here is strictly a business decision. I'll always do what's best for the hotel."

He stared at me, and I tried not to shift my feet. "What's best for this hotel, Mrs. Grady, is not to get on my bad side. Do we understand each other?"

"I fear we do."

"Glad to hear it. I think I will have a mosey around. Check on Francis, see he's settling into his new job okay. Then I'll want to make sure everything here's up to code. We wouldn't want any complaints made to the town, now would we?"

"We would not," I said.

"I hope I don't hear any more of that communist talk here, either. I assume a garden job pays more than a kitchen helper?"

It didn't. I said nothing. We looked at each other. We might have stood there all day, engaged in a battle of wills, had not Charlie cleared his throat and said, "While you're here, Chief. What about me leaving? Nice as this place is, I've got engagements in other hotels, and I'd like to be on my way."

Monahan broke eye contact with me. "Why you asking me?"

"Thursday you told me I wasn't to leave."

"I don't care what you do," Monahan grunted. He
walked away, leaving his car blocking the driveway at the
top of the circle.

"Good thing I asked," Charlie said. "Otherwise, I might
have been here until Christmas. My act's good, and I try to
keep it fresh, but I don't have that much material. My engagement scheduled for tonight's been canceled, so I'll
leave in the morning, if that's okay with you."

"What? Oh yes. That's fine. We've made alternate arrangements to put up tonight's act. But didn't you find that
a bit weird? How Chief Monahan suddenly lost interest in
searching for communists, never mind murderers?"

"That guy can't hold two thoughts in his head at the
same time. Right now he's only interested in making sure
his son still has a job. As I'll be here one more night, I'm
happy to perform this evening, as we discussed."

"We'll put you on after the magician. Two sets?"

"Sure. Will I see you there?"

"I'll try to catch it."

He threw his towel over his shoulder and headed toward
the beach.

Y

MY MIND WHIRLED AS I WATCHED CHARLIE SETTLE HIM-
self comfortably into a lounge chair. I didn't know what I'd
do if Francis Monahan didn't work out as a gardener's assistant. Would I have to keep shifting him endlessly from
one department to another, just to keep his father from ha-
rassing us? I might have to. So far, as far as I knew, Francis

had been guilty only of being clumsy, and that as a result of being egged on by some of the other staff, but he'd been dishonorably discharged from the army, supposedly for theft. What would I do if I believed he was stealing from the hotel or, worse, from our guests?

Nothing like that had happened, I told myself. No point in worrying about it until it did happen, which, hopefully, it wouldn't. My attention was caught by a great deal of noise coming from one of the cabins close to the main building. Doors slammed, a man yelled, children wailed, a woman shouted. Three bellhops emerged from cabin two, laden with luggage. The Berkowitz family followed, dressed in traveling clothes, apparently about to prematurely check out of our mountain paradise.

"I don't wanna go!" a little girl, her black hair tied in yellow ribbons, screamed as her mother dragged her down the porch steps.

"I don't care what you want!" Mr. Berkowitz bellowed at her, which got the other girl, identical to the first but for the blue ribbons in her hair, to join in the screaming.

"Now see what you've done!" Mrs. Berkowitz yelled.

"I don't want to hear another word out of you," her husband replied in a voice loud enough to have birds lifting off the trees lining the lake. It certainly was loud enough to have every person in the lake, in the pool, on the courts, on the veranda, or walking along the path stop whatever they were doing to stare. "Not until I've dropped you at your mother's, where you can spend the rest of the summer."

"No!" wailed Yellow Ribbons.

The bellhops dropped the mountain of luggage on the edge of the driveway, and one of them ran toward the parking area.

"It's all right, dear," Mrs. Berkowitz said to her daughters as they climbed the steps and walked past me. "We'll have such a lovely time at Granny's."

"I hate Granny!" Blue Ribbons yelled. Those girls had impressive pairs of lungs. She stared at me. I gave her a smile. She narrowed her eyes and stuck out her tongue.

🍸

WHILE MR. BERKOWITZ INFORMED THE RECEPTION CLERK they were checking out and the Berkowitz children wailed, Mrs. Berkowitz spotted a friend and headed toward her. "My mother's taken ill suddenly," she explained. "The doctors say the end is near, and I'm rushing to her side. I only hope I'm not too late."

Leaving them to their family drama, I crossed the lobby, grabbed a copy of this morning's *Summervale Gazette* from the newspaper box next to the reception desk, and glanced quickly at it without slowing down. A picture of a fire-blackened building surrounded by woods filled the top half, and I didn't bother to read the article. I flipped the paper over to see a small box in the bottom corner, below the fold, which said the police were continuing to investigate the "mysterious death" at Haggerman's Catskills Resort and an arrest was expected soon.

As I knew nothing about any imminent arrest, I dared to hope the whole affair would turn out to have nothing to do with us, or with anyone staying here. I threw the paper onto a low table and walked through the outer office to the sound of the clerks giggling. I stopped at my door and turned to face them. "What?"

"Nothing, Mrs. Grady. Nothing at all." Heads bent back to their work. Giggles continued.

I unlocked my own office door and stepped inside. An

elaborate display of long-stemmed red roses in a glass vase sat on my desk. A card addressed to me was tucked into the foliage, and I picked it up and opened the envelope.

Sorry things ended on an unsatisfactory note. Try again soon??? J

I reached out and ran my index finger over a velvety petal before sticking my head into the outer office. "How did that delivery get in here?"

"Darlene at reception called Mrs. Rostov," a clerk said. "Mrs. Rostov accepted the flowers and unlocked your door."

"Thank you." Satisfied that no one had broken into my office, I dropped into the chair behind my desk. I plucked a freshly sharpened pencil out of the overflowing container and took the topmost message slip off the pile. My eyes wandered to the flowers. They were lovely, deep red, long-stemmed, and perfectly fresh, and they must have cost a fortune. I'd ruined Jim's night out, and I felt bad about that. Then again, he got away without paying the bill.

Thinking of last night made me think once again about the Kennelwoods, father and son. I had to admit to myself that I found it hard to believe Richard would kill a stranger for no other reason than to put Haggerman's in a bad light. But what if Harold Westenham was not a stranger to Richard or Jerome Kennelwood? Jim had said his uncle was the most pedantic person he ever knew. If that was so, Harold likely did research on the area before coming here. Did he learn something about the Kennelwoods? Or did he already know something and came here intending to confront them over it?

That line of thought, I realized, could apply to anyone at

Haggerman's, staff or guests. It was not my problem. I swiveled my chair so I was looking out the window and chewed at the end of my pencil.

"Those are gorgeous," Velvet said.

I swung around. "Nice enough."

"Oh yeah, play it cool." She snatched the card off my desk. "*J.* Jim, I assume. What happened last night that he has to apologize? Don't tell me he—?"

"No, nothing like that. I had a run-in with the Kennelwoods. Junior and Senior."

"The delectable Richard? Do tell."

"Is he delectable? I never noticed. I haven't had breakfast. Didn't even finish my coffee. I need a change of scenery. Let's go into town." I stuffed the pencil into its container and threw the message slip on top of the pile.

"Now?"

"Do you have something going on?"

"I'm free for a while. The teen girls exercise group in the pool is at one. At three I have to join a mixed-doubles tennis game. Hottest time of the day, what a great idea. One of the players tripped last night and twisted his ankle, so I've been asked to be the substitute. Randy and I are supposed to be the judges at the beauty pageant at four, but I'm hoping to get Olivia to take my place."

"You should be in the pageant," I said. "You'd win."

"That's not happening. I have evening calisthenics at six, the bingo game to call at eight, and dancing in the ballroom until midnight."

I grabbed my purse. "Let's go. I'll have you back in time."

"Might as well. I'll come with you, wherever you're going, if you agree to talk to Olivia about the beauty pageant.

I was on my way to your house when I decided to pop in and ask how your date went."

"I will, and it was not a date."

"So you keep saying. I'd say those flowers say otherwise." She bent over the roses and breathed in deeply. She lifted her head, her face crossed with disappointment. "No scent."

"The Berkowitz family in cabin two left very suddenly. Do you know what happened?"

"Oh yeah." Velvet gave me a wicked grin. "Everyone's talking about it. Mrs. B. slipped away from the family breakfast table and cornered Luke in the hallway. She told him her husband was going back to the city on Sunday evening and thus the coast would be clear that night after the children were in bed. One of the ladies at the Berkowitz table, who just happened to be lingering around the corner of the same hallway, overheard and rushed to tell Mr. B. about it. Mr. B. was still enjoying his scrambled eggs and toast, and although the lady should have tried to keep her voice down, she didn't, and the entire table heard. Whether Mr. B. cares or not what his wife does for entertainment when he's away doesn't matter. He cares—a lot—about being the subject of gossip, particularly as some of the husbands at their table had the bad manners to chuckle."

"Never a dull moment at Haggerman's Catskills Resort." I reached for the phone. "Before we go, I'll let the booking agencies know we have a three-bedroom luxury cabin in a prime location that has unexpectedly become available."

WE ARRIVED AT THE RED SPOT DINER AT TEN THIRTY. THE restaurant was about a quarter full, breakfast rush over, lunch crowd still to arrive.

"You again," Mrs. McGreevy said when she saw me.

I gave her my most dazzling smile. "I told my friend here about your egg creams, and she said she had to try one. Didn't you, Velvet?"

"I did? I mean, I sure did. Nothing I love more than an egg cream."

Mrs. McGreevy's face cracked, just a fraction. "Best in the Catskills." She waved her arm in the air. "Sit anywhere you like."

"Is Lucinda in?" I asked.

The face stiffened. "Lucinda's working."

"Lucinda is always working." My friend came out of the kitchen, wiping her hands on her apron. "In fact, Lucinda has been working so hard, she's going to sit down and have an egg cream and a good gossip." She brushed her lips across her mother's cheek. "You don't mind, do you, Mom?"

Mrs. McGreevy struggled to contain a smile.

Lucinda led Velvet and me to a vacant booth at the back of the diner, calling, "Three egg creams, please."

"I'll have a grilled cheese sandwich, too, if that's okay," I said.

"Of course," Lucinda said. "How about you?" she asked Velvet. "Would you like something to eat?"

"Not for me, thanks. The egg cream will be enough. I'm Velvet McNally, by the way."

"Oh, sorry." I introduced them as we slid into the red vinyl-covered benches of the booth. Overhead the fans turned, doing not much more than stirring the hot, humid air.

Lucinda pulled off her hair net with a contented sigh and wiped beads of sweat off her brow as her black hair tumbled around her face. "It's nice to take a break. We had a line out the door this morning, and as soon as they were all served, we had to start getting ready for lunch in case it's more of the same. What do you do at Haggerman's, Velvet?"

"I play all day long. I swim." Velvet pretended to do a doggy paddle. "I do exercises." She lifted her arms and twisted from side to side. "This afternoon I'm playing tennis." Imitation of a serve. "Tonight, I'm dancing until midnight." She spread her fingers and moved her hands back and forth as though catching a beat. "The rest of the time, I look beautiful." She put her hands to her chin and fluttered her eyelashes. "Believe me, it's as exhausting as your job. I'm Elizabeth's outdoor activities director."

Lucinda laughed.

"Have you heard any more talk about the death at Haggerman's?" I asked.

"Not a word. Yesterday's news, I guess. You heard about the fire at the Shady Pines Bungalow Colony?"

"I saw a picture in this morning's paper, but I didn't read the article. What happened?"

"It started in the middle of the afternoon yesterday, and everyone was down at the lake, so no one was hurt, but one of the cabins burned to the ground. People say the fire was set deliberately."

"Why would anyone do that?" Velvet asked.

"The guy who owns that place owns a handful of the cheaper bungalow colonies around. Shady by name, shady by nature, I've heard. They say he has some debts back in the city. Debts to the sort of people you don't want to be in debt to. A couple of old-timers were in here this morning, talking about it when I served them their eggs and hash browns."

"Do you get much of that sort of thing around here?" Velvet asked. "Trouble from the city, I mean?"

"No, we don't. Must have been an extreme case. Chief

Monahan came in for breakfast earlier, and all the guys in here wanted to ask him about it. Chief's never one to keep quiet, not if he can be the center of attention. He can only concentrate on one thing at a time, Elizabeth. I'm afraid your murder will go on the back burner. Not that he's ever going to catch the person who torched that cabin. He'll be long, long gone."

"How about the FBI guys? There were two of them at Haggerman's Thursday morning. Have you had them in here?"

"Not that I've seen. And that lot stand out around here like a bunch of sore thumbs in winter mittens."

I pondered that for a moment. Charlie had also said Monahan couldn't think of two things at the same time, and it would appear the fire, plus Francis's employment situation, now occupied all his attention. But surely the FBI wouldn't just lose interest and wander away. Would they?

Three egg creams arrived. Velvet's eyes opened wide. "Oh, my goodness, that looks good." She picked up her long-handled spoon and dug in.

"What do you know about Richard Kennelwood?" I asked Lucinda after I'd enjoyed my first taste of the drink.

Lucinda grinned at me around her straw. "I'm starting to get the feeling you're friends with me only as a source of gossip."

I grinned back. Next to me Velvet slurped happily away.

"That's not it," I said. "It's the egg creams."

"Anything to keep customers coming in."

"Here you go, hon." The waitress dropped my sandwich in front of me. Gooey orange cheese leaked from between slices of grilled bread oozing melted butter. I hadn't asked for a side of fries, but she'd added a mountain of them anyway. Velvet helped herself to a potato slice.

"I told you about the history of Kennelwood Hotel," Lucinda said. "Family place, Jerome's father opened it."

I nodded.

"It does pretty well, has a steady base of people who've been coming since their grandparents' day. The staff are not a particularly happy bunch. They say Jerome's a slave driver, but what can they do? It's a summer job. Jerome and his only son, Richard, never got on. Five years or so ago, Richard up and left. He got a job running a big hotel in New York City, I heard. Jerome had a bad heart attack a few months ago, and Richard came back to manage their place."

"What's their reputation around town?" I asked.

"Like I said, the staff complains, but there are worse places to work, let me tell you."

"Like Haggerman's," Velvet mumbled through sunken cheeks as she sucked at her straw.

"Most amusing," I replied.

"There are three levels of hotel in the Catskills." Lucinda lifted her left hand and spread the fingers. She pushed down her index finger. "One, the big, expensive, famous places: the Concord, Grossinger's, Kutsher's, Kennelwood." Down went the middle finger. "Two, the smaller, less famous but still nice hotels with good reputations, like yours." Ring finger. "Then the bungalow colonies and the small, cheap hotels." She spread both hands in the air. "Jerome Kennelwood is friends with the owners and managers of the first group, and he pays not the slightest bit of attention to anything to do with the last lot. The middle group? There are stories. He can be ruthless about undermining what he sees as the competition."

"Why is Haggerman's his competition?" Velvet plucked another fry off my plate. "Aside from being next door. Aren't the Concord and those places competing with him for the same guests?"

"Partly because the owners are his cronies, and he knows that if he attempts to undercut them, they'll gladly return the favor. Also because people who come to the Catskills year after year tend to be loyal to the place they like. Not many families who've stayed at the Concord are going to move to a place like Kennelwood, not if they're happy with the Concord. But undermine the less well-known places, and their guests might take a look at Kennelwood Hotel for next year's stay."

"Nasty," Velvet said.

"That's business. It's because my parents are such nice people they owned a single diner in Summervale and don't have a restaurant empire. Tony and I"—she grinned—"intend to have that restaurant empire one day."

"Who's Tony?" Velvet asked.

Lucinda explained, and Velvet said, "what about Richard Kennelwood? Is he like his dad when it comes to business? But more important, is he married?"

"You interested?" Lucinda asked.

"Not for me. He likes Elizabeth."

Color rushed into my face. "He does not." I put my crumpled napkin on the table.

"He does, too. Are you going to eat the rest of that sandwich?"

"Help yourself," I said, and she did so.

"Richard isn't married, far as I know," Lucinda said. "I've never heard anyone say anything bad about him, but early days yet. He just took over this season. The staff seem happier, though. A bunch were in here the other night, and they said the hotel was ramping up hiring. Jerome's famous for not taking on enough staff and then expecting the workers he does have to do more than they think's reasonable for a day's work."

I thought of the uncleaned swimming pool and stale dinner rolls.

"Which brings us full circle," Lucinda said, "back to Chief Monahan. He knows which side his bread's buttered on, and he makes sure he keeps himself on the good side of Jerome Kennelwood and the other big owners. The little guy—or girl—like you and me? Not so much. Lois, who works in the office at the police station, says the chief and Deputy Dave have been known to argue about that."

"Do you know everything that goes on in this town?" I asked.

"Pretty much," Lucinda said. "Not many places around here stay open all winter, so the locals are used to coming here. Helps that the police station is on one side of us and the newspaper office on the other. Lois, for example, comes in here for lunch every Tuesday and Thursday all year round. Thursday is hot-turkey-sandwich day, and that's what she has. She sometimes comes on Fridays also, depending on what's the day's special."

While we'd been talking, people had been coming and going. Lucinda had taken the seat facing into the room, and I noticed her continually checking out what was going on behind me. I heard a burst of chatter as the door opened, bringing with it a wave of warm sticky air as a group came in and asked for a table for six. Lucinda dipped the spoon into her glass and scooped up the last drops of soda and chocolate syrup. "I'd better get back at it. You might work hard in that swimming pool, Velvet, but I'd exchange it for a hot kitchen at this time of year in a flash."

"My offer's still open," I said. "Dinner and dancing. Any night."

"Thanks." She scooted across the bench seat. I opened my purse.

"Your money's no good here," Lucinda said.

I slapped bills onto the table. "It most certainly is."

Y

"SHE'S NICE," VELVET SAID AS WE DROVE OUT OF TOWN.

"She is nice, and her fiancé, Tony, is an absolute doll. If she doesn't take up my invitation for them to come to the hotel one night soon, I'm going to call him and order him to bring her." When we got back, I was pleased to see that the police car was gone from the front of the hotel. We didn't need our guests to keep remembering that a man had died here under suspicious circumstances.

Then again, a man had died here under suspicious circumstances. I'd like to know what the police were thinking about that, but Monahan definitely wouldn't tell me, and Deputy Dave would be unlikely to.

It was entirely possible the police had hit a dead end and no one would ever know what happened. Streams of people pass through our doors all the time. Taxis come and go, deliverymen drop off supplies. We employ enough people to populate a small town, hundreds of guests are in residence at any one time, and people from other hotels come to Haggerman's for dinner or to enjoy the entertainment and then leave at the end of the evening.

It was terrible what had happened at the Shady Pines, but no one had been hurt, and the fire had taken police and newspaper focus off Haggerman's, so that was a good thing from my point of view. Though not from that of the employees and guests at Shady Pines.

"That was fun," Velvet said. "We need to get away from this place more often. I'll catch you later. Don't forget to tell Olivia about the beauty pageant."

"I'll do that now, before I forget."

Velvet ran off, skipping lightly down the path, her long ponytail streaming out behind her. I watched her go, as the grains of an idea for an advertisement began forming in my mind. The sun shone on her golden hair and bounced off the lake in front of her, full of swimmers and paddleboaters. To Velvet's left sat cabins one and two, fresh white paint, wide-pillared porches with comfortable chairs. To her right were the lush flower beds and freshly mowed grass in front of the main building. At this time of year the gardens were at their absolute best. A photograph taken from this spot, particularly if it was in color, would be marvelous. Expensive, yes, but fabulous advertising for the delights to be found at Haggerman's Catskills Resort. Who wouldn't want to spend their summer enjoying this view?

An overall-clad figure was bent over a bed of red and white geraniums, moving slowly through the plants. A trash can was on the ground next to him, and he tossed weeds and dead foliage into it as he worked. As I watched he straightened, put one hand to his lower back, and leaned backward in a nice stretch. He caught sight of me and immediately returned his attention to the plants.

"Good morning, Francis," I said.

"Miz Grady. I wasn't s-slacking off. I was—"

"Enjoying your surroundings. I also like to take a moment out of a busy day simply to enjoy being here."

He blinked in confusion, and when he realized I wasn't reprimanding him for breathing, he grinned at me.

"I hope you enjoy your new position," I said.

"Hurts my back." He had a slight stutter, and the words came out slowly as he selected them with care.

"You'll get used to it eventually. You should wear a hat to keep your head covered. That sun gets hot."

"Yes, m'm." He returned to his work.

He seemed nice enough. His father hadn't needed to threaten me not to fire him. I couldn't forget that Francis had spent time in prison, but I could hope the stint in jail had cured him of whatever bad tendencies he might have had.

Instead of going to find Olivia, as I'd originally intended, I took a back path to the staff cabins. I heard rustling in the trees, and I spun around, holding my breath. A moment ago, birds had been chirping. Now, all was quiet. A branch snapped. Wide-trunked oaks and maples, branches heavy with leaves, edged the path; the undergrowth was thick with struggling saplings and forest decay. Inside the forest all was dark except for a few patches of dappled sunlight breaking through the canopy. I could see no further than the first line of trees.

"Who's out there?" I called. "I'm sorry, but this area is out-of-bounds to guests."

Dead leaves rustled. A deer probably. Maybe not. "If you're a staff member, you shouldn't be lurking in the woods, either."

All was quiet. In the distance I could hear the laughter of children. Usually at this time of day, staff would be coming and going, up and down the path. At the moment, I might have been the only person left in the world. I thought of Harold Westenham, taking a moment to enjoy a quiet cigarette. I'd briefly suspected Louis Frandenheim of killing the man. Louis had left Haggerman's—I'd seen him off myself—but had he left the Catskills? Was he watching me now, wanting revenge for throwing him out? Was he hoping to be able to comfort my mother after my . . . death?

My heart pounded, my hands were clammy. I cast my eyes around me, looking for something I could use as a weapon if needed. The forest floor was littered with dead twigs, nothing that wouldn't snap in a mild wind.

I told myself to calm down. It had been a deer, and it had slipped silently away when it sensed my presence.

I let out a sigh of relief and turned to continue on my way. Behind me a branch snapped, dead leaves crunched, and I whirled around to see something large and solid hurling out of the woods.

Chapter 16

"WINSTON! FOR HEAVEN'S SAKE."

The dog leapt on me, eyes bright, tongue flapping, stubby tail wagging with sheer delight. Dead leaves and broken twigs were trapped in his short fur, and his paws were covered in mud. I reached out and plucked a twig off his ear. "You scared me half to death."

I'd have to have a word with Aunt Tatiana. Again. We couldn't have her dog running wild on the hotel grounds. Fortunately, he seemed to know he had to stick to the back trails and the edge of the woods, but I dreaded the day he'd frighten an elderly lady into a heart attack or steal an ice cream cone from a child. "You'll have to come with me," I said. "I'll take you home."

"Elizabeth, is that you? I thought I heard your voice. What are you doing out there?" Jim Westenham stood on the porch of the repurposed guest building.

"I'm wrestling with this vicious beast," I said. "Come on, Winston." I slapped the back of my leg, and the dog fell into step beside me.

"A bulldog." Jim said. "A handsome one, too, probably a purebred. I'm not surprised his name's Winston. He looks like Churchill. Where'd you get him?"

"He's my aunt Tatiana's dog, and I've no idea where he came from. He arrived when she did." I climbed the steps to the porch. "Do you know much about dogs?"

Jim held out his hand for Winston to sniff. Clearly he met with the dog's approval, as Winston then permitted Jim to scratch the top of his head. "My parents are dog lovers. We always had a mutt or two running around when I was a kid. I miss having a dog, but a Greenwich Village walk-up's no place for one, particularly not with the schedule I keep." He straightened and leaned against the railing. Winston sniffed his shoes and trouser legs. "Dare I hope you're here to see me?"

"I am. Thank you very much for the flowers, they're gorgeous, but you had nothing to apologize for. Instead, I should be apologizing to you. I let Jerome Kennelwood and his son get under my skin, and that wasn't fair to you."

"Apology accepted," he said.

Winston wandered around the porch, sniffing in every corner. With all the people coming and going in this building, he must have a lot of wonderful new scents to catch up on. Too bad he couldn't tell me who he'd smelled down at the dock on Wednesday night.

"Have you heard anything more about your uncle's case?" I asked.

"No. It's gone very quiet. I was planning on going into town after lunch to try to talk to the chief. I need to know when I can take my uncle's body to White Plains. No one in the family lives there anymore, but that's where my grandparents are buried, so I guess . . ." His voice drifted off. "My parents are driving up from Florida, and they'll want to have a funeral."

I told him about the arson at Shady Pines and what that would do to the resources of our town's tiny police department. "I find it odd that the FBI haven't been back. I'd have thought they'd have questions. But nothing, as far as I know."

"That is odd," he agreed. "They've not bothered to contact me again, either."

"I need to know when I can open that cabin, and you'll want to get the last of your uncle's things. Can you ask the chief when you talk to him? He was here earlier, and I didn't think about it at the time."

"He was here? So he is still investigating?"

"He came on a personal matter, and he came alone. Can I ask a favor of you, if you have the time?"

"Shoot."

"You have resources, at the paper I mean. I'd like to know what Francis Monahan did in the army that got him jail time and a dishonorable discharge. I've heard vague rumors, but no details. He's my employee and . . . I like to think I'm a good judge of character." I pushed aside a thought of Ronald Grady. "I've learned to be. The hard way."

"There's a story there," Jim said.

"One you'll never hear. Everyone probably thinks they're a good judge of character. I like Francis Monahan; he's polite and shy, and I don't sense any trouble in him. Maybe the army didn't, either. Until trouble happened."

"I can do that. Won't take more than one or two phone calls."

I was about to ask Jim to also find out what he could about Richard Kennelwood and his dealings in the New York hotel world, but I bit my tongue. One favor was more than enough.

"Thanks. Come on, Winston, let's get you home. I'm supposed to be talking to Olivia about something, but I can't remember what."

"It'll come to you," Jim said.

"Probably too late to do anyone any good." I called the dog again. He lifted his head from a close examination of the overflowing ashtray on the low, wobbly wooden table. "Will you let me know what you find out?" I asked.

"Sure," Jim said.

Winston trotted happily at my heels as we took the staff shortcut through the woods. Olivia wouldn't want to baby-sit Winston, but she'd have to until I could find Aunt Tatiana. I didn't have a key for her rooms.

"Winston was running wild through the woods," I said as I walked into our house. "He can't be doing that."

My mother was waving her hands in the air, a bottle of red nail polish open on the table in front of her. "Tell Tatiana, not me."

"I'm telling you both. I'm also telling you he'll have to stay here until she can come and get him."

"Why don't you look after him?" She blew on her nails.

"Because it's past noon, and I have a full day's work still to do, and I am not walking through the lobby with him tagging along behind me."

"Very well. Winston and I will have a pleasant afternoon. Won't we, Winston?"

He woofed in agreement.

I began to leave, but I stopped. I was supposed to ask Olivia to do something. The acrid scent of the nail polish remover and the freshly applied polish reminded me. "Oh, right. Velvet thinks it would be better if you judge the beauty pageant this afternoon, rather than her."

My mother eyed me. "Better for who?"

"For whom. Better for our guests, better for the reputation of our hotel."

"I detest those things. No matter what happens, the end result is one preening girl and a pack of humiliated, tearful ones who consider themselves to have been insulted."

"It's adult women. Ages eighteen to twenty-nine."

"One preening adult woman, then." She sighed heavily. "If I must."

"You must."

"What time?"

"Four o'clock on the dock. Randy will be the other judge."

ONCE AGAIN, WHEN I ARRIVED AT MY OFFICE I FOUND the clerks giggling and watching me out of the corners of their eyes.

"What is it this time?" I said.

More giggles. My office door was open, which it shouldn't have been, and I went tentatively in. To my considerable surprise I found Aunt Tatiana arranging a glass bowl of freshly cut flowers.

More flowers?

"Where did those come from?" I asked her.

My aunt turned to me with a smile. "You are popular

today, *lastachka*. Which is as it should be. A young woman should have admirers. When we were courting, Rudolph would often present me with flowers. Or give them to my mother, which is the same. He had no money for such frivolities, so he'd pick a wildflower out of a crack in the pavement. I sometimes suspected he raided the public gardens as well." She smiled fondly at the memory.

"That's lovely," I said, "but no one's courting me." Unlike the perfect long-stemmed red roses of earlier, these ones were a brilliantly colored varied assortment of what was available right now in our flower beds.

"Where did those come from?"

"Kennelwood," Aunt Tatiana said. "I was once again called to the front desk to accept them for you. These appear to have been picked by the gentleman himself or his gardener. No bows and fancy ribbons. Just flowers in a vase." She handed me an envelope, and I opened it.

The message was handwritten in blue ink on stiff white card stock with the logo of Kennelwood Hotel stamped in gold on the top.

> *Please accept my apologies for last night. I hope to see you here again and soon. Richard*

I looked up to see Aunt Tatiana smiling at me.

I threw the card onto my desk. "He's just trying to get on my good side."

"Is it working?"

"No."

"Let it work, *lastachka*. There are good men in the world. My Rudolph was a good man. Your father is a good man."

"I know that."

"Do you? I wonder. You deserve happiness."

"I'll be happy in September," I said, "when I have the time."

My aunt shook her head and took her leave.

EVERYTHING AT HAGGERMAN'S RUNS BY THE CLOCK. EVerything except my job, most of which can be done whenever I get around to it. For the occasional time when promptness is important, I keep a small wind-up alarm on my desk. At quarter to four, it buzzed. I wasn't the least bit interested in watching the beauty pageant, but Olivia had a bad habit of "forgetting" to do things she didn't particularly want to do.

When she first told me she'd inherited a resort in the Catskills and wanted me to manage it for her, I imagined spending my days wandering through the grounds, dressed in a beautiful fresh summer frock and huge beribboned sun hat, perhaps with an icy drink in hand, pointing out to obsequious staff which flowers needed deadheading, visiting the kitchen to suggest roast chicken for dinner one evening, or assuring gracious, well-heeled guests I'd see that someone attended to their needs immediately.

I hadn't foreseen myself stuck behind a desk in a hot stuffy office all day, every day, juggling temperamental staff; bidding on hard-to-come-by or overly expensive resources; negotiating between competing department heads; putting out the myriad fires, large and small, that were continually popping up.

I've never worked in the hotel industry before, but still, I should have known better. I'm a bookkeeper by training, and I've balanced some very large accounts. I was working at a Midtown department store as head of female staff when Olivia inherited Haggerman's. A department store's also an extremely demanding environment, but at least it closes at a reasonable time every day and I got actual days off.

Haggerman's never closes, and I am never off.

Then again, I reminded myself, it was only for a couple of months of the year. The autumn and winter up here are so quiet and beautiful they make every mad summer's day worthwhile.

In the outer office, Randy was picking up the microphone that led to the loudspeakers dotted around the property. "Attention, everyone! Only ten more minutes until the Miss or Mrs. Haggerman's pageant begins down by the dock. You won't want to miss this, gentlemen."

"Mrs. Haggerman's?" I said.

"Not enough single women, so we had to expand to invite the married ladies." He had the pink-and-blue sash that was the prize tossed over one shoulder.

"Better take that off," I said. "Or people will think you won."

"I'll vote for you, Randy," one of the clerks called.

"Not me," someone else said. "Luke the waiter has my vote."

The women burst out laughing. Luke's reputation was getting around.

Randy grabbed the portable bullhorn, and we left the office. I almost bumped into Jim Westenham coming in.

"Are you busy, Elizabeth?" he asked.

"Sort of. The beauty pageant is about to start, but I don't need to be there if it's important."

"Important enough."

"Let's walk, and you can tell me what you learned. Randy, go on ahead, please. If my mother's not there, send

someone to the house to get her. Do you have another
judge? There should be three."

"I have someone in mind. I'll make a big show of picking him out of the crowd. They always like that." He gave
me a nod and hurried away shouting, "Beauty pageant is
about to start, everyone. Down by the dock."

Guests streamed out of the lobby, and Jim and I walked
slowly among them.

On the porch, staff were setting up small square tables
for the regular four o'clock bridge game and throwing a
white cloth over the long table on which afternoon tea
would be laid out for the players. A gray Chrysler New
Yorker and a bright red Buick Roadmaster were parked in
the circle, while a flurry of bellhops unloaded piles of
trunks and suitcases for the new arrivals.

"The chief wasn't in when I stopped at the police station," Jim said, "but I had a talk with the deputy."

"He speaks?"

"When the chief's not around, anyway. He didn't have a
lot to tell me. He's been in touch with the police in Newburgh, where Uncle Harold's been living the last couple of
years, and they said he's never been in any trouble. I could
have told him that, saved him some time. He asked me if
Uncle Harold had ever been known to gamble, and I said
no. He lived modestly on his writing income and his sav-
ings from when he taught college. I think Deputy Dawson
was hoping this somehow tied into that arson case, so the
police could wrap up two cases in one bow, but that's not
on, either."

"Did he say anything about when they'll release your
uncle's remains?"

"Not up to him, Dawson said. I have to talk to the chief.

I left a message for Monahan to call me here at the hotel, but I don't have high hopes of him bothering to do that. I'll have to keep trying to chase him down."

"I hate to sound mercenary, Jim, but I don't want to keep that cabin closed off if the police don't need it anymore."

"That cabin contributes to your livelihood, Elizabeth. Don't apologize for wanting to use it."

We walked among the excited crowd heading to the beach. Rows of chairs had been set up for the audience, and a handful of rowboats and paddleboats bobbed on the clear, placid waters of the lake, waiting for the show to start.

"I asked Dawson what was happening with the FBI investigation," Jim said, "and he can't say."

"Can't or won't?"

"Can't. He hasn't heard anything from them since that first day, when they came here. Monahan says the FBI are still interested in what Uncle Harold had been up to and have asked them to keep an eye out for any contacts he might have made while he was here. Dawson told me I'd have to speak to Chief Monahan for more details, as the chief hasn't confided in him on what he calls matters of national security."

"Rubbish."

"Your chief of police is overly fond of grandstanding, and I get the feeling the deputy's tired of it. He asked me if I had any contacts in the NYPD he could tap into."

"Do you?"

"Sure I do, and plenty of them. But I'm a newspaperman. I'm not going to start calling in favors to help a small-town cop get out from under the thumb of his overbearing chief. After I left the police station, I found a pay phone and called the FBI regional office. I didn't expect to find anyone to talk to, but I wanted to leave a message to have them call me back. To my considerable surprise, one of the agents who'd been here, Kowalski, not only was in the office but was willing to talk to me."

"Five minutes!" Randy boomed. "Five minutes until the beautiful ladies of Haggerman's Catskills Resort strut their stuff."

Jim and I stopped at the top of the small hill that leads down to the beach, the guest dock, and the lake. Francis Monahan had done a good job of weeding the flower beds. I wondered what Kennelwood's gardeners had to say after someone plucked their best blooms. I pushed my thoughts away from Richard Kennelwood. Better not to go there. This summer, like last, had to be all about getting the hotel established under its new management and keeping it profitable. Next year, if all goes well, maybe I'll be able to afford to hire an assistant manager to take some of the load off me. Next year, I might be able to think about flowers and romance. But not this year.

"The FBI have closed their involvement in this case, saying it has no merit," Jim said. "Kowalski told me I can come in anytime and pick up my uncle's papers. They've examined the documents and discovered nothing that would indicate my uncle was doing anything other than writing a work of fiction. Essentially Kowalski implied the whole thing was a waste of their time."

That snapped me out of thoughts of handpicked flowers fast enough. "But the deputy told you they were still investigating."

"Might be the FBI never bothered to tell Chief Monahan otherwise, or if they did, the chief never bothered to inform his deputy. Telling people the FBI are involved gives your chief gravitas, in his eyes anyway. Regardless of the FBI's interest, or lack thereof, the murder case is still open, don't forget."

I waved my arms around me, encompassing the peaceful surroundings and the cheerful crowd gathering to watch the pageant. "I don't see much investigating going on."

"A small-town police department doesn't have a lot of resources, Elizabeth. Other things happen, and they move on."

"Aren't you interested in finding out what happened?"

He turned his head and looked at me. His eyes, the same lake blue as his uncle's, were sad and serious. "I am. I'm very interested, but I don't think it has anything to do with Haggerman's. Someone wanted my uncle dead, for reasons I can't begin to understand, and they followed him here. When I get back to the city, I'm going to start asking some questions. It's also possible it was a case of mistaken identity. I had a look at that spot where it happened. It's dark there, away from the bright lights of the hotel and paths. Did someone mistake Uncle Harold for another man? Stranger things have happened. Here comes your mother."

Olivia strolled down the footpath, practically screaming summer glamour in a dress of a check print of red, pink, and cream, with a bell skirt, a wide red belt, elbow-length sleeves, and a high collar turned up to frame the sharp bones of her face. Large sunglasses covered her eyes, and her hair was fastened into a chignon. Randy, bullhorn in hand, hurried to greet her. The pageant contestants were lined up along the shoreline, hands on hips, smiles in place, ready to be presented. All except one wore bathing suits of some sort and shoes with heels. Most of them had had their hair done in a variation of a flip, and their makeup carefully applied.

I spotted Velvet, crouched down, balancing on her heels,

while she chatted to two old men who'd snagged front-row-center seats.

"You asked me to find out about Francis Monahan's service record," Jim said. "I put one of the girls in the newspaper office on it. She'll call me when she has something to tell me."

"Thanks."

Jim nodded toward the crowd. "See that short guy in the cheap suit and dusty hat over there approaching your mother?"

"Yes. Dressed like that, he doesn't look like he's a guest here."

"He's not. That's Martin McEnery, from the local paper."

"The one who wrote that verging-on-slanderous article."

"The very one. He's brought a photographer, so they must be intending to do a story on the pageant. That's his excuse for being here anyway."

"Thanks, Jim," I said. "If you'll excuse me, there's something I need to do."

I left him and made my way through the crowd. "Pardon me," I said to the men talking to Velvet. "I need to borrow Miss McNally."

Velvet pushed herself to her feet. "What's up?"

I pointed out the newspapermen. "I'd like you to keep an eye on those two, under the pretext of being friendly. If they are here to write about our beauty pageant and take photos of the contestants, that's good publicity for us and they're welcome. If they start asking questions about Harold Westenham or any supposed communist activity, or poking around where they don't need to go, let me know."

She gave me a quick salute and hurried away. I was

about to head back to the top of the hill when I saw a man push his way through the crowd and approach the newspapermen. He thrust out his hand to McEnery, and they shook. He was dressed in casual clothes, beige trousers and a short-sleeved brown-and-yellow-striped shirt. Chief Monahan, out of uniform. Velvet slid up to them and said something to the newspaperman. Monahan left them and found himself a seat at the edge of the circle.

I wondered what he was doing here. Interested in the pageant? Enjoying a day off at the lake? Or had he come for other reasons and found a crowd assembling?

Olivia and Randy walked together to stand at the bottom of the dock. An excited hush fell over the audience. The contestants shifted nervously. Some patted their hair, one stuck her hand into the top of her two-piece bathing suit and made some adjustments. This wasn't exactly Miss America. One or two of the women were moderately attractive, but none of them were as pretty as Velvet. The oldest looked as though she would have preferred to be just about anyplace else. She hadn't put on her bathing suit, instead she wore pink-and-yellow shorts with a white shirt and scuffed sneakers. Her shoulders were hunched, and she kept her head down and her eyes on her feet. Her dark blond hair was long and thick, she had a nice figure and good legs, but if she didn't smile she'd never win. I assumed she'd been pushed into this by her husband or her mother. She might have been signed up without her knowing.

"Ladies and gentlemen. Boys and girls. Haggerman's guests all. Welcome. I'm Randy Fontaine, and I'll be your host for this afternoon's pageant."

The crowd cheered, the sound echoing off the hills, and Randy took a deep bow. "I'm joined this afternoon by none other than the fabulous, the famous"—Randy swept his arm before him—"the fantastic star of stage and screen, Miss Olivia Peters."

Loud cheering.

Olivia stepped forward and gave the adoring audience a bright smile and casual wave. "What a marvelous group you are, and so kind to come out on this beautiful day." She looked absolutely radiant, with the blue lake behind her, the blue sky above. I had a glimpse of my mother, the star, and—to my considerable surprise—felt a touch of pride. Olivia's job here was to provide the glamour, the excitement, the star element, in the way only she could. My job was to keep the place running. We might make a good team after all.

"Miss Peters and I will be your judges," Randy said. "But we'll need a third."

I was pretty sure I knew who the third would be. Mr. Hart, who'd taken cabin one, our most expensive, for the entire month of July, and was accompanied by a family group large enough to overflow into the main hotel. Mr. Hart sat proudly in the front row, his hands crossed over the top of his cane.

"Chief Monahan," Randy said. "Would you be so kind as to do the honors for us today, sir?"

The chief stood up, beaming from ear to ear. He walked through the crowd, pausing now and again to say something to an onlooker or to shake a hand. He arrived at the front and greeted my mother with a light kiss on the cheek. Perhaps only I knew her well enough to recognize her displeasure.

"Let's have a quick photo." The newspaper photographer put one knee on the ground and held up his camera. Chief Monahan placed himself between my mother and Randy.

He threw his arms around their shoulders. Olivia edged away, although her smile didn't falter.

"Big smile, Randy," the photographer called. "Chief. That's great."

So that was why Monahan had come: to get his picture in the paper. Not to investigate a brutal murder.

Randy should have asked me before he invited the chief to be a judge, but he likely thought he was helping Hagger-man's get on the man's good side. He was probably right, but I still thought the honor should have gone to Mr. Hart.

Still, there would be plenty more pageants as the summer went on and the guests turned over.

I was pulled out of my thoughts by a low voice in my ear. "Elizabeth, might I have a word?"

"Oh, hello, Charlie. Here to get material for your act?"

"Plenty of material, Elizabeth, but I'd never dare use it. See the one second from the end?" He pointed to the oldest of the women, the one I'd noticed earlier. "I'll bet her husband pushed her into this, and she looks as happy about it as if she were facing a firing squad. The one in the front expects to win, but she won't. Your mother will never vote for a girl who's so obviously desperate."

"You're a good judge of people."

"I try to be. So I can make fun of them. Are you interested in this or—"

"Let's walk," I said.

We headed for the footpath. A shadow broke away from a patch of shrubbery next to the side of cabin one and slid around the building. I stopped.

"Everything okay?" Charlie asked.

"Yeah." I started walking again, and he fell into step beside me. "Someone's watching the pageant who should be at work. I've scared them off."

Charlie chucked. "You're a formidable boss, Elizabeth."

"Don't tell anyone, but it's all a front. I'm a softy beneath."

"Your secret's safe with me." He was dressed in knee-length green shorts and a Hawaiian shirt splashed with orange and purple flowers. The grease in his hair sparkled in the sun.

The tennis courts were empty, and only one handball game was underway. "Joan Rosenberg hails from Brooklyn," Randy said into the bullhorn, and the Brooklynites cheered.

"I was with you this morning," Charlie said, "when the police chief came to talk to you about his son Francis."

"Yes, and?"

"Something started niggling at me. It's been bothering me all day, and finally it came to me. I was a lawyer in my past life and in the army, which is where I knew Harold Westenham."

"So you told me."

"The name Francis Monahan is what was niggling at me. Seeing Chief Monahan just now, in his civvies, I remembered. In late 1944, I worked briefly on a case in France. Minor stuff, and I was given a major case not long after, so I forgot about it. Until now. As we moved through France following D-Day, the people were so happy to see us. Parties in the streets, invitations to their homes, cafés and restaurants thrown open. Nothing but joy and goodwill. In some small town whose name escapes me, one of our GIs stole a necklace. Middle-class family—they didn't have a lot before the war and even less after, but they did have a gold necklace that had been an heirloom from earlier days when the family was well-off. They'd hidden it all through the war. And then, after liberation, they invited a bunch of GIs to their house for what they could scrape together by way of a meal."

"And one of our soldiers took their necklace."

"Yup. The homeowner brought it out to show his guests, and the next morning it was gone."

"Francis Monahan."

"That's not an uncommon name. Might be someone else entirely. I'm only telling you what I remember, Elizabeth. As the guy's working here, and some of your guests have valuable things, I figured you needed to know. I've seen several nice pieces of jewelry on display in the evenings."

"Thanks for telling me. People can change, and I'm not going to judge Francis. But you're right, I needed to know."

"One more thing. Monahan's commanding officer was none other than Harold Westenham."

"Really?"

"Really. And what makes me remember this, among all the other stuff we had to deal with in those days, is that Harold was in a rage. A total and complete rage. As far as he was concerned, it was a disgrace to the entire American army that one of our guys blatantly abused our guests' hospitality and stole from people we were supposed to be rescuing. The war was still going on, we were always on the move, but Westenham wanted nothing less than a full-scale trial and court-martial."

"Which is what happened, right? Francis went to jail."

"It's all coming back to me now. Thing is, Elizabeth, there'd been some doubt that Monahan acted alone or was even primarily responsible for the theft. The necklace was found in his kit, and so he was the one charged. He wasn't the brightest soldier in the army, by far, and there were whispers that he had a pretty hard time of it from some of the other guys."

I thought of the waiters here, laughing at the shy, awkward dishwasher struggling with a stutter. Maybe even causing accidents he'd be blamed for.

"Westenham and I talked it over," Charlie said. "I thought the case wasn't solid enough, but Westenham was determined to see it through. And so Francis Monahan was arrested. As it happened, I moved on before the trial, and I never thought about the matter again. Until ten minutes ago, when I realized how the names were connected. Westenham. Monahan."

We'd reached the end of the public path long ago, and we stood at the edge of the woods. The sound of Randy's bullhorn and the cheering of the crowd was a faint noise in the background. Closer to, I could hear the rustle of the wind in the trees and the gentle babble of the brook as it tumbled over rocks and gravel toward the lake.

We began walking back. "Thanks for telling me this," I said.

"I'm sorry Harold didn't come up to me that night. Say hi. Maybe if we'd gone for a drink . . . Maybe what happened wouldn't have happened."

"Perhaps. Or perhaps it would simply have happened at another time. In another place."

We arrived back at the dock in time to see Chief Monahan and Olivia presenting the beaming winner with her sash. Most of the other contestants pretended to smile, but their faces were frozen in anger. The one Charlie'd said was being too obvious about wanting to win threatened to burst into tears. The older woman, who hadn't wanted to take part in the first place, looked pleased not to have been centered out.

Monahan put his arm around the shoulders of the winner and they, along with Olivia, posed for the newspaper photographer while the crowd slowly dispersed.

Back to work for me. I turned around quickly, and there he was, standing at the top of the hill, staring at Olivia with openmouthed adoration.

Chapter 17

LOUIS FRANDENHEIM, WHO'D BEEN BANNED FROM THE property. I marched toward him, my blood boiling. So intent was he on Olivia he didn't see me coming.

"What are you doing here?" I yelled.

Louis jumped. His watery eyes blinked rapidly. "Goodness, Miss Peters. You frightened me."

"I'll do a lot more than frighten you. I told you if I saw you here again I'd have you arrested."

He tucked his chin into his chest and hunched his shoulders, like a child who's been caught with his hand in the cookie jar. "I . . . I . . . I'm here to see my sister and her family. You can't keep a man from his family."

"I can. And I will. You were spying on me earlier today, weren't you? By the path near the woods."

"Not spying, Miss Peters. I . . . I was looking for my sister's girl."

"You were hiding in the woods until you could track

down my mother. The bulldog chased you off. You're lucky he didn't attack. He's very vicious, particularly if he thinks my mother's being threatened."

Louis blanched.

I looked around, hoping to see a hotel security guard. Instead, I saw something better. Chief Monahan and the newspaper guys heading my way. Randy was taking the bullhorn back to the office; the pageant contestants had dispersed, some openly weeping, the winner, as Olivia had predicted, preening as she showed off her sash. Down by the dock, Olivia and Velvet were chatting to a group of women.

"Chief Monahan." I waved. "Can you come here for a moment, please? Randy!"

"Now, Miss Peters, there's no need . . . ," Louis whined.

"Great show, Mrs. Grady," the chief said. "I was proud to be part of it. Tomorrow's front page, Martin here says, above the fold. Provided we don't have any more murders or fires set, right?" He slapped Martin McEnery on the back.

"That's nice," I said. "This—"

"What did I tell you, Mrs. Grady? Haggerman's can be an asset to the town, and the town'll return the favor. We all help each other out 'round here, right?"

"Right," McEnery said.

"I trust that means you won't continue going around saying we're a bunch of communists." I momentarily forgot why I'd called him over.

The chief of police narrowed his eyes. He studied my face. I held my ground and didn't flinch. McEnery glanced at Monahan, and I realized he was waiting for a clue as to how to react.

"Two-way street, Mrs. Grady," Monahan said at last. "Do we understand each other?"

"I believe we do. As for more immediate matters . . ." I

indicated Louis, who'd started edging away. "This gentleman has been ordered to leave my property, and he refused."

"So?" the chief of police said.

"'So'? What do you mean, 'so'? I'm asking you to escort him off the property and order him not to return."

Monahan chuckled, and then he indicated his shirt. "I'm off duty. Dropped by to help judge your little beauty contest. Call my office and make a complaint. Let's go, Martin, I've got stuff happening back in town. Can't spend all day lazing around." They walked away. My mouth might have flapped open.

"See, Miss Peters," Louis said with a smirk, "nothing to get yourself worked up over."

"I—"

"There you are! When Mr. Fontaine told me you were back, I couldn't believe it." Louis's sister strode down the path, wagging her finger in front of her. "Will you never learn, Louis? I gave you money for the bus to New York."

"Wasn't enough," he whined.

I almost expected her to grab him by the ear. "I'll give you enough!" Instead of his ear she grabbed his arm. "Do you want to see us all kicked out? I'm not having my vacation ruined because of you. My apologies, Mrs. Grady. This will not happen again. I'm going to send my son with him this time. He'll see Louis gets to New York. Once there, he won't be able to afford the bus fare back." She marched off, dragging the protesting Louis with her.

Chapter 18

BACK IN MY OFFICE, I IGNORED THE TOWERING STACK OF papers on my desk, shoved aside the mountain of pink message slips, leaned back in my chair, and thought over the events of the past few days. It seemed like we'd had one disaster after another, everything from a busboy dropping a room-service tray to the murder of a guest.

I called the switchboard and asked them to locate Rosemary. She returned my call a couple of minutes later from the ballroom. In the background I could hear sounds of the room being set up for the Saturday evening cocktail party. "One of the bartenders up and quit on me, Elizabeth," she said. "I can't manage tonight with only one. I'm going to help out behind the bar. If Olivia doesn't like it, I'll tell her to find me a replacement herself."

"Okay. Whatever you need. Why'd he quit?"

"Fool wants to be an actor, and he heard about an audition in New York. He'll be on the next bus to the mountains tomorrow, but I'm not taking him back. I need reliable staff. What's up?"

"I want to ask you about something that happened earlier in the week."

"Elizabeth, I can barely remember what happened earlier in the hour, but I'll try."

I asked my question, and she told me what I needed to know. I thanked her, and said I'd handle Olivia regarding the matter of Rosemary working behind the bar.

AT 6:25 I LOCKED UP AND LEFT THE MAIN BUILDING. IN THE pool, hotel nannies or mothers were trying to coax protesting children out of the water. At the lakefront, Velvet had fifteen women of all ages spread out along the dock, bending and stretching. A couple of men lounged in chairs, smoking, sipping glasses of whiskey or bourbon, and watching the women while arguing about the state of the world. On the beach, Randy was leading a substantial crowd in an enthusiastic game of Simon Says. Mrs. Brownville and several of her friends had pulled a circle of chairs together and were enjoying a cocktail before dinner. They also, I assumed, were arguing about the state of the world. Or the tiny part of it that is Haggerman's Catskills Resort, at any rate.

"There she is now! Yoo-hoo, Mrs. Grady!" Mrs. Brownville began waving.

I was too late to pretend I hadn't seen her, so I put on my professional smile and approached their group. "Good evening, ladies."

"I was telling my friends here how thrilled MarySue is at being crowned runner-up Miss Haggerman's this afternoon. Of course runner-up isn't the same as winning, but

I'm confident that with some further instruction in deportment, she'll be a winner next time."

"Uh, yes."

"MarySue's my niece. My sister's youngest. Such a nice girl, I can't understand why she isn't married yet." Mrs. Brownville smiled at me. I smiled back. I did not tell Mrs. Brownville why I had not remarried.

"Anyway, I wanted you to know that I never believed you were a communist." She sipped at her drink. Liquid in shades of orange and yellow, much like a sunset, filled a long thin glass.

"That's nice. I guess."

"I'm an excellent judge of character. I told everyone what they were saying about you and your mother was absolute nonsense, didn't I, girls?"

Eyebrows were raised and glances exchanged, but no one out and out contradicted Mrs. Brownville.

"I hope you enjoy your evening," I said. "Try to catch the show later. It's Charlie Simmonds's last night with us."

"Such a marvelous comedian," Mrs. Brownville said. "He can be a tad risqué for those with less sophisticated tastes, but I always say you don't have to go to his show if you don't approve."

I excused myself as Velvet's class ended and the women headed back to their rooms and cabins to get ready for the evening.

Velvet picked up a towel that had been thrown over the railings of the dock and wiped at the back of her neck. I waited for her at the bottom of the dock, and she soon joined me.

"Good class?" I asked as we started to walk.

"Good enough. The beauty pageant went well. It'll be a boost to the hotel if a picture gets into the paper. I was surprised to see Chief Monahan here, in his civvies, acting all jovial and friendly."

"I suspect our chief never passes up the chance to be the center of attention. He certainly wasn't here to do any work. I need you to do me a favor."

"Sure. What?"

I told her, and she stopped walking and turned to face me. "You aren't serious?"

"Deadly serious."

"Okay, Elizabeth. You're the boss."

I FOUND MY MOTHER AND HER SISTER RELAXING ON OUR porch, icy drinks and a tray of deviled eggs and smoked oysters on toast on the table between them. Winston peered through the porch railing, alert for wildlife that needed to be taught to keep to their assigned places. I'd decided not to tell Olivia I'd encountered, again, the dratted Louis. Hopefully, his sister was right, and once his nephew had deposited him in New York City he wouldn't find his way back.

"Are you planning to go to the show tonight?" I asked her.

"I thought I would. You have that magician appearing, don't you?"

"Yes. He's here tonight and tomorrow. We have two acts tonight, as Charlie Simmonds is still here, singing for his supper. On Monday that dance couple you got for us arrives for the entire week."

"Good."

"I'm going to drop in later."

"Why?"

"Why not? We've had to make a change in the bartenders. One of them quit on us."

"Why are you telling me this?"

"No reason," I said. "Aunt Tatiana, you should come to the show one evening."

"Pff," she said.

"You'd enjoy it. Get yourself gussied up, have a few drinks, a couple of turns around the dance floor." I winked at her. "Maybe meet an eligible gentleman. We do get a few staying here now and again, you know. Widowers with their children and their families."

"I work hard all day," she said. "I have no desire to gussy up, as you put it."

"All the more reason to have fun at night. Put some glamour into your life." This was an old conversation. I knew she wouldn't come.

"The glamour," Aunt Tatiana said, patting her clean but well-worn and several times mended housedress, "I leave to Olga."

"Olivia," my mother said.

Aunt Tatiana popped a deviled egg into her mouth. "There is a leak in the ceiling of cabin nine, Elizabeth. The wallpaper in the main bedroom is beginning to peel."

"Have you told George and the maintenance crew?"

"Yes."

"Then you don't have to tell me." I took the last egg, reminded, as though I needed to be, that the resort business is not about glamour.

"You caused a scene in the dining room at Kennelwood last night," Aunt Tatiana said. "I was telling O about it."

"What do you know about that?" I asked.

"Everything." She chuckled. "Irena sent a boy over this morning with a note for me. After you left, Richard and Jerome got into an argument. Richard said Jerome had been out of line, and Jerome said if that snip of a girl—his words, not mine—can't handle the cut and thrust of business, she needs to go back to her kitchen. And then Richard said personal insults and underhanded maneuvers are not part of any business he's in charge of, and Jerome said—"

"I can't believe they had an argument like that in public," I said.

"Really, Elizabeth. Will you never learn? This did not happen in *public* but in the kitchen, and one of the cooks, who is Irena's nephew, overheard. If it had been in public, word would not have spread so quickly, and not to me." Aunt Tatiana threw back the contents of her glass.

I harrumphed and went inside. I dressed for the evening with some care and not a small amount of trepidation, as I mentally went over everything I'd learned this afternoon. I knew who'd killed Harold Westenham, and I knew why, but I had no way of proving it, and no court would be interested in my conclusions, no matter how convinced I was that I was right. Tonight I intended to lay a trap.

I could only hope I didn't fall face-first into the blasted trap myself.

Chapter 19

THE MAGICIAN WAS A DISAPPOINTMENT, TO PUT IT mildly. Rather than a tuxedo or a costume, he wore a business suit the color of milky oatmeal that had seen better days, far better days. He sounded like he was giving a speech to the board of directors of a bank, not entertaining a demanding audience. Worst of all, his magic tricks fell flat. They would have bored an audience of ten-year-olds.

From my post at the back of the room, I saw guests exchanging rueful glances with one another. I hoped he'd spice things up a bit for the second show. Olivia, sitting at the Hart table, actually yawned.

At last, the so-called magician gathered up his tall hat and his numerous scarves and bowed to unenthusiastic, scattered applause. Randy bounded onto the stage and tried to work up some enthusiasm for the man's next appearance. When that failed, he introduced Charlie Simmonds. "Held over at Haggerman's by popular demand!"

Randy didn't mention that the popular demand was from the police, but that didn't matter. A couple of people cheered, and the crowd picked up their applause. I couldn't help but notice that some of the most enthusiastic clapping was coming from the Brownville table. Mrs. Brownville leaned over and whispered something to her niece, the runner-up at today's beauty pageant. The girl laughed heartily. I also couldn't help but notice that she'd positioned her chair so she pointedly had her back to the pageant winner, who was proudly sporting her wide pink-and-blue sash across her low-cut dress.

The small elderly lady I'd seen last night at Kennelwood Hotel, the one with all the diamonds who didn't appear to have much time for Jerome, had come with a good-size party. She'd taken a few turns around the dance floor with men the right age to be her sons and sons-in-law, laughed heartily at Charlie Simmonds, and chugged back a substantial number of brightly colored cocktails as the evening progressed.

The waiters and activities staff who'd been pressed into service as dance partners lined the wall, waiting for the band to retake the stage. The newly famous Luke stood alone, apart from the rest of the waiters who clustered together. His eyes casually swept across the room, and I wondered if he was seeking out his next conquest, or if he waited for the women to approach him. At that moment, he turned his head and looked straight at me. I tightened my lips and gave him what I hoped was my best steely-eyed no-nonsense-boss glare.

He turned quickly away. I'd noticed him once before, on Wednesday, when Rosemary and I were admiring the food ready to be taken upstairs for the cocktail party. He'd gone into the kitchen moments before Francis Monahan had dropped a tray of plates and came out right after, laughing as if it was the funniest thing he'd ever seen.

Luke, I guessed, was a self-entitled, privileged bully. Personal relations between the members of staff were hardly my concern, but someone would have to keep an eye on our Luke. I might have a word with Rosemary and Aunt Tatiana.

I put Luke out of my mind and took advantage of the brief lull at the bar to talk to Rosemary. "Everything going okay?"

Her cheeks were flushed and her eyes bright. "Going great. Olivia saw me, but she pretended not to."

"She's saving her choice comments for when she and I have a quiet moment." I studied the rows of bottles behind the bar. "What do you recommend tonight? What's good?"

"Everything's good," Rosemary said. "When I make it. If you're looking for a suggestion, how about a sidecar? Pretty orange color and slightly sour."

"Sure."

"And before you ask, yes, I can manage the dessert buffet, supervise the staff, and also work the bar. I was in the kitchen when we had a slow couple of minutes, before people starting falling asleep at that awful magician, and everything's ready." Her hands flashed as she scooped ice and poured streams of colored liquid out of bottles. Next to her the other bartender served up two scotch on the rocks.

He gave me a grin. "She knows what she's doing." He was a good two decades younger than Rosemary, and her neck stiffened at the supposed compliment.

I accepted my drink, served in a coupe glass with a twist of orange and a light sugar rim, and took a sip. "This is great."

Rosemary smiled her thanks and said, "What can I get you, sir?" to the next customer.

"I'll have two of those, thanks," he said.

Charlie's act ended, and the band returned to the stage and struck up the next tune, a lively Benny Goodman swing. Couples rose from their seats and took their places on the dance floor while men rushed for the bar and ladies headed outside for a breath of air. As he always did, Charlie slipped quietly away. The magician joined the line at the bar and ordered a double bourbon.

I checked my watch. Almost ten o'clock. It would be full dark outside now.

Randy was dancing with an elderly lady, and Velvet, dressed in her pink tulle, stood by the door. She also checked her watch and then she glanced over at me. A cluster of women returned from the ladies' room, sweeping Chief Norm Monahan along with them. He was in uniform tonight.

Velvet stepped in front of him and spoke in a low voice. He nodded and looked around the ballroom.

I took a sip of my drink, which had suddenly lost all flavor, and wiped my hands on my skirt.

Velvet and the chief left the ballroom. I put my glass on a table and rapidly crossed the room. Randy excused himself to his partner and also made his way to the door.

"Mrs. Grady. May I have the honor of this dance?" A gentleman stood before me, immaculately dressed in a dark suit and thin black tie, and enough grease in his silver hair to lubricate my car.

I brushed past him. "I'm dreadfully sorry. Emergency in the kitchen. Another time."

"The judging this afternoon wasn't at all fair." The runner-up plucked at my sleeve. Her eyes were glassy, her words slurred, and tendrils of hair were coming loose from her bun. "It's obvious Olivia Peters was going to pick an older woman, and of course Randy will do whatever she does. You need to have—"

I stepped around her and kept walking.

"I've had a complaint about the value of your judging," I said to Randy when I reached him, waiting for me by the door.

"I'm not surprised. MarySue didn't like coming in second. I've heard all about it, from her as well as her aunt."

We walked quickly down the sweeping staircase. Randy slipped around the reception counter and found the flashlight he'd left there earlier, and together we crossed the lobby and stepped outside. Lights lining the pathways, on cabin porches, and above the hotel's veranda had come on. Groups of people were gathered on the veranda, catching the air or having a nightcap before turning in. In one corner, an enthusiastic game of canasta was in progress.

Randy and I hurried down the steps and took the path running along the lakefront. Behind us, the hotel was a blaze of lights and laughter. To our left, people called to one another in the cabins or sat on their porches enjoying the end of the day. The swimming pool was quiet, the tennis and handball courts empty. To our right, the lake lay dark and silent, the boats taken to the service dock for the night. A bat flew overhead. The moon was full tonight, but clouds had been gathering.

I could see Velvet and Chief Monahan ahead of us. Randy and I hurried after them, trying to keep up while being unnoticeable about it. They reached the end of the public path and turned up the hill, heading for cabin nineteen. They walked quickly, Velvet setting the pace, Monahan trying to keep up. Randy and I followed. The lights over the side path were dimmer and the space between them larger. On one side the dark woods crowded in, and the undergrowth rustled as the passing people disturbed whatever was in there. Cabin nineteen was shrouded in darkness. This afternoon, after the beauty pageant, I'd instructed maintenance to remove the police tape, asked Aunt Tatiana to have her staff pack up Harold Westenham's possessions and prepare the room, and told the reservations clerk the cabin would be available as of the day after tomorrow. If the police or the FBI wanted to argue with me, I'd play dumb and say I thought their investigation was finished.

I heard old planks creak as Velvet climbed the stairs to the porch.

"Okay," Chief Monahan said. "Let's see it."

"Sorry." Velvet's voice was low and soft in the night. "I forgot to bring the key."

"You forgot? You're the one who told me you'd found something. What are you playing at?"

"You don't really care, do you?" I tried to keep my voice strong and steady, but it might have cracked just a little.

Monahan whirled around. "Who's out there? What's going on?"

Randy switched on his flashlight. It was a small thing and didn't cast much light, but I could see the face of the angry man staring at me.

I took a deep breath and tried to stay calm. "You came here tonight in response to Velvet's call because you have to keep up the fiction of believing that rubbish about communists gathering at Haggerman's and meeting with Harold Westenham. But you know that's not true. You've always known that."

"This one said—"

"Sorry." Velvet's voice was calm. "I don't know anything about any communist cell meeting here earlier today and leaving evidence behind that you needed to see. I lied."

Monahan came down the steps, his eyes fixed on me. "What are you playing at?"

"I know Harold Westenham was responsible for your son Francis being court-martialed and jailed and then dishonorably discharged during the war. I also know Francis wasn't guilty, or if he was it was because he'd been set up by the other guys. I suspect Francis is the butt of a lot of jokes."

"You know nothing," Monahan said.

"You look out for him. Your late wife asked you to, and so you should. It's what fathers are supposed to do. But when Francis was in the army, you couldn't be there for him. And so he ended up disgraced."

"That happened nine years ago."

"So it did. But the fallout wasn't over. It never will be, not in your mind. Harold Westenham, the person who'd gone after Francis because he was furious at what he thought your son had done, showed up here. Obviously doing well in life. Well enough to rent cabin nineteen for five weeks. Francis recognized him. It came as such a shock he dropped the tray he was bringing with Westenham's dinner and ran back to the kitchens without even cleaning it up." When I spoke to Rosemary this afternoon, she'd confirmed it had been Francis who'd fled from cabin nineteen, which I guessed after hearing about the wartime history between him and Harold Westenham.

"What of it?" Monahan said.

A plank creaked as Velvet shifted her weight. Randy held the thin beam of light steady. Neither of them said a word. I could see Monahan, his face set in tight lines, his fists clenched at his sides, his body stiff. And he could see me, a dark shape outlined against the light coming from behind me.

"I understand why you killed him," I said. "For your son."

"Francis. He's a good boy."

"I know that."

"He wouldn't have stolen any necklace. What does Francis know, or care, about the value of a piece of jewelry? That pack of bullies he called his friends put him up to it, and when he got caught they let him take the fall. If I'd known, if I'd been there, I'd have put a stop to it, right enough." Monahan's voice began to rise. "That Westenham! A university professor, of all the useless people. What did he know about the law? What right did he have to persecute my boy! To ruin his life. A dishonorable discharge! I searched for him, after the war, when Francis came home, and I learned what had really happened. My boy had a hard time in jail, and he couldn't get a decent job after. Westenham didn't go back to his college, and I couldn't find him. I put it out of my mind. I tried to forget, and I helped my boy move on. Then he showed up here, Westenham, bold as brass. Francis saw him. Francis came home that night, upset, shaking like a leaf. Frightened. It all came back to him."

"You decided to get it out in the open. To confront Westenham," I said.

He said nothing. My heart pounded. I needed to hear him say it.

"You love your son. I admire that so much. You'd do anything for him, wouldn't you? I can understand that. My own mother wasn't a large part of my life when I was a child, but she always knew I was in good hands. She knew my aunt and uncle loved me as much as she did. She knew they could be counted on to look out for me. Always. I can't imagine how hard it must have been for you, when Francis had to leave and you knew the world would be a hard place for a boy like him."

"Francis told me Westenham was in cabin nineteen. I came here the next night after dark. I found Westenham standing by the lake, having a cigarette. Not a care in the world, but my son's life ruined. It made my blood boil."

"You wanted to talk things over with him, make him understand what he'd done, all those years ago."

"Talk?" Monahan spat onto the planks of the porch. "Lady, I don't *talk* to the likes of him."

"You didn't mean to kill him," I said.

"Sure I did. Pick up a good-size rock, quick blow to the back of the head, and then roll him down the hill into the lake. Splash. Over and done with. Guy didn't even know what hit him." He grinned at me. "What do you think you're going to do about this? You and your city friends? I'm the chief of police here, lady. You're a suspected communist."

"I have a newspaperman listening to this entire conversation," I said. "Jim, you can come out now."

Silence.

"Jim?"

"You think Westenham's nephew's hiding in the woods." Monahan laughed. "Think again, lady. Last I saw him, he was on his way to Rock Hill. As is my deputy. Seems the staties have made an arrest in the arson at Shady Pines. Imagine, the New York mob in the Catskills.

"I'll be on my way now. It seems you forgot our little deal. You help me out, and I'll help you. That deal's over. Your days are numbered here, lady. You and your mother."

I swallowed. My hands were shaking. I'd counted on Jim to be here, to be my witness. No court of law would take my word or that of Velvet and Randy, who were, after all, my employees, over that of the chief of police.

What on earth had I been thinking, not to just get on with my life and forget what I'd figured out?

Monahan stepped off the stairs. He stood in front of me, smirking. Randy's light threw deep shadows across his face. His eyes were small and dark.

"Get that blasted light out of my face," he snapped.

Randy lowered the light, and all I could see were our feet.

An animal roar emerged from the line of trees, a solid shape flew through the air, and a hard body landed between Monahan and me. I screamed, Monahan screamed, Velvet and Randy screamed. Monahan threw up his hands and stumbled backward, crashing into the steps.

Randy raised his flashlight, giving me enough light to see Monahan reaching for his gun. He pulled it out of its holster and aimed it at the creature crouching at his feet. Not a vicious wild animal but Winston, tongue lolling, chubby tail wagging, here to join the fun.

"No!" I screamed. "Don't shoot!"

Velvet had remained where she was, on the porch, above Monahan. Realizing what he intended to do, she swept an ashtray off the table and brought it down on the chief's head the moment he pulled the trigger. His arm jerked and the shot, thankfully, went wild. Wide-eyed, shocked at what she'd done, Velvet stared at the ashtray in her hand. The light wavered as Randy dove for cover, and then all went dark. Winston barked. For a brief moment Monahan stood still. His gun was in his right hand, and he lifted his left to touch the back of his head. "You'll pay for that. Both of you."

"I didn't mean—" Velvet said. "I . . . You can't shoot Tatiana's dog."

Monahan appeared not to hear her. His eyes fixed on my face, he lifted the gun, and pointed it directly at me. I sucked in a breath, but once again he'd turned his back on Velvet. Before he could fire, or not, she threw the ashtray aside, let out a mighty yell, and leapt onto his back. Monahan jerked and twisted, trying to throw her off, and I was reminded of a movie I'd seen some time ago, a cowboy taming a wild horse. Velvet's golden hair flew out behind her, and she kept screaming, but she held on. He raised his hands and clawed and swatted at her arms, and I heard a clatter as something hard fell to the ground. I leapt toward them, intending to grab Monahan from the front, pull him forward, and help Velvet bring him down. Instead, I tripped over Winston, who'd set up a chorus of furious barking, and I crashed into one of the pillars supporting the porch. My head spun, and stars danced in front of my eyes, but I kept enough of my wits about me to grab wildly for one of Monahan's legs. He kicked out at me. The blow had been aimed at my head, but I'd ducked in time, and he got me in the side of my shoulder. Pain sliced through me.

"Randy!" I yelled. "Help."

"I can't find the flashlight!"

"Never mind the flashlight. We need help."

The old wooden boards of the porch shook as Monahan threw Velvet off him and she crashed hard into them.

"What's happening out there?" a young woman's voice called.

Another joined it. "Do you need help?"

"One of you, call the security guards," I yelled. "The other, stay where you are. Don't let him get past you to the hotel." I braced myself for another kick, but it didn't come. Instead, footsteps pounded on the ground and shrubbery rustled. In the weak light illuminating patches of the path, I could see Monahan running down the trail.

Winston took off after him in a streak of brown and

white. I had no idea the chubby, short-legged dog could run
so fast. Without thinking, I took off after them.

"Get help!" I yelled.

I ran. I don't quite know why I ran. But Monahan was
running, Winston was running, and therefore I was running. A befuddled young dance instructor stood in the center of the path. She held out her arms, blocking access, and
said, "What's going on here?"

"Get outta my way," Monahan roared.

But the girl knew who signed her paycheck, and she
asked, "Mrs. Grady? What's happening?"

Rather than stop and try to explain, or to push his weight
around, Monahan veered off the trail and crashed into the
woods, into the dark forested spaces where the lights of the
lamps didn't reach. It's hard, if not impossible, to run without making a sound, in the dark, in the woods. I stopped
running and listened. My heart was pounding, and not from
that brief moment of exercise, and I tried to control my
breathing. Branches groaned as they bent, twigs snapped,
undergrowth crunched beneath heavy boots. Winston
barked once. I didn't know what had happened to Monahan's gun. I'd heard something fall when he fought off Velvet. Had he dropped it? Or did he have it in hand, ready to
shoot me when I came in sight?

"Mrs. Grady?" the dancer called.

"Stay here. Tell the security guards where I've gone and
to follow me." I stepped on a branch, and I bent over and
picked it up. It was about two feet long, as thick as my
thumb. The best I could do by way of a weapon. Ahead, the
creek splashed over rocks as it meandered downhill toward
the lake. I gripped the branch, held it in front of me, gathered what little courage I possess, and slipped into the
woods. Like the creek, we were going downhill, and in no

more than a dozen strides, the black mass of the lake appeared in the gaps between the trees. I felt the slippery rocks at the creek bottom beneath my feet, and I stepped cautiously into the cold water. My shoes would be ruined, but that wasn't something I'd worry about now. I broke out of the forest to emerge on the service path the moment the clouds separated. A huge round full moon came out and threw a long line of white light across the dark water. Rowboats were tied to the dock, paddleboats pulled up on shore, and at this time of night no workers would be around.

Perhaps foolishly, I didn't fear that Monahan would spring out and attack me. Far too many people had seen him running and me giving chase. He'd want to get into town, to the police station, where he could sit behind his desk, call the state police before I could, and give his side of the story. He'd try to present me as some sort of deranged female, burdened by too much responsibility. And they'd believe him.

The moonlight illuminated the dock and the man and dog running along it. Monahan reached the end, and whirled around. His hands were empty: he'd lost his gun. He saw me step out of the trees, brandishing my branch.

"You can't get away, Norm." My voice broke, and I took a deep breath to try to control it. I needed to sound calm, reasonable, as though I was in control. "Look, it's late. Why don't you come up to the hotel and have a cup of coffee, maybe some sandwiches or cake, and we'll talk things over. My staff are waiting for us; I'll get someone to call Francis and have him come down. How does that sound?"

He stared at me for one brief moment, and then he turned toward the water and, without hesitating, jumped. Winston leaned over the edge of the dock and stared down, still barking.

I put on a burst of speed and ran toward the dock. I

hadn't heard the loud splash I would have expected as Monahan's considerable bulk hit the water, but a moment later I heard a soft one as he untied a rowboat and slipped the oars. The boat pulled out onto the calm, moonlit water.

I hit the dock running and skidded to a stop next to Winston. In the far distance I could hear the babble of voices, rising in intensity as people asked one another what was going on. Close to me—nothing.

What had happened to Velvet? Had she been hurt when she fell? Had Randy stayed with her, trying to help?

Out on the water, Monahan faced in my direction as he rowed steadily away, but I couldn't see if he was looking directly at me or not. Winston barked one last time, and then, show over, he wandered back to shore.

For the briefest of moments, I considered grabbing a boat and going after Monahan, but I dismissed the idea. He'd grown up around here, among the hills and trees and lakes of the Catskills. I'd grown up among the pavement and corner stores and traffic of Brooklyn. Other than a couple of trips on the Staten Island Ferry on outings with my dad when I was a child, I've been in a boat exactly once in my life. Shortly after Olivia and I arrived to take over Haggerman's, a staffer took me out in a paddleboat to tour the lake and see our property from the water.

Delayed Lake is a small body of water, but around the bend to my left, toward which Monahan was heading, a narrow channel leads to a progressively larger series of lakes. Where the channel opens into the next lake sits Kennelwood Hotel.

Was Monahan heading for Kennelwood? Did he expect to find a friendly welcome there? Would he have them call the state police to come and arrest Velvet, Randy, and me?

I was about to turn and head back when movement on the water caught my eye. A boat was emerging from the channel. A canoe, moving fast, low in the water, a single person seated in the rear paddling steadily and efficiently.

I jumped up and down, waving my arms over my head. "Stop him! Stop him! He tried to kill me." My shouts skimmed across the water and echoed off the hills.

The canoe slowed, and then it turned slightly and moved to intercept the rowboat. I heard men's voices, but I couldn't make out the words. The voices started out low, and then Monahan began yelling and gesturing wildly. The rowboat pulled away, heading out into the lake. The canoe followed. The canoe was sleeker, faster, and the man at the paddles younger and fitter.

"Someone came running into the hotel yelling at the top of their lungs that shots had been fired and calling for a doctor. What on earth is going on? Elizabeth, have you lost leave of your senses?"

I turned to see Olivia standing in a group of elegantly dressed people, many still holding their cocktail glasses, all of them watching me. Curious staffers, some fresh from the kitchen or the ballroom, others in casual clothes or even their nightwear, peered out from behind trees.

Randy ran down the dock. His hair stood on end, the right knee of his pants was torn, and he'd lost his tie, as well as the flashlight. "She's okay. Velvet's okay. She was knocked unconscious, but only for a moment, so I stayed with her until help came. What do you want me to do?"

"Get me a boat," I said. "Where the heck is our security guard?"

"Here, Mrs. Grady," Eddie said. "I came as fast as I could when I heard there was trouble."

The dancer I'd sent for him peeked over his shoulder.

Deputy Dave pushed his way through the crowd. Jim Westenham was with him.

"What's going on?" the deputy called. I could barely hear him over the hubbub of everyone asking one another the same question.

"Your chief killed Harold Westenham, fired his gun at me, and is trying to get away." I pointed to the lake. "We need to get out there. You need to get out there, I mean. Can you row?"

He jumped onto the dock and came to stand beside me. Jim joined Olivia as Eddie suggested—in vain—that everyone go back to the hotel.

"I see Norm in the rowboat, but who's in the canoe?" Deputy Dave asked me.

"I don't know. It came out of the channel. They spoke, and then Monahan rowed away." I waved my arm in the air.

Deputy Dave ducked. "Why don't you put that down before you take out someone's eye?"

"What? Oh, sorry." I tossed the branch into the water. Winston appeared out of nowhere and leapt in after it.

The dock swayed as more people began to join us. Another rowboat was untied, and Bradley, the night clerk, and a waiter jumped in and began rowing.

We watched as the canoe caught up to Monahan's boat, both craft caught in the line of moonlight as though it were a spotlight. The canoeist put his hand out and grabbed the side of the rowboat. Shouting voices drifted across the smooth water. Monahan stood up. Even from here, we could see the boat tip to one side, right itself, and tip to the other side. The man in the canoe shouted at Monahan to sit down. Monahan stared over the side, down into the dark water.

"Norm, don't do it!" the canoeist yelled. I recognized the voice: Richard Kennelwood.

The second rowboat paddled steadily toward them, but they were still a good distance away. The boats at Haggerman's are intended for bobbing gently in the shallow waters at the edges of the lake or in the nearby marsh while guests fish for their supper. They are not built for speed.

One of the young staffers handed a bullhorn to Deputy Dave.

The deputy lifted it to his mouth and called. "Norm! This is Dave Dawson. You have to come in. Let's talk it over."

Randy untied another rowboat. He held the rope and looked at me. I looked at the boat. It didn't appear to be entirely seaworthy. I can swim, but I'm not comfortable out of reach of shore. I shook my head, and Randy got in and picked up the oars.

Winston ran down the dock, drippling wet, proudly bearing the branch. He dropped his prize at my feet, and smiled up at me, asking me to continue the game.

On shore Velvet, a cloth pressed to her head, had joined my mother and Aunt Tatiana. A man, nattily dressed in a pristine white dinner jacket, hovered beside her. When she saw me watching she gave me a crooked smile and a thumbs-up. A considerable number of the people behind her had cocktail glasses in hand, and the hems of long dresses and expensive shoes were sinking into the soggy ground at the edge of the lake. A young man had the pink-and-blue sash awarded to Miss Haggerman's tied around his neck.

Bradley and the waiter were about halfway to the canoe and rowboat. Randy had barely cleared the dock. Richard Kennelwood held Monahan's boat with one hand and extended his other, asking Monahan to take it. The rowboat shifted from side to side, Monahan swayed. His legs were apart, his arms extended to his sides. As I watched, he dropped his arms, and turned to his left. Again, he looked down into the depths. Delayed Lake isn't deep. But it's deep enough.

"No!" Richard shouted.

"Francis is waiting for you at home, Norm." Deputy Dave's calm voice bounced across the lake and echoed in the hills. "Come on in and let's talk things over."

Monahan didn't move for several long seconds, and then he dropped onto the boat's wooden bench and buried his head in his hands. Richard pulled his canoe alongside the rowboat, hand over hand. When he reached the side of the other man, he stretched out his arm and touched Monahan's bent back.

They stayed like that, the two watercraft caught in the moonlight, moving softly on the swell of the lake, until the next rowboat arrived. Bradley clearly had some experience with boats as, after exchanging a few words with Richard, he swiftly but carefully transferred himself from his boat to Monahan's. He settled himself in his seat, picked up the oars, and began rowing toward the dock with steady, confident strokes. Richard followed, and Randy slowed his own boat, waiting for them.

I let out a long breath.

Deputy Dave turned to the onlookers and lifted his bullhorn. "Show's over, folks. Please return to the hotel."

Not believing him, no one moved.

Olivia marched onto the dock, her black gown trailing behind her, her long white gloves glowing in the moonlight, her mouth a slash of red in her pale face. Jim Westenham followed her. I glared at him, and he gave me an embarrassed shrug.

"Give me that!" My mother snatched the bullhorn out of Deputy Dave's hand.

"Wasn't that a marvelous show? Let's have a hand for the inaugural performance of the Haggerman's Catskills Resort dramatic club." Still holding the bullhorn, Olivia began to clap. Jim Westenham joined her, displaying as much enthusiasm as if he were front-row center at the Metropolitan Opera, and one by one the onlookers joined in. I blinked, struggled to recover some of my wits, and then sunk into a deep curtsy.

"Bow!" Olivia growled to Deputy Dave.

"Yes, ma'am," he said. He bowed.

I doubt anyone believed Olivia, but she'd spent a good part of her life making people want to believe.

Out on the lake, the little convoy was getting closer.

"I need these people to disburse before the chief lands." Deputy Dave held out his hand for the bullhorn.

"If I must," Olivia said quietly. Then she spoke into it again. "Today I assigned a lady to the position of bartender. This is a first for Haggerman's, and I need to see what she's capable of. Drinks in the ballroom are on the house, but for the next thirty minutes only. Starting now. Elizabeth, set your watch."

Half the onlookers bolted. As for the other half, Olivia said, "Any staff member still here in one minute will be required to account for their presence to Mrs. Rostov."

Aunt Tatiana, housecoat thrown over her nightgown, bare feet thrust into fuzzy slippers, pink rollers in her hair, waved.

The other half of the onlookers bolted. Luke scrambled to follow, lost his footing, tripped over a rock, and fell to his knees into the creek. No one stopped to help him up. He pushed himself to his feet and limped after them.

A handful of nonstaff and nondrinkers remained. Aunt Tatiana and Eddie, the security guard, began politely suggesting people return to the hotel, and gradually, reluctantly, they did so.

"Nicely done," I said to my mother.

"I know," she replied, handing the bullhorn to Deputy Dave.

"Can you check on Velvet, please?" I asked. "She had a bad fall, and she doesn't look too good."

My friend had sunk to the ground, eyes closed, head thrown back against a tree truck. The man in the white dinner jacket crouched next to her.

"That gentleman's a doctor. I'll take her to our house and ask him if she should go to the hospital." My mother smiled at me. "Also nicely done."

I turned at the splash of oars and the sound of something thumping against the dock as Randy's boat pulled up. Bradley and Norm Monahan came next, followed by Richard Kennelwood in his canoe, and last the rowboat with the waiter.

Deputy Dave stretched out his arm to Norm Monahan and helped him climb out of the rowboat. And then, one at a time, the others clambered onto the dock and tied up their boats. Winston presented his branch to each of them, but no one took him up on his request to play.

Monahan's head was down, his shoulders slumped.

"Let's go, Norm," the deputy said. "We can sort this all out in the morning."

"Yeah," Monahan mumbled.

"You can't just walk away as though nothing happened," I protested.

"We all need to take some time to calm down," Dave said.

"Calm down! I'm not calming down! I am calm. He—"

At that moment we heard a shout from the direction of the public path. "Over here!" The deputy shouted back, and two men stepped gingerly over the creek and walked to the bottom of the dock. They were both bulky, with square heads and thick necks, dressed in cheap suits and dusty hats. I guessed they were not Haggerman's guests.

"Better late than never," the deputy said.

"Got lost on the road," one of the new arrivals said. "It's dark out there."

"Why don't you take Chief Monahan into town? I'll follow."

One of the men grabbed Monahan's arm. "Let's go, buddy." He led the chief away. All the fight had gone out of Monahan, but I had no doubt it would be back tomorrow with a vengeance. I turned on the deputy. Randy, Richard, Jim, Bradley, the young waiter, and the second of the new arrivals watched us.

"You can't pretend nothing happened," I said. "He fired his gun at us. He killed Harold Westenham."

"I know," the deputy said.

"You have to believe me. You— You know?"

"I don't know exactly what went on here tonight, but it looks as though you interfered in police matters, Mrs. Grady. For once, I'll overlook that. Please don't let it happen again."

"I—"

"That was Detective Stanford and this is Detective Flynn from the New York State Police. They were intending to question Norm tomorrow morning in the matter of the death of Mr. Harold Westenham. When I realized what was going on here tonight, I had one of your employees call them and let them know things had to be moved up, but they got lost on the way out of town."

"Sorry about that," Detective Flynn said.

"They'll want to talk to you in the morning, Mrs. Grady," Dave said. "As will I." He and Flynn started to walk away.

"Wait!" I said. "You can't just leave like that. You say you knew. How?"

"Boot print. Norm needs a new pair of boots. He's been going on for weeks about it, but he hates shopping, particularly when the summer visitors are in town. The sole of his left boot is almost worn through on the left side. It leaves a distinctive print. I saw that print in the mud next to Westenham's body, where you and your friends had pulled it onto the shore. That meant nothing, as Norm got to the body before me. Norm had a quick look at the body, and then he went up to the man's cabin to search it. After he'd gone, I saw that print again, on the hill, under a tree, on the far side of the body. Where Norm didn't go."

"That's all you have?" Jim said. "Not much."

"I thought I was imagining things. Offhand, I could think of absolutely no reason Norm would kill a total stranger. I took a picture of the print anyway, in case it proved to be important. Yesterday morning, I dropped by his house on another matter. Francis was home, but Norm was in the shower. While I waited, I had a brief chat with Francis. He's an emotional boy—man, I should say. Makes it easy for some guys to bait him. He was sad, he told me, because the man who'd been his commanding officer in the war had died at Haggerman's. He didn't say any more, but it got me thinking. I know the story, and I know Norm blames that man for everything that happened to Francis since. What Francis told me was enough for me to call in the state police. Enough to get an investigation started. I asked Francis for a glass of water, and while he was doing that, I grabbed Norm's work boot from the mat by the door and took a photo of the sole. It matches the one at the scene."

"He told me he did it," Richard said. "Out on the lake. He was about to jump, and then Dave reminded him of his son."

Chapter 20

"I HAVE TO BE GOING," DEPUTY DAVE SAID. "WE'LL BE back tomorrow to take everyone's statements."

Once again, he began to walk away, but then Randy remembered something and called him back. "Forgot I had this." He stuck his hand into his waistband and brought out a gun. "Chief Monahan dropped this."

When Dave Dawson and Detective Flynn had disappeared into the trees, I turned to the men around me. "I have to get up to my house and see how Velvet's doing. You two"—I indicated Bradley and the waiter—"please come to my office in the morning." They'd leapt in to help, and I intended to reward them for that.

"Yes, ma'am," they said.

The men trailed along behind me. When I turned up the path toward my house, Jim, Randy, and Winston followed. Richard, I couldn't help but notice, came with them. He caught my eye and gave me a soft smile. I ducked my head and hurried up the trail.

Velvet, Olivia, and Aunt Tatiana, the latter still in her nightwear, were in the living room. Velvet sat on the couch in a cloud of pink tulle. She had a thick blanket thrown across her shoulders, her hair had come out of its pins and tumbled in a golden river over her shoulders. A patch of hair was wet, and the makeup on one side of her face had been scrubbed off. She clutched a cup of hot tea in both hands. Winston ran across the room and rested his muzzle on her lap. She smiled at him and gave him a pat. Olivia and Aunt Tatiana were not drinking tea but what looked to be champagne. I plucked the bottle out of the ice bucket. Yup, champagne. And not the cheap stuff, either.

I raised one eyebrow in question.

"A successful conclusion to a difficult week," Olivia said. "The culprit apprehended, no one harmed."

"Except me," Velvet said. "My head hurts."

"Which is why you do not get champagne," Aunt Tatiana said.

I swung my right arm in the air, testing my shoulder. It hurt, but not too much. Not enough to stop me having a glass of champagne.

"Are you sure you don't need to go to the hospital?" Randy dropped onto the couch next to Velvet, crunching the fabric of her skirt. "Here, let me see."

She turned her head and let him separate strands of her hair. "Bleeding's stopped," he said. "You've got a heck of a lump there, though. Going to be a lot worse tomorrow."

"A doctor was in the ballroom," Olivia said, "when some idiot of a guest came running in to yell that we were all about to be murdered. He came with me and tended to

Velvet. He left a moment ago. He said she'll be fine, provided she rests."

"Which she will," I said. "I'll get someone to lead Velvet's classes tomorrow."

"But—" Velvet began.

"No buts," I said. Even if I had to take the classes myself. Perish the thought. I tested my shoulder again.

"What about you, Elizabeth?" Richard asked. "The doctor tended to Velvet. He should have stayed to have a look at you."

"I'm fine. Really, I am. I'll probably wake up in the night and realize I had a close call, but nothing more than that." I refrained from obviously moving my sore shoulder.

"May I offer you gentlemen a drink?" Olivia asked. Without waiting for an answer, she said, "Elizabeth, fetch more glasses, and bring another bottle. It's in the fridge."

I went into the kitchen as instructed and got glasses out of the cupboard. As I turned around, I caught a glimpse of myself reflected in the dark windows. My hands flew to my hair. My lovely poodle cut was now more of a sheepdog, several scratches crossed my right cheek, and traces of dried blood marked the skin. A deep gash ran through my right sleeve. I scrubbed furiously at the blood on my face and plucked a twig out of the curly depths of my hair. I kicked off my ruined shoes, pulled up my dress, unclipped my stockings, shredded into rags, and yanked them off. I tossed them into the kitchen trash. As long as I looked this bad, I might as well go all the way and be comfortable. I wiggled out of my girdle and hid it in a drawer, in case one of our visitors wandered into the kitchen in search of a glass of water. I then put champagne glasses and the bottle on a tray and carried it out.

"While Tatiana brought Velvet here and the doctor tended to her, I followed our guests to the ballroom," Olivia was saying. "I rightly suspected that Rosemary wouldn't believe it if they told her I'd opened the bar. For the second time in a week. While I was there, I took the opportunity to select a couple of nice bottles for expected guests." She lifted her glass in a toast.

"Because I know Rosemary's fully capable of serving the thirsty hordes you let loose on her, I'll take it as done that she can tend bar from now on, shall I?" I said as I wrestled with the cork on the bottle.

"Along with her other duties," Olivia said.

"With a commensurate increase in pay."

My mother looked at me.

The cork popped, the champagne fizzed, and I served the drinks.

When everyone, including me and excluding Velvet, had a glass of champagne, I turned to Jim. "What happened to you? You were supposed to be in the woods listening. I set the trap so carefully and timed the whole thing so we'd all be in place at five after ten."

"When I called Monahan with my supposed information," Velvet said, "I told him I couldn't get away until ten so he was to meet me then. Which he did."

Jim had the grace to look embarrassed. "All I can say is I'm sorry. Why didn't you tell me what you needed me for?"

"I wanted you to be an impartial witness," I said.

"Sorry," he said again. "I got an anonymous tip that a mob hit man was about to be arrested over the Shady Pines arson, so I went to check it out. Turns out, nothing was happening. Nothing at all. Dawson was there, too—"

"Who?"

"Deputy Dawson."

"Oh, Deputy Dave. I forgot he has a last name. Go on."

"We got to talking. Looks like we'd both been fed a line,

and we started wondering who would have done that, and why. I remembered what you'd asked me to do, so we came here, to find out what was going on. We arrived in the nick of time."

"Arrived almost too late, you mean," Velvet mumbled.

"While we were waiting for the rest of you," Olivia said, "Velvet told me what happened at cabin nineteen. Really, Elizabeth, don't you have enough to do around here without doing the police's job for them?"

"That's the thing," I said. "I thought I had to do the police's job for them. I never thought Deputy Dave, I mean Deputy Dawson, had the initiative to start an investigation of his own."

"We talked about that," Jim said. "He's new here, and at first he thought Monahan was being a typical small-town, old-time cop. Son of the previous chief, friends with all the important people in town, still doing things the old way. Then he started to think it might amount to more than that. That Monahan was"—he glanced at Richard Kennelwood, who'd scarcely said a word all night—"in the pockets of the big-hotel owners."

"He is," Richard said. "Or I should say he was. My dad and I had our disagreements about his way of running the hotel and doing business in the community, but what finally had me packing up and leaving was one incident in particular. Five years ago, a guest drowned in the lake. She'd gone out for a paddle late at night with an off-duty staff member. They'd both had far too much to drink, the boat capsized, and the guest drowned although the staffer made it to shore. We could have been sued, and the publicity would have done us no good, so Dad and Monahan covered it up. The police report said the guest took the boat out by herself. Not long after that Monahan bought himself a nice new car, and

I went to the city. When I came back I told Monahan, although not in so many words, the arrangement he had with my father would not continue."

"How did he take that?" I asked.

"He pretended not to know what I was talking about. He also told me I had a few things to learn about how things work in a town like Summervale."

"Dave Dawson was starting to have his suspicions about Monahan's involvement in my uncle's murder," Jim said. "When he found out the FBI said the communism angle had no merit but Monahan hadn't bothered to tell him, that cinched it. He realized Monahan was deliberately trying to muddy the waters, instead of clearing things up, and what he heard from Francis the other night told him why. He called the state police and told them what was what. You did him a big favor, Elizabeth."

I harrumphed. "I put my life in danger, and the lives of my friends." I smiled at Randy and Velvet. Randy, I noticed, hadn't moved from Velvet's side since checking the state of her head, She hadn't shifted over, either. "Not to mention Winston's."

"Winston!" Aunt Tatiana said. "What happened to Winston?"

The dog, who'd been snoozing happily at Velvet's feet, woke with a bark.

"Monahan shot at him," I said. "He missed because Velvet clobbered him with an ashtray and spoiled his aim."

"Heroine that I am," Velvet said modestly.

Randy smiled at her. "When Elizabeth took off after Monahan, I had a tough decision to make. To follow her or to help Velvet. Velvet had been knocked down and momentarily lost consciousness. I knew Elizabeth was capable of taking care of herself."

I harrumphed again. "How did I do Deputy Dave any favors?" I asked Jim.

"He didn't have enough to charge Monahan. He hoped the state police would be able to dig up more evidence, but that was only a hope. If they'd arrived, started investigating Monahan, and left without finding anything, Dave's career would have been finished. Instead, you got Monahan to confess."

"He'll deny it tomorrow," I said.

"Probably," Richard said. "But I can, and will, testify he told me out there that he killed Westenham in revenge for Westenham having Francis arrested in forty-four. That, plus what Dave's come up with, will probably be enough."

"There'll be more, Elizabeth," Jim said. "Once the investigation gets going. And now it will, because you set it in motion."

"All of that's well and good," Olivia said. "I want to see an article in the newspaper retracting that ridiculous claim that Haggerman's is a communist hot spot."

Jim laughed. "I suspect you'll get it. Martin McEnery at the paper and Monahan are mighty close. 'You scratch my back; I'll scratch yours' sort of thing. McEnery won't be able to backtrack fast enough once he hears Monahan's being disgraced. That's provided the editor at the *Gazette* doesn't throw him overboard first for writing a spurious story that had not one shred of merit."

"So all that communist stuff was made up out of whole cloth?" Olivia said.

"Yes, and I should have recognized it for what it was," Jim said. "I was there, with Elizabeth, when Monahan walked into Uncle Harold's writing room. He was absolutely delighted when he saw that book on the desk. What a great excuse it gave him to divert attention from what was just a sordid little personal murder and try to make it look like a big deal. Unfortunately for him, the FBI dismissed his communist talk as soon as they had a proper look into Uncle Harold's papers."

"If he ruined the reputation of Haggerman's in order to save his, too bad," I said.

Velvet had fallen asleep, her head on Randy's shoulder. Randy made no attempt to move it.

A knock sounded at the door, and Olivia called, "Come in."

Rosemary and Charlie Simmonds did so.

"What the heck has been going on?" Charlie said. "There I was, onstage, top of my form, telling my best jokes, and not one person was paying any attention. Never mind the sudden line at the bar and people coming running from all directions, with something they absolutely had to tell everyone at their table in their loudest possible voice."

"Another day in which we've almost run out of liquor," Rosemary said. "Another rush order on Monday."

Velvet snored lightly. Jim stood up. "I'll tell you about it on the way back to the hotel. We need to let these people get to bed."

Rosemary looked at me. "Everything okay, Elizabeth?"

"It is now," I said. "We'll talk tomorrow."

"Come, Winston," Aunt Tatiana said. The dog stretched every fiber in his pudgy body before ponderously getting to his feet.

"He deserves a special treat," I said. "If Winston hadn't arrived when he did and frightened Monahan, I don't know what would have happened."

"We'd all be in jail, most likely," Randy said.

"Velvet should spend the night here," I said. "We need to keep an eye on her. She can have my bed, and I'll take the couch."

Randy stood up and swept the sleeping woman into his arms. His eyes opened wide and he grunted softly, saying, "Heavier than she looks." I laughed and pointed the way to my bedroom. He laid her on my bed and rejoined us. I'd see that she was comfortably tucked in for the night. "I have to be heading back to New York City first thing in the morning," Jim said to me in a low voice. "Stuff's happening at the paper I can't keep putting off, and my parents are arriving from Florida. We'll be back when the cops release Uncle Harold's remains. I'm hoping that won't be too long. Can I . . . pop in and say hi?"

"You're always welcome," I said. "As are your parents. Let me know the date, and I'll try to get you a room. One not in the old building, either."

He smiled at me. I smiled back.

"Off you go, Randy," I heard Olivia say. "Elizabeth and I will take care of Velvet."

"I can stay. If you need—"

"We do not," Olivia said firmly.

Jim hesitated. For some reason I was aware of Richard Kennelwood watching us.

"Anytime you need help solving a murder," Jim said at last. "I'm your man."

"Believe me," I said. "That will not be necessary. Good night."

They headed out into the night. Only Richard Kennelwood remained.

"I'll get you some blankets," Olivia said to me.

I walked with Richard to the door.

"Thanks for your help," I said. "Your arrival was timely. Do you often go out for a late-night paddle?"

"When I can. The nights are so peaceful on the lake." He stared into my eyes. "Elizabeth?"

I breathed. "Yes?"

"I didn't simply happen to be passing. I was . . . I mean, I was on my way here. To Haggerman's. To your house. I was hoping to talk you into coming for a turn around the lake with me. I should have called ahead, but the night was warm, and the moon was full, and I . . ."

"Oh," I said.

He gave me a crooked grin. "Another time, maybe?"

I grinned back, my cheeks burning. "Yes, yes. I'd like that."

"Elizabeth!" my mother called. "What on earth is your girdle doing in the cutlery drawer?"

ACKNOWLEDGMENTS

Developing a new series is a lot of fun, and this one was no exception. I'd particularly like to thank Kim Lionetti for working with me on the concept and the good people at Penguin Random House, particularly Miranda Hill, for loving the idea. Cheryl Freedman helped smooth out early drafts. Thanks to Rick Blechta, who plays in a big-band orchestra called the Advocats in Toronto, for helping with the music and dances.

If some of my knowledge of the places and scenery of the Catskills is off, you can blame the blasted pandemic for the fact that I haven't been able to travel there to do the location research I might otherwise have done. Someday soon, I hope.

Ready to find
your next great read?

Let us help.

Visit prh.com/nextread

Penguin
Random
House